I, MICHAEL BENNETT

JAMES PATTERSON

& MICHAEL LEDWIDGE

arrow books

Published by Arrow Books in 2012

5 7 9 10 8 6

First published in Great Britain in 2012 by Century

Arrow Books
Random House, 20 Vauxhall Bridge Road,
London SW1V 2SA

www.randomhouse.co.uk

Addresses for companies within The Random House Group Limited can be
found at: www.randomhouse.co.uk/offices.htm

The Random House Group Limited Reg. No. 954009

A CIP catalogue record for this book
is available from the British Library

ISBN 9780099550037
ISBN 9780099576792 (export edition)

Typeset in 12/16 Berkeley by SX Composing DTP, Rayleigh, Essex

Penguin Random House is committed to a sustainable future for
our business, our readers and our planet. This book is made from
Forest Stewardship Council® certified paper.

MIX
Paper from
responsible sources
FSC® C018179

Printed and bound in Great Britain by Clays Ltd, St Ives plc

To the people of the most beautiful city on the Hudson, one of the most beautiful rivers in the world. Live in peace.

For Bob Hatfield, Mick Fescoe, and the rest of the gang from St. Patrick's.

One

STARTING TO GASP AS she climbed the increasingly steep slope of the tangled hiking trail, Mary Catherine was about to take a breather when the tree line opened. Glancing out over the open ridge, she immediately halted in her tracks, as what was left of her breath was suddenly taken.

Off to the right, the flat lake and majestic foothills of the Catskill Mountains glowed in the soft morning light like a priceless Hudson River School landscape come to life. Mary Catherine stood for a moment, mesmerized by the exhilarating vista, the distant golden hills, the mile-long expanse of silvery blue water, smooth and perfect as a freshly tucked-in sheet.

Only for a moment.

Two geese floating by the near shore of the lake took frantic, honking flight as a large projectile landed in the water beside them with a tremendous, booming slap.

"Youkilis tries to tag from third!" Eddie Bennett yelled as the baseball-size rock he'd just chucked sent violent ripples over the serene water. He dropped to his knees as he threw his arms up in dramatic triumph. "But the Yankees' new center fielder, Eddie the Laser Beam Bennett, throws him out by a mile. Ball game over. Pennant over. Thuuuuh *Yankees* win!"

"Mary Catherine!" protested one of the girls from the front of the long, single-file line of children already on the move through the trees farther down the trail.

There were ten of them in all, six girls, four boys. Being a mix of Spanish and Asian, black and white, and ranging in age from seven to sixteen, they were often mistaken for a small Montessori school.

But they weren't, Mary Catherine knew. They were a family, believe it or not. A large, raucous, often aggravating, but ultimately always loving family. One she found herself smack-dab in the middle of again and again for some reason.

Who was she kidding? she thought as she hauled Eddie up and sent him scurrying ahead of her along the forest path. She knew the reason, or at least the main one. His name was Mike Bennett, the NYPD detective father of these ten crazy kids, stuck back in the city on a case. Which meant she was on riot patrol without backup here at the Bennett family lake house. At least until the weekend.

This latest frenzied fiasco of an outdoor adventure was actually courtesy of the two littlest ones, Shawna and Chrissy: a first-ever Bennett family vacation breakfast picnic. But it was Jane, the Girl Scout, who had turned it into a full-blown nature walk with her Orange County field guide. An activity Ricky, Eddie, and Trent were determined to tease into oblivion at every turn, of course.

Less than a minute later, Mary Catherine

watched helplessly as, midway down the hiking line, Ricky Bennett suddenly hopped up on a rock and began making drumbeat sounds with his mouth. It was a rap beat, Mary Catherine knew. The very same one the thirteen-year-old had driven them all crazy with on last night's two-hour ride up here.

"Uh-oh. Here we go. More dissension in the ranks," Mary Catherine mumbled as she hurried forward through the column of kids.

His brother Trent, seizing the moment, immediately jumped up beside Ricky and joined in the fun with a manic, high-pitched, scratching-squeaking sound.

"Y'all, I'm sick of this wood. Get me back to my 'hood," Ricky rapped in a bellowing voice before the two knuckleheaded boys collapsed in bursts of laughter.

"Mary Catherine!" fourteen-year-old Jane shrieked this time.

Mary Catherine finally arrived from the rear of the file, forcing a scowl across her face to hide her smile.

She thought the boys were actually pretty funny but, of course, being an experienced nanny and nobody's fool, she would take that secret to her grave.

"Boys, you will cease this instant," Mary Catherine said to them as sternly as her lilting Irish brogue would allow. "Nature walks are about relaxation. We'll not have your human beat-bashing nonsense."

"It's beatboxing, Mary Catherine," Ricky said helpfully, between giggles. "Human beatboxing."

"I'll box you about your human head and shoulders in about three seconds," Mary Catherine said, pulling his hat down over his face. She whirled around and busted Eddie making faces over her shoulder.

"And for you, Eddie Andrew Bennett," she said, poking his chest, "another rock near one of Orange County's fine feathered friends and we'll see if that portable PlayStation of yours can throw Youkilis out from third!"

Two

HEADING BACK TO THE rear of the line, Mary Catherine looked pleadingly at the two oldest Bennett kids, Juliana and Brian, for some much-needed assistance, but they avoided her gaze—eyes expressionless, zombielike, as if they were sleepwalking. Wasn't looking like any help was on the way from the teen ranks this early in the a.m. She was on her own and surrounded on all sides, she thought, flicking a drop of sweat from her nose.

After they got up here late last night, maybe this was a bit too much too soon. But then again, wasn't the entire point of vacation to get these kids out of the concrete jungle of Manhattan and up here into the clean, fresh country air? They would happily laze around in their pajamas until noon if she let them. Like all good Marine Corps drill instructors and nuns, she knew it was better to get an ironclad routine going straight off the bat, and then get them used to it, no matter how painful it was at first. If she'd learned anything in the last few years as the world's hardest-working nanny, it was that.

And despite all the tomfoolery, Jane was making the best of it, at least. The head of their expedition thumbed through her guidebook as they continued along the path. She brought the party to a halt as she came upon some small gray birds making creaking chirps as they bathed in a forest creek. She lifted the binoculars from around her neck.

"Is that a dove?" Fiona whispered as she crouched alongside her. "No, wait. A plover, right?"

"Yes, very good, Fiona," Jane whispered back, flicking and stopping on a page to make a notation. "That is a plover. A semipalmated plover, I believe."

As they continued on, a loud croak began echoing through the trees.

"Is that a bird, too?" said seven-year-old Chrissy, looking around excitedly.

"No, Chrissy," Jane said, patting her little sister on the head. "I'm pretty sure it's a frog."

"I believe it's a semipalmated frog, to be exact, Chrissy," called Ricky from the back, to the snickering delight of the boys.

That's when it happened. Trent saw it first. He stopped as if he'd hit an invisible wall and began jumping up and down as he repeatedly stabbed a pointing finger toward the undergrowth to the left of the trail.

"Yeah, well, what the heck is . . . . that?" he screamed.

Arriving at the scene of the commotion, Mary Catherine took a couple of seconds to piece together what was going on. Between the shafts of sunlight, sprawled along the forest floor beside an elm tree, was a large gray silhouette. When the form snorted out a breath, Mary realized it was a deer, a large doe, lying on her side. She also realized there was something on the loamy forest floor beside her, a bulbous gray-green form, slick with moisture. Wisps of steam were rising off the curious blob. It was moving slightly.

As the prone deer turned and began to lick at the form, Mary Catherine realized what they were witnessing. The deer had just given birth.

"Ugh!" Trent said.

"What?" Ricky said.

"Ewwwwww!" Eddie said.

"Quiet, children. Hush!" Mary Catherine said, urging them all to crouch down.

As they kneeled, watching from the trail, the mother deer suddenly stopped licking. The wet gray caul of the newborn deer bulged and then split and a tiny face emerged. The wet creature wriggled and blinked furiously as it rolled out of the steaming birth casing and onto the forest floor.

Mary Catherine glanced from the wonder they were witnessing to the rest of the crew around her. Every one of the kids was floored, absolutely astonished. Even the boys. Especially the boys. She'd never seen them so wide-eyed. The miracle of life had utterly silenced the peanut gallery.

They all gasped in unison a moment later as the mother deer suddenly rose in a long, graceful, almost regal movement, her head and ears cocked directly at them. The fawn, still on its side, blinked at its mother and then began to rock, trying to roll over and get its long legs underneath it.

"Come on. You can do it. Come on," Chrissy prompted.

As if hearing Chrissy's encouragement, the newborn finally stood on all fours. They all watched as it wobbled in place, its legs trembling, its wet eyes wide, its fur in the shafts of light as fuzzy as a bumblebee's.

"Oh, my gosh! It looks like a bunny, a long-legged bunny," Shawna said, clapping with delirious excitement. "It's the cutest ever, ever, ever."

No, that's you, thought Mary Catherine as she kissed the bouncing little girl on the top of her head. The miracle of life, indeed, she thought, looking from the fawn to the surrounding crowd of crazy sweet kids who had somehow become her life.

DETECTIVE
MICHAEL BENNETT

Book One

TO CATCH A KING

Chapter 1

THEY SAY THE NEON lights are bright on Broadway, but from where I sat, beside an upstairs window of the Thirty-Fourth Precinct's brown brick pillbox on Broadway and 183rd Street in Washington Heights, I was seriously having my doubts. In fact, the only illumination I caught at all as I stared out that cold predawn morning was from an ancient set of cheap Christmas lights strung across the faded plastic awning of a bodega across the street.

And they weren't even blinking.

Yawning down at the grim street, I knew it could have been worse. Much worse. Back in 1992, the year I started in the NYPD up here in the Heights—once one of northern Manhattan's most notorious, drug-riddled neighborhoods—if you saw any twinkling lights in the sky, it was most likely a muzzle flash from a gun being fired on one of the rooftops.

I was twenty-two back then, fresh out of the Police Academy and looking for action. I got it in heaps. That year, the three-four stacked up a staggering 122 murders. Death really does come in threes, the precinct detectives used to joke, because every three days, like clockwork, it seemed someone in the neighborhood was murdered.

In the early nineties, the neighborhood had become a wholesale drug supermarket, an open-air cocaine Costco. At 2:00 a.m. on Saturdays, it looked like the dinner rush at a McDonald's drive-through, as long lines of jittery customers idled in the narrow, tenement-lined streets.

But we had turned it around, I reminded myself as I looked out at the still-dark streets. Eventually, we locked up the dealers and boarded up the crack houses until the cokeheads and junkies were finally convinced that the Heights was back to being a neighborhood instead of a drugstore.

And by "we," I mean the veteran cops who "raised" me, as they say on the job—the Anti-Crime Unit grunts who took me under their wing, who showed me what it was to be a cop. A lot of them were actual Vietnam veterans who'd traded a foreign war for our unending domestic drug war. Day in and day out, we cruised the streets, making felony collars, taking guns off the street, putting bad guys behind bars.

Sitting here twenty years later, working my latest case, I kept thinking more and more about those fearless cops. As I sat looking out the window, I actually fantasized that they would arrive any minute, pulling into the special angled parking spaces below and hopping out of their cars, ready to give me some much-needed backup.

Because though we'd won the battle of Washington Heights, the war on drugs wasn't over. Not by a long shot.

I turned away from the window and looked back at the pages of an arrest report spread across the battered desk in front of me.

In fact, the war was just getting started. It was about to flare up bigger and badder and deadlier than ever before.

Chapter 2

I SIFTED THROUGH SOME photographs until I found the reason why I was up here so early. I propped the color shot over the screen of my open laptop and did what I'd been doing a lot of in the last few weeks—memorizing one of the faces in it.

The photograph showed three men standing in a rundown Mexican street beside a brand-new fire-engine-red Ford Super Duty pickup truck. Two of the men were wearing bandannas and baseball caps to cover their faces and gripped AR-15 assault rifles with extended magazines. Between them stood a bareheaded, broad-shouldered, light-skinned black man. A gold Cartier tank watch was just visible above the cuff of his dark, tailored suit as he smoothed an Hermès tie.

I stared at the man in the middle—his pale blue eyes, his cropped salt-and-pepper hair, his expensive attire. Smiling as he glanced in the direction of the camera, the handsome dusky-skinned black man had the casual grace of a model or a sports star.

He was a star, all right.

A death star.

The man's name was Manuel "the Sun King" Perrine, and he was the notorious drug kingpin who ran the Tepito drug cartel, the most violent in Mexico. Two years earlier, Perrine had had two U.S. Border Patrol agents and their families murdered in Arizona and burned their houses to the ground. Though the ruthless killer and *Forbes* magazine–listed billionaire had been in a Mexican prison at the time of the ordered hits, he'd promptly escaped and gone on the run when the proceedings for his extradition to the U.S. had begun last year. It was as though he had disappeared into thin air.

It turned out he hadn't. Manuel Perrine was

coming to New York City today. We knew where, and we knew when.

The ten-page arrest package I'd been working on spelled it all out in exhaustive detail. It had surveillance photos of the meeting place, building descriptions, Google maps. It even had the location and directions from the planned arrest site to the trauma unit of the New York–Presbyterian Hospital emergency room, which I was praying we wouldn't need.

If all went well today, by five o'clock, I'd be at a bar, surrounded by cops and DEA and FBI agents, buying rounds as we toasted our success in taking down one of the most dangerous men on the face of the earth.

That was the plan, anyway, and it was a good one, I thought, staring at the pages. But even with all its detail and foresight, I was still wary— nervous as hell, to be perfectly frank.

Because I knew about plans. Especially the best-laid ones. If the Heights had taught me any- thing, it was that.

It's like the wise sage Mike Tyson once said: "Everybody got plans . . . *until they get hit*."

Chapter 3

"HEY, FIRST ONE IN. I like that in a team leader. You deserve a gold star *and* a smiley-face sticker," someone said five minutes later, as a massive cup of coffee thudded down beside my elbow.

"No, wait. I take that back," said the bearded, long-haired undercover cop who sat down across from me. "I forgot that Your Highness doesn't have to drive in from the ass end of the Bronx, but actually lives nearby, here in the glorified borough of Manhattan. Forgive me for forgetting what a yuppie fop you've become."

I smiled back at the grinning, wiseacre cop. His name was Hughie McDonough, and his egregious chop-busting stemmed from our days at Saint Barnabas Elementary School in the

Woodlawn section of the Bronx, where we grew up. In addition to being school chums, Hughie and I had been in the same Police Academy class and had worked together in a street crime unit here in the three-four for a couple of years.

We'd lost touch when I went on to the five-two in the Bronx and he transferred out of the NYPD and into the DEA. Over the course of the last fifteen years, McDonough had built a rock-star reputation as a fearless undercover agent. He was also one of the foremost experts on Colombian, and now Mexican, cartels. Which was what had us working together after all these years on a joint NYPD-federal task force, hoping to nail Perrine.

"Late again, huh, McDonough?" I said shaking my head. "Let me guess. You were blow-drying that Barbie hair of yours? No, wait. You ran out of Just For Men for your Jesus beard."

"Tell me. What does it look like below Ninety-Sixth Street?" Hughie said, ignoring my dig and continuing the trash talk. "And what about those cocktail parties, Mike? I mean, you are one of NYC's top cops, according to the latest *New York* magazine article. You must be on the cocktail party circuit."

I glanced across the table thoughtfully.

"Cocktail parties are pretty much like keg parties, Hughie, except they're indoors and the cups are different. Crystal instead of the plastic ones you're used to."

"Indoors?" Hughie said, scratching his head. "How does that work? Where do you put the Slip'N Slide? And don't you get holes in the walls when it's time for the strippers to shoot the beer bottles?"

"McDonough, McDonough, McDonough," I said as I Frisbeed my coffee-cup lid at him. "Such sinful talk. And to think once you were such a nice little church boy."

McDonough actually cracked up at that one. Church Boy was what the black and Hispanic public school toughs called us on the subway when they spotted our Catholic school dress shoes and ties. In Hughie's case, that was about all it took for him to start swinging. He wasn't a big kid, but his crazy fireman father made him and his four older brothers compete in the citywide Golden Gloves boxing tournament every year, so he had no problem at all mixing it up. One time, as high school legend had it, he knocked a huge mouthy kid from Pelham down the back stairs of a city bus and out the door onto East 233rd Street with one shot.

"To church boys," McDonough said, leaning over the desk and touching his coffee cup to mine in a toast. "May we never run out of ugly plaid ties and white socks to wear with our black shoes."

I toasted him back and smiled at the old-school crazy cop over the rim of my cup.

Considering the danger inherent in what we were about to do, it was good to have my pugnacious old friend here now. He was as cocky and brass-balled as ever. There wasn't anyone else I'd like to be partnered with for this major arrest—or to have watching my back, for that matter. Even with his seriously warped personality.

I smiled as I glanced back at the window. Then down at the photograph of Manuel Perrine. Seems like maybe my backup had arrived after all.

Chapter 4

"SO: HAVE YOU FINALLY got this arrest plan sussed out, Fearless Team Leader?" McDonough said, fingering through the papers covering the desk.

"Just finishing up," I said. "I was working on an ass-covering rider at the end in case the Sun King doesn't stick to the script. How does this sound? 'If necessary, we will immediately alter from the original plan and effect as safely as possible the arrest as referred to herein.'"

"That's good," McDonough said, squinting up at the ceiling tiles. "But also add something like, 'We will neutralize the adversary in the quickest, most effective, most efficient, and safest manner that presents itself at that point in time.'"

I shook my head as I typed it into my Toshiba.

"I like it, Church Boy," I said. "If that's not some prime slinging, I don't know what is. You're actually not completely witless, which is saying something for a guy who went to Fordham."

Having gone to Manhattan College, I couldn't let a chance to get a dig in on any graduate of Manhattan's rival, Fordham—the Bronx's other Catholic college—slip by.

McDonough shrugged his broad shoulders.

"I wanted to go to Manhattan College like you, Mike, but it was so small I couldn't find it. And silly me, I looked for it in Manhattan, when all along it was inexplicably hidden in the Bronx," he said. "But my impeccable Jesuit training has got nothing to do with slinging it. I'm a DEA agent, baby. I have a BA in BS."

"A bachelor's degree in bullshit? You must have gotten a four-point-oh," I said as I continued typing.

"This is true," McDonough said, closing his eyes and leaning his broad-shouldered bulk back in the office chair until he was almost horizontal. "And yet somehow I find myself unable to hold a candle to your law enforcement prowess. Seriously, bro, I've tagged along on some of these rides, and this is as major-league as it comes. This is one world-class bag of shit we're about to grab, and to think it's all because of little old you."

I took a bow as I typed.

"Stick around, kid," I said. "Maybe you might learn something."

This crazy case actually was mine. It had started out as a real estate corruption probe, of all things. My Major Case Unit had been brought in when the board president of a new billion-dollar luxury high-rise on Central Park West suspected that the building's real estate manager was getting kickbacks from the contractors he was hiring.

When we got up on the manager's phones, we learned that the kickbacks weren't the only thing he was into. He was a sick pervert who frequented prostitutes on a daily basis, despite the fact that he was supposed to be a pious Hasidic Jew with a large family up in Rockland County. What he liked best were Hispanic girls—the more under-age the better—from a Spanish Harlem brothel.

When we swooped down on the building

manager and the brothel, we also arrested the pimp running the place. It was the pimp, a Dominican named Ronald Quarantiello, who turned out to be a gift that kept on giving. The jittery, fast-talking criminal was extremely well connected in New York's Hispanic criminal underworld. And staring at a thirty-year sentence for sex trafficking, he'd cut a juicy deal. He agreed to flip against his business partner, Angel Candelerio, the head of DF, Dominicans Forever, the city's largest Dominican drug gang.

And boy, did he flip. Like a gymnast during an Olympic floor exercise. Ronald helped us bug Candelerio's house, his Washington Heights restaurant, where he did all his business, and his encrypted phone.

I thought the pimp was high when he told us that Candelerio was a childhood friend of the globally notorious drug kingpin Perrine. But a wiretap on Candelerio's phones and bugs confirmed it.

Once the transcripts of his conversations with Perrine were obtained, my boss told her boss, and the DEA and FBI were brought in to form a task force with yours truly as the team leader.

The icing on the cake came a month ago, when Perrine and Candelerio started talking about a visit Perrine was going to make to New York.

A meet that was going down at noon today.

As McDonough stood up to take a cell call, I went over the arrest papers for a final time. I double-checked the mission statements and interior layouts and maps. Lastly, I went over the grisly crime-scene photos of the Border Patrol agents and their families whom Perrine had murdered.

The most gruesome shot, the one I couldn't forget, showed a Dodge Caravan sitting in the one-car garage of a suburban house. Where its windshield had been, there was just a bloody, jagged hole. The front end was riddled to Swiss cheese with hundreds upon hundreds of bullet holes.

I studied the picture and took in the violence it displayed and wondered if being put in charge of this arrest was a blessing or a curse.

I glanced up at the yellow face of the wall clock above the window, which framed a slowly lightening sky.

I guess I'd soon see.

Chapter 5

BY 8:00 A.M., THE upstairs muster room was crowded with our FBI, DEA, and NYPD joint task force.

Joint task forces usually comprise about a dozen agents and cops, but for this international event, a total of thirty hand-picked veteran investigators were present and accounted for. They stood around, joking and backslapping, buzzing with caffeine, anticipation, and adrenaline.

As the final prearrest meeting got started, I spotted about a dozen or so big bosses from each of the represented agencies. Bringing them in at the last second was a courtesy, an opportunity for them to say they were part of things when the TV cameras started rolling.

Of course, that's what they'd say if it all turned out okay, I thought as Hughie and I went up to the front of the room. If it all went to hell and heads needed to roll, the honchos were never there.

"Morning, ladies and gents," I said. "We've been over this a number of times, but I see a few new faces late to the party, so here's the lowdown."

I turned to the whiteboard beside me and tapped the Sun King's picture.

"This, as everyone knows by now, is our main target, Manuel Perrine. He runs the Tepito Mexican drug cartel, which has been tied to as many as seven hundred murders in the last three years."

"That guy's Mexican?" said some white-haired NYPD chief whom I'd never seen before. It was always the upper-echelon tourists in these meetings who busted the most chops.

I rolled my eyes toward Hughie, prompting him to take the question.

"Actually, he's from French Guiana originally," McDonough said. "In the nineties, his family moved to France, where he became a member of the Naval Commandos, France's version of the Navy SEALs. In the early aughts, he returned to South America and did a stint as a mercenary, training guerrillas for FARC, the narco-terrorist group in Colombia. He's been linked to dozens of FARC kidnappings and murders, as well as a 2001 truck-bomb assassination of a Colombian regional governor, which killed fifteen people."

I jumped in before the chief could interrupt again. "Around 2005, after the Colombian military crackdown, Perrine ended up in Mexico again, working as a mercenary, this time for the various cartels to train their drug mules and enforcers."

Hughie added, "He's one of the guys personally responsible for the escalation of the hyperviolence we've seen over the last few years among the cartels. He militarized these scumbags and has planned, and personally taken part in, several dozen Mexican law enforcement ambushes and assassinations."

"That's why when we make contact, we need to take him down as soon as possible and use wrist and ankle cuffs," I said to the people who would actually take part in the arrest. "This guy might dress like Clinton from *What Not to Wear*, but he's a stone-cold special forces–trained psychopathic killer. You give him a chance, he'll embed a chunk of lead in your brain like he's picking out a silk tie."

"Why is he in New York, again?" said another tourist, a short, pasty FBI lifer who was sitting like an overgrown cave troll on the edge of a desk. "He run out of people to kill in Mexico?"

"Because of this man," I said over the chuckles.

I pointed to a photo of a smiling, heavyset Angel Candelerio on the whiteboard beside the photo of Perrine.

"Candelerio is the head of the Dominicans Forever drug gang, which runs most of the drugs, sex trafficking, and gambling north of Ninety-Sixth Street. Not that you could tell by the image he likes to front. He lives up in Bedford next to Mariah Carey and Martha Stewart and has a chauffeur-driven Lincoln limo and a daughter in NYU law school.

"The FBI Special Surveillance Group is on Candelerio's house as we speak. They're going to follow him to the arrest site here," I said, pointing to a third photograph, which showed Margaritas, Candelerio's Washington Heights restaurant, where the reunion with Perrine was to take place.

"I didn't ask where," the old FBI troll said as he twiddled his thumbs. "I asked why."

"NYPD received info that Candelerio and Perrine are old friends from the same village in French Guiana," Hughie said, taking my back. "Candelerio has connections in the Caribbean and Europe in addition to the city, so we think that with Perrine taking so much heat down in Mexico, he's going to make another move with the help of his old friend."

"But isn't the guy a billionaire?" said the little agent as he lifted a rubber band off the desk and started playing with it. "I mean, Perrine's— what? Late forties? He's financially set. Why not retire? Also, why risk your ass coming into the U.S. at all? Crafty bastards, even evil ones like Perrine here, don't usually act stupid, as a general rule."

"Who knows?" I said to the annoying devil's advocate with a shrug. "He hates America? He thinks he's bulletproof? He's rubbing our noses in it?"

I pointed to the photo of the restaurant again.

"Whatever the reason is," I said, "at noon today, two blocks from where we're sitting, Perrine is due to meet Candelerio. We're going to let Perrine sit down and get comfy, and then we're going to crash the party. We all know our jobs. It's time to do them."

"Sounds good. How's the legal situation?" asked a young, bored-looking FBI SAC as he checked his BlackBerry.

"We already have the paperwork," I said, lifting up the yellow envelope containing Perrine's sealed indictment and the warrant for his arrest, which had been signed by the U.S. District Court.

"All we need now is to deliver it," Hughie said.

Chapter 6

SWEATING UNDER HEAVY Kevlar in a Saint Nicholas Avenue tenement stairwell, I panned my binoculars over a C-Town supermarket and a cell phone store onto Candelerio's restaurant, Margaritas.

It was cold and windy outside, the sky over the jagged skyline of five-story walk-ups the color of a lead pipe. As in all stakeouts, the minutes were going by in geologic time, as if everything in the world had hit slo-mo.

I checked my phone for the hundredth time. The screen said 10:40. Another hour or so to go until noon. A depressing thought came as I remembered the photos of the armed-to-the-teeth Mexican drug dealers and the shot-to-pieces minivan: *High Noon*.

I certainly didn't want the arrest to turn into a showdown, but considering the person we were arresting, I was ready if it did. Like the rest of the task force, I was packing heavy firepower—an M4 assault rifle with a holographic sight, along with my Glock. New York cops aren't necessarily Boy Scouts, but we do like to always be prepared.

The DEA SWAT team, bristling with ballistic shields and MP5 submachine guns, was hidden in a bakery van around the corner, and there were another half dozen backup cops and FBI agents in the building across the street, watching the alley at the restaurant's rear.

We were settled in our blind with the trap set. Now all we needed was for Perrine to walk into it.

"Hey, what's that?" Hughie said, suddenly sitting up at the windowsill beside me.

"What? Where?" I said, frantically swiveling my binoculars left and right, down toward the sidewalk.

"Not the street," McDonough said. "The sound. Listen."

I dropped the Nikon binocs and cocked an

ear out the open stairwell window to catch the heavy driving thump of a dance song coming from somewhere in the wilderness of tenements around us.

"Someone's having a morning disco party. So what?"

"Don't you remember?" McDonough said, bopping his head up and down to the beat. "'Rhythm Is a Dancer.' That's the same song they played that summer we worked together in the nineties. I used to vogue to this jammie."

"Growing up just flat-out isn't going to happen for you, is it, Hughie?" I said, passing my shirtsleeve over my sweat-soaked face.

We continued to watch and wait. A vein twitched along my eye when Hughie's cell phone trilled at eleven on the dot.

The thumbs-up he gave me confirmed it was the FBI operations team up in Westchester County that was surveilling Candelerio. Aerial and ground teams had been covering the Dominican for the last week. This morning we'd brought every local PD from Westchester and the Bronx into the loop in case there was some unforeseen detour and we had to do a traffic stop.

"Candelerio is rolling, headed out toward the Saw Mill River Parkway right on schedule," Hughie said, ending the call. "ETA in thirty. Get this, though. Our spotter said his wife and three girls are with him, and they're all dressed up."

I frowned. We were already doing the arrest in a public place. Having Candelerio's family around would only make things even more complicated.

"Dressed up?" I said. "He's bringing his *family* to meet Perrine?"

McDonough shrugged.

"Who knows with a family of drug dealers?" he said. "Maybe meeting the Sun King is like meeting real royalty to them. How many opportunities do you get to have an audience with a king?"

I went back to my window perch. I pinned the glasses onto every car that slowed, onto every pedestrian who walked past on the sidewalk. With Candelerio on the way, it meant that Perrine would be coming along any moment now.

My heart fluttered into my throat as a kitted-out black Escalade suddenly pulled up in front of the restaurant. A back door popped open, and out came three men. I tried to spot faces, but all I caught were Yankees baseball caps and aviator sunglasses before the three were inside.

"Did anybody see? Is it Perrine? Can anyone confirm ID?" I frantically called over the radio.

"Negative. No confirmation," called the DEA SWAT.

"Not sure," called a cop from the team at the restaurant's rear. "They went in too fast."

"Damn it," I said as Hughie whistled by the window.

"Mike, movement. Six o'clock," he said.

I panned the glasses back to the restaurant, where a dark-skinned Dominican waitress with big silver hoop earrings and short black hair was stepping out onto the sidewalk.

The attractive Rihanna look-alike was named Valentina Jimenez, and she was a cousin of the informant who was helping us out on the case. She'd come out to give us the signal. If Valentina lit a cigarette, it would mean that she had spotted Perrine.

I watched her intently as she stood in front of the restaurant, looking up and down the street.

"Stand by," I said into the radio, ready to give the other teams the green light.

That's when it happened.

Valentina did something, but it wasn't lighting a cigarette.

She glanced back into the restaurant and then bolted in her high heels at top speed down Saint Nicholas Avenue as though she were running for her life.

Chapter 7

"WHAT IN THE NAME of God?" Hughie yelled, giving voice to my thoughts.

"Have her picked up," I said into the radio.

"What does it mean? It was Perrine who just went in there? Did she forget the signal?" Hughie said.

"We still don't know. We have to wait and talk to her," I said. "She could have just gotten spooked."

My cell phone rang a second later.

"I'm sorry. I didn't know what to do, okay? I'm so sorry," Valentina said, sobbing.

"It's okay, Valentina. I'm having you picked up. You're safe. Just listen closely. Was it him? Did Manuel Perrine just come into the restaurant?"

"No. Those men were members of Candelerio's crew. They were just laughing with the manager about how much partying they would be doing today since Candelerio is away. Candelerio isn't coming to lunch. I knew I had to call you, but I was afraid they'd see. You know what they would do to me if they saw me calling a cop? That's why I left. And I'm not going back. I don't care what you do to my cousin. These guys are killers. I can't take working there anymore."

I stared down at the restaurant in disbelief. Candelerio wasn't coming? Which meant Perrine wasn't coming. What did that mean? They were onto us? Were the drug dealers meeting somewhere else?

"Why isn't he coming? Did you hear anything?" I said as calmly as my racing pulse would allow.

"They said it was a family thing. A graduation? Something like that."

A graduation? I thought. This early in the year it would have to be Candelerio's oldest daughter, Daisy, the one at NYU law school. That actually made sense. It explained why Candelerio had brought his family, and why they were all dressed up. Except on the phone for the past month, the drug dealer had said he wanted to meet Perrine at noon today at the restaurant. How did that make sense?

The answer was it didn't. Exactly nothing was going the way we'd expected. I couldn't believe this was happening.

"A squad car is pulling over. Can I please, please, please go home?" my informant said.

"Of course, Valentina. You did good. I'll call you," I said, hanging up.

The metal clang of a passing garbage truck bouncing over potholes in the street rang off the gouged walls and dirty marble steps as I stood there trying to figure out what was happening.

"So?" Hughie said, holding up his hands.

"We were wrong," I said. "Candelerio isn't coming. He's going to his daughter's graduation."

"How is this happening?" Hughie said, speed-tapping the barrel of his M4 as he paced back and forth. "You heard the transcripts. Perrine said the meet's at Margaritas! This is Margaritas. Candelerio is a silent partner in the place. He eats here three times a week."

I slowly went over the case in my mind, especially the telephone transcripts. They were written in a weird mix of Spanish and Creole that had been translated by two different FBI experts. But Hughie was right. In the calls, Perrine kept talking about being at Margaritas. Margaritas at noon.

"Maybe Margaritas isn't a place," I said.

"What is it, then?" Hughie said. "You think Perrine wants to meet Candelerio for a margarita?"

"Maybe it's a code word or something. Does *margarita* mean anything in Spanish?"

"Um . . . tequila and lime juice?" Hughie said, lifting his phone. "I'm the Gaelic expert. Let me ask Agent Perez."

"It's a name of a flower," Hughie said, listening to his phone a moment later. "It means . . . daisy."

We both did a double take as the realization hit us simultaneously.

"Candelerio's daughter!" we said at the same time. "Margarita must mean Daisy, then," Hughie said. "Has to be. But how does that make sense? Perrine wants to see Candelerio's daughter graduate? That's why he came to the States?"

I thought about it. "Maybe he wants to meet in the crowd, or—"

I snapped a finger as I remembered something from the surveillance photographs, something that was out of place. I immediately called our control post back at the precinct.

"There's a picture of Candelerio's family on my desk. Text it to me pronto," I said to the detective manning the shop.

Less than a minute later, my phone vibrated, and Hughie and I looked at the photo, which was tagged with the family members' names. I looked more closely at the oldest daughter's face and smiled.

"I knew it. Look at the oldest one. She has darker skin than the others. And her eyes—she has blue eyes. Both Candelerio and his wife have brown eyes, and she has light blue eyes. That's impossible. How did we miss it?" I said.

"You're right. She even looks like Perrine!" Hughie yelled. "Shit! That's it! That's goddamn it. You're a genius. Daisy must be *Perrine's* daughter."

"That FBI lifer was right," I said. "Perrine isn't

risking his ass coming to the States for money. It's to see his daughter graduate."

Hughie answered his ringing phone.

"Candelerio just passed the exit for Washington Heights and is continuing downtown," he said. "Aerial is staying on him. SWAT wants to know what's what."

"Tell them to saddle up and move 'em out," I said excitedly as I started down the stairs. "We're jumping to plan B now. Looks like we have a graduation to attend."

Chapter 8

TEN MINUTES LATER, OUR four-car task force caravan was gunning it south, sirens ripping, down the West Side Highway.

Hughie was at the wheel as I worked the phone and radio, coordinating with my bosses and the other arrest teams. I don't know which was flying faster, the frazzled cop-radio traffic or the highway's guardrail, zipping an inch past my face at around ninety.

"Thank God you added that ass-covering rider to your arrest report, huh?" Hughie shouted as he tried to set a new land speed record. He gave a rebel yell as the traffic cone we clipped sailed over the guardrail into the Hudson River.

My partner seemed to be enjoying himself, but I wasn't feeling it. Not even close. I'd called NYU law school and learned that graduation was to take place at 12:30 today, but not at the law school.

It was taking place at Madison Square Garden!

Thousands of people were supposed to be there, and we were somehow supposed to pluck Perrine from the crowd? Safely? The towers of midtown began to loom on my left. I didn't know how or even if that could be done.

We killed the sirens when we got off the West Side Highway at Thirty-Fourth Street. It took a few minutes to weave through the heavy Manhattan gridlock to the Garden, on Seventh Avenue at Thirty-Second Street. As we turned the corner, we could see that people were already pouring into the famed arena—smiling, well-dressed families holding balloons and video cameras, surrounding twentysomethings in black-and-purple gowns.

Even if we spotted Perrine at this thing, there had to be a million ways in and out of the Garden, I thought, rapidly scanning faces. It was way too porous. We needed a way to box in the cartel head. But how?

I still hadn't figured it out as we circled the block and pulled in behind the disguised FBI SWAT van onto the apron of a fire station driveway on Thirty-First.

"Bad news, Mike. We don't have the go-ahead to do this. Not even a little," Hughie said after he got back from a quick powwow with the SWAT guys. "The bosses are going nuts because there are thousands of potential lawyers and lawsuits in there, not to mention the mayor, who's actually the keynote speaker. What do you think?"

I took a long moment to do just that, given that this was the biggest arrest in my career. Taking down a suspect in the middle of a graduation would certainly make a lot of waves. Especially at the notoriously *über*liberal NYU law school, where they probably had courses called Cops: Friend or Enemy? and The Art and Science of Claiming Police Brutality.

But NYU or no NYU, if Perrine was in there, the time to strike was in the middle of the ceremony. Safe in the crowd, he'd only be thinking about his daughter and how proud he was. We'd need to use that. Use his vulnerability. Because afterward, he'd only be thinking about one thing. Getting away.

"So what's up? You want to wait?" Hughie said.

"Hell, no!" I finally said.

"Good," said McDonough, rubbing his hands together, his Irish eyes a-smiling. "Me, neither, Church Boy. What do we do?"

I thought about it for another minute. Then I had it. It was a crazy idea, but this was a crazy time. Not to mention a crazy, extremely violent criminal we were up against. We needed to grab this guy. Badly. It had been a while since the good guys had put one up on the board.

"We have all the phones for all the Candelerios, right? The wife and the kids?" I said.

"Control does," Hughie said, scrolling through his phone.

"Get me Daisy Candelerio's number, then," I said, giving one of my own smiling Irish eyes a wink as I took out my phone. "Least I could do is send the graduate a congratulatory text."

Chapter 9

AFTER RISING FROM THE dregs of a third-world hellhole called Kourou, French Guiana, Manuel Perrine, a.k.a. the Sun King, vowed to never again go anywhere near its poverty, its filth, its putrid stink.

Promises, promises, Perrine thought as he vigorously washed his hands inside a crowded Madison Square Garden men's room.

Too many mimosas and cappuccinos on his chartered Global Express jet into Teterboro Airport was the reason for this unfortunate pit stop. Or is it an enlarged prostate? he wondered with a stab of depression as he remembered his upcoming forty-eighth birthday.

Like many men of means, Perrine obsessed

over germs, disease, his general health. With more money in accounts scattered throughout the world than even he could possibly spend, the only thing that could curtail the full, well-deserved enjoyment of his accumulated riches was illness. Which was why he and his personal physician were constantly on guard.

To dispel his morbid thoughts, and take himself away from his even more morbid current surroundings, Perrine closed his eyes and envisioned his luxury penthouse suite in the Fairmont Le Château Frontenac in Quebec City, where he had been staying since fleeing Mexico. In his mind, he saw white everywhere. White furniture, white towels, white bubbles in the pristine white marble bathtub.

Hearing the clamor of coughs and wall-mounted dryers and flushing toilets all around him, he truly couldn't return soon enough.

The Sun King winced as he glanced at himself in the mirror. He was completely bald now. He'd had some work done on his eyes to change their shape, and was wearing brown contact lenses to disguise their color. To further alter his appearance on this trip—which he hoped was his last ever to the U.S.—he'd intentionally put on an unhealthy thirty pounds, which gave him a disgusting double chin.

But, because he was known for his style, the greatest offense to his sensibilities was that he could wear no Prada, no Yves, no Caraceni hand-tailored suits today. The suit he wore now was an ill-fitting, off-the-rack, green gabardine atrocity from a New Jersey Kohl's department store that made him look like he drove something for a living. He needed to *not* stand out for once, and in his puke-colored American rags, he'd succeeded beyond his wildest dreams.

Coming back out into the buzzing Madison Square Garden concourse, Perrine exchanged a glance with Marietta, who was leaning against the wall, watching his flank and rear. In Mexico, he rode with a rolling armada of men and trucks, but that might look a little conspicuous here in the country where he was wanted for double murder, so today he had Marietta, and a few handpicked men, with him.

Thankfully, Marietta was as good as a small army. She was deadly with a gun, a knife—even her hands, if it came down to it. The tall, thin brunette looked about as dangerous as a kindergarten teacher, and yet she was an expert in the Brazilian martial art capoeira, and had the strongest and quickest hands of any woman he'd ever come across. He'd seen more than once the surprise and pain in an unmannerly cartel soldier's eyes after she was forced to show him who was truly boss. His lovely Marietta never hesitated to give new meaning to the term "bitch slap."

Now she, too, was sporting a garish American getup—a loud flowered print dress, also courtesy of the Paramus Kohl's—that hid those amazingly long legs of hers. Perrine allowed himself a chuckle. So different from the all-white Chanel and Vuitton and Armani ensembles that were the dark, statuesque beauty's signature. They were truly slumming here in New York City.

But all in all, his daughter Margarita—or Daisy, as she liked to be called, now that she was an American—was worth it, Perrine reminded himself. She was the only one of his many children who could make him feel . . . what? Tenderness? Admiration? Hope? Love?

That's why he had sent her away at the age of

seven to live in America with his friend Angel. He never wanted her to know the ugly reality of what he did for a living. He'd been a frog his whole life. His daughter Daisy would now be a princess, even if it killed him.

Perrine followed the crowd of clueless American bourgeois sheep into the arena. He was sitting on the left side of the cavernous theater, as far away from his friend Angel Candelerio as possible. He knew his old friend Angel was smart and loyal and discreet, but there could be no room for risk now. Perrine would hear his daughter's speech and be gone. His waiting car would take them directly out to Teterboro, where the jet was gassed and ready. He'd be back in Quebec City by dinner, and Marietta would be back in her white Armani, showing off those legs. For a little while, at least. Until he tore the dress off his brutal, beautiful bodyguard.

As the lights of the dark, wide theater dimmed, and "Pomp and Circumstance" began to play, Perrine allowed himself a moment of long-awaited pride. Though he had money and was intelligent and well read, he had no illusions about the fact that the nature of his work and the general hypocrisy of mankind would always cause him to be seen as a thug. Daisy would rise above all that, he knew. With all his resources at her command, she would ascend above all the savage but necessary things he had ever done, just as a butterfly rises from a swamp. She was his one pure and sure thing.

Sitting here among the American-educated elite, he couldn't help but note what a far cry it was from his hometown, Kourou, near Devil's Island, the place made infamous by the film *Papillon*. Some said his mother's people were actually descended from Henri Charrière, the famous escape artist, Papillon himself.

Perrine secretly liked the idea of being a descendant of Charrière, a French navy veteran and criminal like himself, who never took anything from anyone. He even liked the American actor Steve McQueen, who had played Charrière in *Papillon*. Like Perrine, and unlike almost any American after him, McQueen had had some style.

As the tune played on, Perrine looked for his daughter's always smiling face among the ranks of dark-robed graduates filing in. Like most of the happy fathers around him, he took out his video camera and hit the record button before raising it. He panned and zoomed the camera, but he couldn't see his daughter. He wasn't worried. As the valedictorian, she was going to speak. He pointed the camera at the stage. His little Daisy. He couldn't be more proud or eager to hear what she had to say.

The first speaker was the school president, a short, effeminate man who went on and on about modern America's greatest peril, long-term climate change.

Climate change? Perrine thought, stifling laughter. Forget the fact that as the eunuch blathered, corrupt U.S. politicians were busy burying the nation in trillions upon trillions of dollars in debt. Forget the fact that instead of getting a job or having families, bands of young faithless and clueless American citizens wandered around the dilapidated remnants of its once-bustling cities, so usefully "occupying" things. No, no. Save the planet. Of course. Bravo!

Perrine was still smiling when a robed student suddenly appeared next to the speaker. The president cleared his throat before reading the paper the student handed him.

"I'm sorry. Excuse me. I have an announcement. Will the family of Daisy Candelerio please come to the medical office out on the main concourse? That's Daisy Candelerio's family. This is a medical emergency."

Perrine sat up, wide-eyed, as a surprised buzz went through the crowd. His video camera rolled off his lap and hit the floor as he looked back. Marietta, sitting behind him, already had her cell phone to her ear, the concerned expression on her face mirroring his thoughts.

Daisy? What was this? Something was wrong with Daisy!?

Chapter 10

PERCHED ON A COLD metal stool at the rear of Madison Square Garden's tiny medical office, I rolled my neck to relieve the tension. I gave up on the fifth try and patted my Glock, tucked under the borrowed EMT shirt I was wearing.

Like the rest of the task force, I was most definitely "Glocked" and loaded for bear by that point. Bagging a grizzly would have been simple compared to the difficulty and danger of trying to take down a lethal billionaire cartel head. In a crowded Madison Square Garden, no less!

Actually, the first part of my plan had gone off hitch-free. By using the podium announcement and false text messages and phone calls, we'd been able to lure Perrine's daughter and the rest of the Candelerio family to the commandeered medical office.

Before they knew what was happening, our arrest teams swooped in and rushed them outside through the office's back door into the guarded driveway of Madison Square Garden's midblock entrance, where all the VIP athletes and performers entered and left. We'd made sure to take all cell phones before we buttoned down each of the loud, aggressively resisting family members into waiting squad cars.

I knew why they were so upset. Once they spotted our DEA and NYPD raid jackets and assault rifles, they knew exactly what was going on. Who we were going after.

Perrine's childhood friend Angel Candelerio was especially emotional, so much so that he had to be pepper-sprayed in order to be subdued. The man knew what he was looking at—if Perrine was caught, he was the one who'd be blamed by the cartel. Probably not the best position to be in, considering he worked for an organization in which reprimands were usually delivered by death squads.

Sitting on the medical office examination

table beside me, wearing a borrowed NYU law school purple-and-black graduation gown, was a female NYPD detective named Alicia Martinez. She rolled her eyes as I put a stethoscope on her wrist for the thousandth time.

"How am I doing? Do I make a convincing doc?" I said.

"Just perfect, Mike," the young cop said with another eye roll. "Like the pre-Darfur George Clooney."

"He's Clooney!?" Hughie said in outrage as he opened the window of the office to get some much-needed fresh air. "No way. I'm Clooney. He's the other one—Clooney's bald, caring, nerdy friend."

With Detective Martinez's back to the medical office's glass front door, we were hoping that someone passing on the interior concourse might mistake her for Perrine's daughter. Our bait was set. Now all we needed was for Perrine to bite. If Perrine had gone to all this trouble to sneak into the States to see his daughter graduate, there was no way he would hear about a medical emergency and leave without trying to find out if she was okay.

Above the examination table on the wall hung a poster of the Heimlich maneuver. I glanced at the first panel, in which there was an illustration of a man holding both hands at his throat to indicate that he was choking.

With our trap set and the biggest arrest in New York City in a decade on the line, the question now was, would *I* choke?

Chapter 11

I GLANCED OUT INTO the hallway of the arena and spotted giant posters of Knicks basketballs and Rangers hockey pucks and boxers squaring off. I couldn't believe all this was going down here at the Garden, of all places, but I guess it was appropriate to have this boxing mecca be the site of the heavyweight fight between the cartels and U.S. law enforcement.

"Hey, Hughie," I said to my partner. "You were in Golden Gloves, right? You ever fight here?"

"Nope," Hughie said. "They only had the finals here. I never made it that far, but my oldest brother Fergus did."

"What happened?"

Hughie squinted at the floor.

"Some monster from Queens knocked him out in the second round," he said. "The beast pounded his ear against the side of his head so hard, I swear to God it looked like a veal cutlet. He couldn't hear for a month."

I shook my head.

"Forget I asked," I said as the tactical radio in my ear squawked.

"Okay, Mike. Heads up. I think I see something," the DEA SWAT team head, Patrick Zaretski, told me in my earpiece.

Zaretski was upstairs in the Garden security office, working the cameras. The other arrest teams were next door in an empty office, waiting to take down Perrine at the first sight of him.

"What's up, Patrick? Talk to me," I said.

"It looks like you're being watched. I can just make out a person on the concourse pointing a video camera at the medical office door."

"Is it Perrine?" I said excitedly.

"I can't tell. It's a big old-style camera. Hold it. The subject just put the camera down and is heading directly for your location. Be advised, the subject is heading right for you."

This was it, I thought as I heard the front door of the office open.

Now or never.

Do or die.

"You just need to breathe, Miss Candelerio," I said in a loud voice as I stood blocking Detective Martinez's face from view of the front door. "Stay with me, okay? The ambulance is coming. It's on its way."

"Excuse me. I'm sorry. You can't come in here now. We're having an emergency," I heard the female cop posing as the receptionist say through the open door behind me.

"I'm here to see Miss Daisy Candelerio. Is she all right? What's happened to her?" said a Spanish-accented voice.

What the hell? Something was wrong. It wasn't Perrine.

It was a *female* voice.

When I turned, I spotted a young dark-haired woman in a flowered dress. She was trying to peek around the receptionist to look at Detective Martinez.

An alarm went off inside my head as I stepped into the front room and saw how tall and striking the young woman was. The dress looked cheap, but the woman wearing it was extremely poised, her lustrous hair expensively maintained. She looked like an actress or a model.

Billionaire bait, I thought. Something told me this tall drink of water was with Perrine. He must have sent his girlfriend in first to scout things out.

We'd bag her and her phone and then bag Perrine. My trap was working. Perrine was even closer now, so close I could almost smell his French aftershave.

"Did you say you're Daisy's family?" I said breathlessly as I rushed toward the woman and took her by the elbow. "Thank God. The poor young woman is having a seizure. We need to stabilize her until the ambulance arrives. You need to come back here. Please, she needs someone she knows to talk to her in order to keep her conscious."

The young woman glanced in my eyes, trying to read my face as I brought her into the room. Her eyes were a light amber, I noticed, almost gold, an eye color I'd never seen before. Her flawless skin glowed like fresh cream and even in flats, she was at eye level with my six-two.

Definitely an exotic piece of arm candy.

She bristled when we stepped into the exam room and Detective Martinez turned around. Hughie stood up from the stool on the other side of the table, dangling a set of handcuffs on his finger.

"Yes, Virginia," Hughie said with a smile. "There is a Santa Claus after all."

She did something weird next. The lovely brunette's gold eyes swiveled to Hughie and then back to Detective Martinez then back to Hughie again and then she burst out laughing.

She must have really thought something was funny because after a moment, she was shaking and cackling, wiping tears of hilarity out of her eyes.

Hughie and I shook our heads at her fevered, high-pitched gigglefest. Was she nuts? I thought. High on her boyfriend's drugs?

Still laughing, she broke my grip on her elbow. She actually doubled over as she leaned against the right-hand wall. That's when I noticed, through her lustrous dark hair, that she had something in her ear. A curious piece of flesh-colored plastic.

A piece that looked just like my tactical microphone.

A stark and paralyzing horror gripped hold of me right then as the woman's laughter cut off in midcackle.

Two things happened next, almost simultaneously.

"Get out!" the doubled-over woman screamed into her purse.

Then her purse exploded.

Chapter 12

IT WAS A FLASHBANG grenade, I learned later.

When it went off in the woman's purse a foot away from my face, I didn't know what had happened. Or where I was or even who I was for a few seconds. I didn't know anything except the burning smell of cordite in my nose, the blinding, vibrating stars of light in my eyes, and an excruciatingly painful ringing in my ears.

As I struggled to keep my balance, I heard a rhythmic, low-pitched thudding through the ringing sound. At first I thought it might have been some construction outside. Then I saw bright licks of light blossoming in my shaky vision and Detective Martinez, her face spurting blood, sliding off the exam table and falling with a crash at my feet.

Still struggling with what I was seeing, I looked up to find the dark young woman holding a gun, a little black polymer machine pistol with a ribbon of smoke curling from its suppressor. As she swung the gun at me from the other side of the table, I yelled incoherently as I tried to draw my own gun. Time seemed to slow, the air itself to change, as if I were suddenly swimming in Jell-O. My eyes focused on one thing as my palm finally grazed the checkered grip of my holstered service weapon—the black bore of the woman's gun as it stopped dead level with my face.

The next thing I knew, I felt a weight slam into me. I thought it was a bullet, but I was wrong. It was Hughie tackling me, taking me down like a linebacker sacking a quarterback. He knocked out my breath as he hit me up top, pushing me sideways, away from the front of the gun.

Gasping for breath, I looked up from the floor to see Hughie rising and turning. He sent the exam-table mat flying as he launched himself upward, reaching out empty-handed for the gun and the girl.

"Ten thirteen! Ten thirteen! Ten thirteen!" I started yelling. Or thought I was yelling, because I still couldn't hear anything, not even myself. Then the violent thudding ripped the air again, and Hughie stopped in his tracks. There was a nauseating, wet, splattering sound as his head snapped back, as if he'd been punched.

I'd finally cleared my gun and was getting to my feet when Hughie's lifeless body toppled back on top of me. As we went down in a heap again, I felt the slugs hit the back of Hughie's vest. I also felt Hughie's blood, warm and gushing, on the back of my neck and down the back of my shirt. I finally stuck out the Glock from underneath Hughie's arm and pulled the trigger—and pulled the trigger and pulled the trigger.

When the slide slapped all the way back after the last round, I poked my head up and saw that the woman was, amazingly, gone. Had she run back out? I thought as I quickly reloaded my Glock.

In the hallway, I could see one of the female detectives screaming into her radio as the gold-eyed woman leaped up from the other side of the exam table, where she'd been crouching.

But before I could move, before I could even breathe, she was past me.

She took three running steps, dove out the medical office's window headfirst, and was gone.

Chapter 13

I ROLLED OUT FROM underneath Hughie. Through the stench of blood and gun smoke, I knelt over my friend on the floor. I reached a hand out above his blood-soaked hair as if to somehow mend the gaping red-black holes there. But I couldn't because he was dead. Detective Martinez was dead. Everyone was dead.

I felt a hand on my shoulder. It was one of the DEA SWAT guys, mouthing something into his crackling radio. Without thinking about it, I holstered my Glock and found myself ripping away the M4 assault rifle he held in his hand. Then I went to the open window and threw myself out of it.

The hard plastic butt of the gun almost

knocked me out as I went ass over teakettle and landed hard on my back on the asphalt. As I got up, I saw a woman's shoe in front of me. Then I looked up and saw the tall pale woman it belonged to running hard in her bare feet fifty feet north of me, down the alley outside the medical office window.

As I started running after the woman, a black Lincoln Town Car screeched off the street and came to a jarring halt at the alley's mouth. A thin Spanish driver got out, calling and waving like a maniac at the woman. I brought the rifle to my shoulder just as the tinted rear passenger-side window of the Lincoln zipped down and the baffled holes of a gigantic gun barrel appeared.

I dropped as if someone had yanked my ankles from behind and rolled behind a fire hydrant as the huge gun opened up. In that narrow alley, the report of it was unreal. Concrete dust stung my eyes as a fluttering deluge of lead chewed up the pavement and ripped at the hydrant like an invisible jackhammer.

As the heavy, deafening rounds pounded and tore apart everything around me, I had what I guess you would call a near-death experience. In the awesomely violent rumble of the gun and the way it shook the air, I detected a God-like message. To keep perfectly still was life. To move even the tiniest part of my body was instant death.

I was thinking how wise the message was and how the post office could forward my mail to Behind the Fire Hydrant, Alleyway, Madison Square Garden, New York City, when I remembered Hughie. In my mind, I saw him get shot again, saw the Heimlich poster on the wall behind him get splattered with his blood.

Lying on my back, I flicked the switch on the M4 to full auto. Then, when there was a pause in the firing, I swung up on my knee in a firing position.

The thin driver was getting into the front seat, right next to the woman who'd killed Hughie, when I shot him three times in the side of his head. Then I put the rear passenger-side window behind the red dot of my rifle's holographic sight and opened up. I poured about a dozen shots into the window, then stood up in the awesome silence and began to run.

Running toward the Lincoln, I noticed for the

first time that there were other people in the alley, construction workers crouched alongside a wall beside a UPS guy.

"Ground! On the ground!" I kept yelling.

I slowed as I circled the Lincoln behind the barrel of the assault rifle. The driver I'd killed had his bloody head leaning out the window as though he were checking the front tire. Under the 30-caliber machine gun in the backseat, I saw the shooter, a pudgy, middle-aged Spanish man in a silk-screened T-shirt. He was on his back, moaning, coughing, and spitting up blood. More blood gurgled out the side of his right hand, where he clutched at the hole in his throat.

It was only then that I noticed that the doors on the other side of the car were wide open.

No!

The woman who'd killed Hughie was gone.

Someone cried out as I backpedaled into the street and swung the rifle east, down Thirty-Third Street. On the north side of the street, between a couple of work vans, I could see a stocky, light-skinned black guy in a dress shirt and green slacks running hard, arms pumping, like a sprinter.

I raised the gun, but the sprinting bastard turned the corner before I could shoot him. Though I'd only caught a glimpse of his profile, I'd studied his picture hard enough to instantly know who it was.

I'd finally laid eyes on Manuel Perrine.

Chapter 14

I COULD HEAR BACKUP approaching hard behind me when I tossed my rifle into the window of the Lincoln over the dead driver. I opened the door of the still-chugging vehicle, pulled out the dead criminal, and let him drop into the gutter. I did the same thing to the dying shooter in the backseat, too. Pulled him out and let him fall facedown onto the street. Not standard NYPD practice for wounded suspects, but I was in a hurry, not to mention in a daze of adrenaline-fueled mental and emotional shock.

I hopped in and slammed the accelerator against the floor as I dropped the Lincoln into reverse.

"Out of the way! Move! Move!" I screamed as

I sped backward with my hand on the horn, knowing what a challenge it was to navigate the impenetrable gridlock of midtown Manhattan in the *correct* direction.

I slalomed around a double-decker tourist bus and a Nissan Altima yellow taxi, then drove on the sidewalk until I finally arrived at the corner of Seventh Avenue, where Perrine had headed.

Through the rear window, I saw Perrine about a block north. He had his head down and was still booking and dodging through the clogged crowd of pedestrians as though he were trying out for running back for the Dallas Cowboys. He moved fast for a big man, I thought as I floored the Lincoln—still in reverse—north up southbound Seventh Avenue.

I was met with a sheer wall of horn blasts as I carved the vehicle through the onslaught of oncoming traffic. I missed three cars before I sideswiped a plumbing van and then an eighteen-wheeler mail truck. A bike messenger actually took a swing at me through the open window after I came within a foot of putting him under the Lincoln's back wheels.

Then Perrine was right there in back of me,

running diagonally across the intersection of Thirty-Fourth and Seventh.

I revved the engine and was almost on top of him as he dove and made the northeast corner. I was still seriously thinking about just jumping the curb and hitting him with the back end of the car, but then I noticed the hundreds of innocent people standing there on one of Manhattan's busiest corners, and I hesitated before slamming on the brake.

I pulled my Glock, cocking it as I jumped out onto the sidewalk. I watched as Perrine disappeared into the store on the corner, underneath a pair of enormous electronic billboards.

"Shit," I said when I saw a giant red star appear on the billboard screen and realized where Perrine had just headed.

"Where are you, Mike? Where are you?" I heard one of the arrest team members yelling over my crackling radio.

"Macy's. Thirty-Fourth Street," I yelled as I ran. "Send backup."

And another miracle while you're at it, I thought as I flung open the door to the world's largest department store.

Chapter 15

IT TOOK ME A couple of moments of blinking like mad to adjust to the store's dim mood lighting. I sprinted up a short flight of stairs, cosmetics counters and jewelry cases blurring on both sides of me. Between the displays, shocked-looking shoppers and tourists stood staring, most of them women and kids.

"NYPD! Get out of the store!" I yelled, waving my Glock as I ran.

I was running past the Louis Vuitton bags into men's sportswear when I heard a scream from the bottom of a wooden escalator to my left. I took its moving stairs down two by two into the Cellar—the food and kitchenware section of the store. The sickly sweet smell of gourmet coffee and candy assaulted my nostrils as I breathed hard, panning left and right with my gun.

There was a clatter of metal behind me, and I turned around to see the glass entrance to the store's basement restaurant. The sound must have come from the restaurant kitchen. I rushed inside the wood-paneled space.

"Oh, my gawd! Oh, my gawd!" a massively overweight blond woman kept saying. She was kneeling beside a slim blond waiter who was laid out on the floor by the bar. The guy's head seemed wrong. It was twisted too far around, almost looking over his own back.

"Where?" I yelled, and saw a dozen shocked customers pointing toward the still-swinging door to the kitchen. I ran past a sizzling flattop grill toward an open door at the kitchen's opposite end. There were dusty metal stairs on the other side of it, with heavy footsteps hammering up them. I followed up the stairs, and as I made the top, I finally saw Perrine again, the back of his dress shirt soaked through with sweat, as he bolted down a corridor piled with folded cardboard boxes.

"Freeze!" I yelled.

He didn't listen. An alarm went off and day-light flashed as he slammed open a fire-exit door on the street level. I was coming through that same exit onto Thirty-Fifth Street a split second later when I got kicked in the face. My right cheekbone felt shattered as my Glock flew from my hand. I watched it ricochet off the base of a pay-phone kiosk before skidding across the side-walk and coming to rest under a sanitation department Prius.

I was diving for it when Perrine dropped from the awning over the door where he was hanging and kicked me in the kidney. I whirled around, swinging at his face. I just missed as he bobbed his head back. He bounced back again on the balls of his feet, and before I knew what was going on, he kicked me on the inside of my thigh so hard I thought he broke it. He made a high kind of karate scream as he elbowed me in the face and knocked me to my knees.

As he grabbed the back of my head and kneed me in the forehead, I remembered something important. My hand went to my ankle, and I pulled free the backup pepper spray canister I always carry. I depressed its trigger and proceeded to mace the living crap out of him. As he backpedaled, clawing at his burning eyes, I reached for the collapsible baton I carried on my other ankle and flicked it open. With a loud, whip-cracking sound, the ball on the metal baton's tip made contact with the bridge of Perrine's nose.

He didn't seem in the mood for any more karate after that. He dropped to his knees, blood from his broken nose spraying the sidewalk, as he screamed and blinked and shook his head.

Chapter 16

I FINALLY BROUGHT HIM all the way down to the concrete with a knee to his back and cuffed him. As Perrine moaned and thrashed around helplessly, I fished my Glock out from under the city-approved, low-carbon-emission sanitation vehicle.

I stood up and looked around. There had been hundreds of people on the corner of Thirty-Fourth Street, but here at the dirty service entrance at the back of Macy's, there was absolutely no one. I knelt on Perrine's neck and jammed my gun in his ear.

I thought about things for a little while then. Mostly about my friend Hughie, back in the medical office, with his head blown apart. Dead.

No more beers. No more Yankees games. No more deep-sea fishing trips on his City Island rust bucket with his twenty nieces and nephews. The life of the party was gone now. Forever gone. Forever cold.

I moved the barrel of my gun to Perrine's brain stem. Two pounds of pull on the trigger under my finger, two measly little pounds here on this dim, narrow, deserted street, was all it would take to avenge Hughie and rid the world of this instrument of evil.

I looked up. It had been overcast earlier in the morning, but now I saw through the gaps of the dark line of rooftops above me a sky of immaculate bright blue. I could also see the top of the Empire State Building, iconic and massive, its constellation of set-back windows like a million square eyes staring down at me, waiting to see what I would do.

But I couldn't do it. I wanted to, but I couldn't. I took the gun off Perrine's skull pan after another second, and then arriving squad cars were screeching behind me. Over the sirens, I heard Perrine say something. He leaned up from where I sat on top of him and craned his neck around to look into my eyes as he uttered one word.

"Coward," he said, and then strong hands were helping me up as the sound of helicopter blades whapped at the late-spring air.

Chapter 17

WHEN THE REST OF the task force team arrived, they were very concerned about me. The line-of-duty death of a close colleague was reason enough by itself to be worried about a person's emotional health, and on top of that, I had shot two suspects. They took away my gun and buttoned me up in the SWAT van until an ambulance arrived.

I listened through the door of the van and learned that the waiter in the Macy's restaurant was dead. When he'd tried to stop Perrine from coming in, the drug dealer had snapped the twenty-three-year-old kid's neck in front of fifty witnesses. That bothered me almost as much as Hughie's death. I should have killed the son of a bitch when I had the chance.

I guess my colleagues were right to be worried about my stability because the second the ambulance pulled away from the curb to go to the hospital, I jumped off the gurney and put the med tech in the back in a headlock until the driver agreed to let me out.

I hit the corner of Broadway and just started walking. It was a nice day for a walk. Three o'clock; in the low sixties with a blue sky; the clear light sparkling off the glass midtown buildings. I didn't know where the hell I was going. I just needed to move.

First, I went up to Times Square, then crosstown, past Bryant Park, then up Madison Avenue.

A dazed couple of hours later, one of the security guys at Saint Patrick's Cathedral gave me a look as I pushed in through the large bronze doors on Fifth Avenue.

No wonder he was concerned. With my friend's blood still flecked on my cheek and my hair standing up, I'd been turning heads all afternoon. Like I was a movie star. Charlie Sheen, maybe. Or Jack Nicholson from *The Shining*.

When I showed the guard my shield, he still

looked worried, but in the end, he let me walk past him up the cathedral's center aisle.

I collapsed in a pew halfway to the altar. I could hear a tourist Mass going on, the soft melodious voice of an African priest. I took comfort in it, in all of it. The still, silent darkness. The jewel-like light of the stained glass windows. I sat there for a long time, thinking about Hughie and about friendship and sacrifice.

Who would take Hughie's place? I thought. But I knew the answer. The answer was no one.

I was tired. My body, my mind, my heart, and my soul so weary. I was not in a good place. I thought about calling my grandfather Seamus up at the lake house, but I was afraid I'd get Mary Catherine or one of the kids. I just couldn't talk to them now. No way—not like this.

I looked up high into the cathedral arches, toward the heaven that no one wanted to believe in anymore. I took out my shield. I turned the golden piece of metal through my fingers before I placed it down on the pew beside me and spun it. "God bless you, Hughie. God bless you, Church Boy," I whispered as it came to a stop.

Then I put my head down on the fragrant wood and I cried like a baby as I prayed for my friend and for the world.

Chapter 18

AFTER ANOTHER TWENTY MINUTES or so of having a nervous breakdown, I wiped my eyes and got the heck out of there before the guys from Bellevue showed.

Outside, I decided to make another pilgrimage through the rush-hour crush. It was to one of Hughie's favorite places, O'Lunney's Times Square Pub. I sat at the bar, watching a hurling game on the TV as I pounded down three pints of bracing Guinness. By the time Sligo beat Waterford by the head-scratching score of a goal *and* three points, I'd managed to avoid crying even once. I was making real progress.

Absolutely shot from the arrest and all my

walking, I took a cab home to my West End Avenue apartment. As much as I love my huge family, I was very happy to find it silent and empty. The day I'd just had and the horrors I'd just seen were things I didn't want to share with anyone. Not ever.

I went back to my room and took the longest, hottest shower in history. Then I did what any self-respecting stressed-out cop would do. I got dressed and made myself a cup of coffee and went back to work.

First on my to-do list was to drive out to Woodlawn in my unmarked PD car to tell Hughie's family. By the time I drove down the street, I knew from all the cars and the lights blazing that Hughie's family had already been told, thank God.

Coming out of the car, I saw two of his brothers, Eamon and Fergus, smoking on the stoop in their FDNY uniforms. I remembered sitting on the same stoop on Saturday mornings in my polyester Little League jersey waiting for Hughie so we could walk up to Van Cortlandt Park for our games. I hugged both brothers and offered my condolences before I explained what happened, how Hughie had saved my life.

"Out like a man," Fergus said, wiping a tear. "He always had balls. Too many, maybe. Well, he's with Pop now."

"But is that such a good thing?" Eamon said, wiping his eyes and flicking his cigarette out into the street. "The crazy old bastard probably already has him training, making him do chin-ups on Saint Peter's gate."

We were laughing at that when a frail and haggard old woman in a flowered housecoat appeared at the door.

"Michael Bennett, is that you?" Hughie's mom said in her thick Northern Ireland accent as she beamed at me.

Hughie had told me that she had recently been diagnosed with Alzheimer's, and the brothers were trying to make arrangements for her to move in with one of them.

"I'm so sorry, Mrs. McDonough," I said, gently taking her tiny hands.

"Don't be sorry," she said, staring at me with her rheumy blue eyes. "The party is just starting. Is he with you? Is Hughie with you? All my boys are here except for my baby, Hughie."

I stood there speechless, holding her skinny hands, until Fergus took them from me and led his poor old mother back inside.

Chapter 19

IT WAS ABOUT NINE o'clock when I finally pulled up in front of the Thirty-Fourth Precinct again. I spotted two news vans on the corner as I went inside. After the broad-daylight midtown shootout and the deaths of three cops, I had a funny feeling I'd be seeing more of them.

Upstairs, the cops on the task force team were filling out paperwork. Every eye in the room swiveled on me as I came through the door, as though I'd just come back from the dead.

"Okay, what's the scoop, troops?" I said, ignoring the gawking.

After someone gave me back my gun, they told me the feds had Perrine in the federal lockup downtown, near Centre Street. He'd already lawyered up and wasn't talking to anyone. Of the attractive young woman who had murdered Hughie, Detective Martinez, and the Midtown South beat cop at the booth, there was no sign.

"Press conference is set for tomorrow down at Fed Plaza," the SWAT leader, Patrick Zaretski, told me. "Everyone will understand if you don't want to be there."

"You kidding me? I love press conferences. I mean, never waste a crisis, right?" I said. "It's just too bad Detective Martinez and Hughie won't be able to make it."

But the longest day of my life wasn't over.

I was at the end of one of the paper-covered tables, filling out incident reports and calling up my various bosses to assure them I hadn't completely cracked up, when we heard the noise. It was from outside, down on Broadway—a loud metal thump, followed by tires shrieking and then a long, wailing scream.

I ran downstairs and saw a form sprawled facedown between two unmarked police department Chevys. It was a young woman, her black skirt completely torn on one side, her white shirt covered in blood. I knelt beside her and then reared back as I saw the short black hair and the face framed by silver hoop earrings.

It was Valentina Jimenez, my informant. After I checked for a pulse that I knew I wouldn't find, I looked at the deep ligature burns along her wrists. There were cigarette holes along her collarbone and two star-shaped, point-blank bullet wounds in her right and left cheeks. She'd been thoroughly tortured before someone had executed her.

Instead of getting angry as I knelt there, all I felt was numbing coldness spreading from my chest to the rest of my body.

This was payback for the arrest, I realized. This was Perrine showing me what he could do.

"Coward" was right, I thought. I should have pulled the trigger when I had the chance. If I had, this girl would probably still be alive.

After a minute, I did the only thing there was left to do. I took off my suit jacket and laid it over the poor girl as I sat down beside her.

Chapter 20

THERE WERE FLOWERS IN the shape of the Yankees logo, flowers in the form of an American flag, and green, white, and gold flowers arranged in the shape of a Celtic cross.

Hughie's casket sat in the center of them, candlelight shining on its closed, varnished pine lid. There was music playing from the funeral parlor speakers overhead—Samuel Barber's Adagio for Strings, that crushing, ineffably sad classical piece from the movie *Platoon*.

Not that any help was needed to produce crushing, ineffable sadness today, I thought as I signed the visitors' book.

I'd been to Irish wakes before, but this one was outrageous. Half the Hibernian people in

New York seemed to have made the pilgrimage to Woodlawn. A three-block-long line of mourners stood on McLean Avenue waiting to pay Hughie their respects. An FDNY fire truck stood outside the funeral parlor next to cop cars from New York and Yonkers and Westchester, their spinning lights flashing red, white, and blue on the regiments of sad, pale faces.

I'd just come from Detective Martinez's wake out in Brooklyn and had another wake for the Midtown South cop to hit before tomorrow's two funerals. I hadn't seen this many funeral parlors since 9/11. Or sadness. Or broken people.

My bosses had forced me to speak to a PD shrink for a psychological debriefing. Though I didn't hear word one of what the nice doctor woman tried to tell me, as I came out of her office, I decided that I wasn't allowed to feel bad about what Hughie had done for me.

His act of courage was so incredible and selfless, all I could do was be happy and in awe of it. All I could do was try to make myself live up to his sacrifice. It wasn't going to happen, but I had to try.

The family had laid out about five hundred

photographs of Hughie around the funeral parlor. Hughie in swimming pools; in Santa Claus suits. Hughie putting his fingers up behind his brothers' heads. I was in a few of the older ones, me and Hughie in graduation gowns. Hughie and me with a couple of young ladies we met on a college trip to Myrtle Beach. I smiled as I remembered how Hughie, a true classic clown, had picked up the two by feigning a British accent.

Then it was my turn at Hughie's coffin.

I dropped to my knees and said my prayer. I tried to imagine Hughie on the other side of the wood right in front of me, but I couldn't.

It was because he wasn't there, I realized suddenly. His spirit was long gone, roaring somewhere through the universe in the same no-holds-barred, awe-inspiring way it had roared through this world.

I finally laid my palm on the cool wood as I stood, and then I turned and gave a hug to Hughie's mother, sitting beside it.

Chapter 21

THE GATHERING AFTER THE wake was held near the funeral home at a pub called Rory Dolan's.

Spotting the Irish and American flags along its facade as I crossed the street, I tried to think of the last time I'd been to my old neighborhood. It looked exactly as I remembered it. The same narrow two-family houses lining the streets. The same delis that sold Galtee Irish sausages and Crunchie candy bars along with cigarettes and lotto tickets.

Staring out at it all, I recalled warm summer nights about twenty years before, when Hughie and I and our friends would grab a gypsy cab and head north, up to Bainbridge Avenue, where the bars didn't look too hard at our fake IDs. We'd usually end up in a loud, smoky place called French Charlie's to try to pick up the girls listening to the New Wave cover bands who performed there. What I would give to be there now, blowing my summer-job paycheck at the bar, laughing as Hughie grabbed some girl and spun her right 'round like a record, baby, right 'round 'round 'round.

Inside Rory Dolan's, it was three deep at the lacquered, wood-paneled bar. As I was waiting my turn, the door flew open and I heard a long, clattering roll of drums. Everyone turned as the DEA Black and Gold Pipe Band solemnly entered, their bagpipes droning.

The song they played was called "The Minstrel Boy," I knew. I remembered my father singing the old Irish rebel song about harps and swords and the faith of fallen soldiers at a wedding when I was a kid. I remembered how embarrassed I'd been to listen to my father sing the corny, old-fashioned song in front of everyone. Now, years later, I thought of Hughie, and I sang along with tears in my eyes, remembering every word.

"Mike?" said a voice as a hand touched my shoulder.

I turned to find an attractive woman with dark tousled hair at my elbow, smiling at me. She seemed vaguely familiar.

"Hi," I said.

"You don't remember me, do you?" she said, laughing. "I'm hurt. But it has been a couple of years—or decades, actually. I'm Tara. Tara McLellan? Hughie's cousin from Boston. You and Hughie came up and visited me once at a BC–Notre Dame game."

My eyes went wide as I took in her blue-gray eyes and radiant skin and really did remember. The drunken kiss I shared with the brunette looker as BC won was one of the highlights of my long-ago romantic youth.

"Of course. Tara. Wow. It has been a couple, hasn't it? How are you?" I said, giving her a quick hug.

It all came back to me. We'd made out a little bit that weekend, held hands. Afterward, we'd even exchanged letters. Which showed how long ago it was. Actual paper letters. In envelopes with stamps. My nineteen-year-old heart was most definitely smitten. We'd planned to meet again the following summer, but a month or so later, Hughie let me know she'd gotten engaged to some Harvard guy and that was that.

She'd been very easy to look at then. Now she looked even better, in a sultry, Catherine Zeta-Jones kind of way.

"The family was happy that you were with Hughie at the end," Tara told me with another smile. "It was comforting that he didn't die alone."

Cold comfort, I thought but didn't say. A traditional Irish delicacy.

I nodded. "I'm sorry we have to meet again under such horrible circumstances. What are you drinking?" I said.

"Jameson on the rocks."

I ordered us a couple, and we sat and drank and caught up.

It turned out that, like pretty much everybody in Hughie's extended family, she worked in law enforcement. She'd worked as a tax lawyer for a Greenwich, Connecticut, hedge fund, but after 9/11, she needed a change and joined up with the government. First with the state's attorney's office and now with the U.S. District Court, Southern District of New York, where she'd just become an assistant U.S. attorney.

"Southern District?" I said, whistling. "Hughie never mentioned he had a big-league ballplayer in the family. So you must already be familiar with Perrine's case?"

Tara chewed at an ice cube as she nodded.

"I'm pulling every string I can pull to get on the prosecution team," she said. "When I get it, I'm going to work night and day to bury that son of a bitch."

"You text me when and where, and I'll bring the shovels and the backhoe," I said, clinking her glass.

Chapter 22

"SO WHAT'S YOUR STORY, Mike?" Tara said, smiling. "I read about you in *New York* magazine. How your wife passed away and about all your adopted kids. You're quite the New York celebrity, aren't you?"

I laughed at that.

"Oh, sure," I said. "Me and Brad and Angelina are heading to George's Lake Como villa tonight on the G6. Doing anything?"

She touched my arm and looked into my eyes.

"You're still as fun and funny as I remember, Mike. That was some weekend we had way back when, if memory serves me right."

I didn't know what to say to that. It was almost embarrassing how attracted we were to each other after all this time. There was a lot of eye and physical contact. So much that even I was picking up on things. That's what funerals did sometimes, I knew. Nothing like the yawning abyss of death to make you want to cling to something—or, more specifically, someone.

Soon the Irish music was replaced with some quiet stuff over the sound system. It was nice being there with Tara as Ray Charles sang, "You Don't Know Me." After a minute or so, I took another sip of Irish whiskey and sat up, blinking. I was here to mourn my friend, after all, not put the moves on his cousin, no matter how attractive she was.

As Ray brought the song to a soft, weepy close, there was another sound from outside. It wasn't so romantic. It was car horns honking, several of them blaring on and on without letup. In addition to the honking, there was loud, manic music and police whistles.

What now?

Chapter 23

THE BAR IMMEDIATELY CLEARED. When I finally stepped out into the street behind the crowd, I could see that the honking was coming from the parking lot of a bank across the street. A couple of dark-colored SUVs, a kitted-out Hummer, and a sparkly-rimmed Cadillac Escalade were leaning on their horns.

As I stepped off the curb, I saw that Hughie's brother Fergus was already across the street trying to pull open the Hummer's driver's-side door.

"Off that frigging horn, jackass!" Fergus was yelling. His face was red with sorrow and drink. He kneed the door. "You crazy or stupid? Can't you see this is a funeral? People are in mourning. Cut that shit off!"

When he kneed the door again, the smoked-glass window slowly zipped down. At the wheel was a small, young, almost pretty-looking Hispanic guy in a wifebeater. There were two older and tougher-looking Hispanic men sitting beside him, and several more in the back.

My radar went off immediately. This felt wrong. The men looked expressionless. What the hell was this? I thought.

"Is this where it's happening?" the pretty-boy driver said, stroking his goatee as he smiled.

"Where what's happening?" said Eamon, now standing beside Fergus with rage in his face.

"The roast," the Hispanic guy said as he placed a large revolver between Fergus's wide eyes. "The Irish pig roast."

There was movement and a bunch of clicking sounds, and suddenly the gangbangers in the Hummer and Escalade were holding guns. Not just regular guns, either. They were tactical shot-guns and AK-47 assault rifles. A guy in the back-seat had an AR-15 with what looked like a grenade launcher attachment. It was completely surreal. How was this happening? Who would threaten people with assault weapons at a cop's wake?

Out came my Glock. Around me, I saw at least half a dozen other cops and DEA guys from the wake draw as well. Even one of the pipe-band guys had a piece out, a .45, pointed at the Escalade's windshield.

"Drop it! Drop it! Drop it!" everyone was yelling.

"Listen to me," the pretty-boy gangbanger said. "We got a warning to you from our king. He's not going to stand for this shit. You want to live? You want your family to live, you better wise up. Bad shit is about to go down. Kind you never seen before. You understand? You got all that? Message received? Now back off before we put you in a pine box next to your friend."

When I turned, I saw Patrick Zaretski, the DEA SWAT guy, with his SIG Sauer leveled at the driver's temple. The safety was off, and his finger was firmly on the trigger. I could tell by the look in his eye that he was more than ready to blow the driver away.

"Not here, Patrick," I said. "Look at the heavy weapons they have. There are too many innocent people here. Better to let them roll, and we'll call it in."

After a moment, he reluctantly nodded and stood down, along with the rest of the outraged cops.

As the gangbanger SUVs pulled out onto McLean Avenue, a motorcycle roared up behind them, a huge black Suzuki Hayabusa. Its rider flicked down the helmet visor as the bike passed. I caught a glimpse of a face—a fine-boned face with black hair and gold eyes—and then the bike was screaming as it streaked away.

That was the worst outrage of all, I thought as I stood there with my mouth open, watching the woman who had killed Hughie roar away.

As the SUVs tore down McLean Avenue behind the motorcycle, we all jumped on our cell phones to call in a car stop. Twenty minutes later, we heard that the local precinct found the expensive cars abandoned five blocks away. It turned out both SUVs were stolen, and the men had probably switched cars.

It had been an elaborate operation. All for what? To warn us? To intimidate us? It had worked. I was definitely shaken up. My friend's wake had come incredibly close to becoming a bloody massacre.

"What does it mean?" Tara asked me back in Rory Dolan's, as I ordered another Jameson's—a double this time. "Why would these men do this? Why come here? Haven't they done enough?"

I shrugged my shoulders. I had been a cop for a long time, but I couldn't deny how scary this felt. It seemed like I was looking at something entirely new.

"I don't know, Tara," I finally said, truthfully. "I have absolutely no freaking clue."

Chapter 24

NOT TOO FAR FROM SoHo and Wall Street, the MCC, or Metropolitan Correctional Center, is a twelve-story concrete bunker located on Park Row, behind the Thurgood Marshall Courthouse at Foley Square.

In a break room on the eighth floor, Manuel Perrine, the Sun King, flicked an imaginary dust speck from the sleeve of his baggy prison jumpsuit as he listened to a phone call. He nodded, and nodded again, then said, "Very good," and thumbed off the iPhone.

With the phone's video FaceTime feature, he'd just watched the whole incident at the cop's wake in the Bronx. The chaos, the baffled-looking cops. In real time, no less. It was as though he'd been there himself. Good com was essential to all operations. What field marshal would have it any other way?

Being in jail was no excuse to avoid strategizing. Already there were planes taking off and packages being delivered, arrangements being set in motion. He was still in a position to put his considerable resources to good use.

Still, the indignity of every moment spent in this place was such an unforgivable offense. The steel grid embedded into an air shaft that passed for a window in his cell; the metal bunk beds and white brick walls. The amount of money he had spent on the operation in bribes alone, so that he could sneak in and out of the country, was insane. And yet here he was, back where he started, in a squalid rat cage. All of it was for nothing.

He'd already ordered the death of his old friend Candelerio and his entire family. He would then kill Candelerio's crew after all was said and done. They needed to be taught, brutally taught. Everyone involved would be held up as an example of what happened when a king was crossed. Every knee would bend for the crime of his being put in this unclean box in this concrete coffin of a city.

He tapped his nose where the cop had shattered it. There was tape over the gauze now, a ridiculous X, like the burial spot on a treasure map. All his life fighting, and no one had ever broken it until now.

He looked up with his heavy-lidded blue eyes when a bald, muscular guard came in. But the guard wasn't there to bring him back to his cell. Perrine wasn't supposed to be in the break room in the first place.

There was another person with the jacked-up guard, a prisoner with a black eye in a baggy jumpsuit identical to his own.

The handsome young blond inmate was named Jonathan Alder, and he was in for running a Wall Street Ponzi scheme. Now, instead of bilking senior citizens out of their retirement savings in his silk moiré suspenders, Jonathan reluctantly provided a whole host of new services to his fellow cons. The soft, freshly turned-out punk bitch had been a gift to Perrine from the jail's current shot caller, a notoriously brutal incarcerated Mob boss. It was a sign of respect. A housewarming present that Perrine—bored, enraged, violent, and incredibly frustrated—couldn't wait to unwrap.

Standing, Perrine grabbed Jonathan Alder's chin and looked him over carefully, like a man inspecting a horse he was about to purchase. He caught one of the jewel-like tears that dropped from the shivering young man's eyes and giggled as he licked it off his palm. Yummy. He turned to the guard.

"Do you have the other item?" Perrine asked in his strange French-like accent.

"How could I forget?" the tan musclehead of a guard, whose name was Doug Styles, said as he reached into his shirt pocket and handed Perrine a fat white wax-paper packet of prime Peruvian coke.

"Anything else, monsieur? Hope you find the service to your liking," the hard-eyed guard said sarcastically. His voice was the deep, rough, not-to-be-trifled-with bark of a drill sergeant.

Perrine looked up at the guard thoughtfully. Every man had his price, and Doug's here was three hundred and twenty-five thousand dollars in tens and twenties delivered to his shit-box split-level in East Brunswick, New Jersey. Doug thought it was just for the phone and other courtesies, but of course that was just the beginning of the arrangements.

"No, thank you, Doug. How long do you think Jonathan and I have to become acquainted? I don't want to make trouble for you."

Doug raised his beefy forearm and checked his watch.

"Twenty more minutes. Night count is coming up."

"Yes, yes. Twenty minutes is nice, but half an hour would be so much better," Perrine said, batting his baby blues at the guard. The deep creases of his dimples showed as he smiled.

"Really? How about eight hours and a mint under your pillow for you two lovebirds? Screw you, you sick bastard. I'm in charge here. You want a phone? I can get you a phone or this worthless punk, that's fine. But if you think you can lean on me, you're going to find yourself down in sub-basement two in twenty-four solitary, drinking your frog's legs through a broken jaw. You don't own me. Don't for a second think you own me."

Chapter 25

PERRINE WAITED A LONG second and then put up his palms in a conceding gesture.

"I understand completely, Doug. I did not want to step on your toes. You are indeed the boss."

"Damn straight," Styles said.

Perrine lifted the iPhone off the table and brought up an app. He showed the screen to the guard.

"Actually, before you go, could I show you something? Won't take a moment," Perrine said.

On the screen was a video of a reddish-haired woman, the back of her head visible over the top of a couch as she sat watching TV. It seemed like the camera was filming from a partially open closet door.

"This little video, Doug, is a real-time feed," Perrine said. "I believe that chubby little morsel on the couch there is your wife, Sharon, correct? No wonder she's taking a breather—watching those twin boys the stork brought you two last year would tire anyone out. And she breast-feeds them, too; I saw that a couple of minutes ago. Talk about double duty. Quite impressive.

"Did you know that with one snap of my finger, instead of watching her watch Real Housewives of Who-Gives-a-Fuck, you and I, Doug, could instead watch that impressive little lady of yours be forced to perform the most startling of things? Things truly beyond your wildest imaginings. It would be an amateur video, to be sure, but sometimes those are the ones that really get the blood pumping the most, don't you agree?"

The guard's face was no longer so tan. He swallowed hard as he stared at the iPhone.

"I'll do whatever you want," Doug said, his command voice not so commanding anymore.

"Whatever. My God. Sharon. Please don't hurt her."

"Please what?" Perrine said, putting a hand to his ear.

"Please, sir?" Doug said, his lips trembling.

"Fuck SIR!" Perrine barked, his smile suddenly gone, his eyes like blue steel. "PLEASE WHAT!?"

"Please . . ." the bald guard said, shrugging his massive shoulders. He closed his eyes as he realized it.

"Please, King," he finally said in a near whisper.

Perrine's smile returned as he lowered the phone and started to unfold the package of coke.

"You're a fast learner, Doug. I appreciate that. Lovely Sharon and your two thirsty little boys appreciate that. Keep up the good work and we're going to get on like gangbusters."

Perrine expertly laid out a fat line of top-shelf cocaine and even more expertly hoovered it off the scarred metal prison table before he thumbed at the door.

"Now, leave us for thirty—and I repeat,

thirty—minutes, Doug. And whatever you do, my large, helpful friend, don't let the door hit you in the ass on the way out."

DETECTIVE
MICHAEL BENNETT

Book Two

SUFFER THE LITTLE CHILDREN

Chapter 26

ONE YEAR LATER

IT WAS AROUND five thirty in the morning and still dark when I passed the ghostly Asian guy doing tai chi. In a misty clearing to one side of the northern Central Park jogging trail, birds were tweeting like mad as an elderly Asian man wearing a kung fu getup straight out of *Crouching Tiger, Hidden Dragon* went through the slow, graceful motions.

I always saw him on my predawn Saturday morning Central Park suicide run and, as always, I wondered what his story was. Was he actually a ghost? Were the Shaolin monks opening a Harlem branch? What did he do when he wasn't being ancient and mystical?

Sweat dripped from my perplexed head as I kept running. A lot of questions and no answers, which was about par for the course lately.

I'd been running a lot in the year since Hughie's murder. I mean, a lot. Twenty-five miles a week. Sometimes thirty. Was I punishing myself? I didn't know. I certainly was pushing the envelope on my knees, though.

It just felt right, I guess. When I was moving, huffing and puffing and slapping my size-eleven Nikes on asphalt, I felt safe, human, okay. It was when I stopped and let the world catch up to me that the problems seemed to start.

The sun was just coming up behind my kids' school—Holy Name, on Ninety-Seventh Street—twenty minutes later as I dropped to its front steps, my tank completely empty. As my face dripped sweat onto the concrete, I watched a guy in a newspaper truck load the corner box. When he left, I saw Manuel Perrine's face on the cover beneath the headline:

SUN KING'S NEW YORK TRIAL
IT'S ON!

It actually wasn't news to me. Hughie's cousin Tara McLellan had been assigned to the trial, as she had wanted to be, and was keeping me up to speed. There had been a lot of back-and-forth to move the trial to Arizona, but in the end, the feds decided to try him first for the murder of the waiter in the department store, maximizing the trial's impact by holding it in the largest, most visible venue possible. The whole thing was very political. National elected officials and even the president had weighed in, everyone wanting to show how serious they were about the Mexican cartel problem and border security.

Even with the politics, I didn't care. I was glad he was being tried here. The son of a bitch had killed my friend, and even after I testified, I was going to go to the trial every chance I got, so that I could see justice done. I was going to do my best to have Perrine put where he belonged, namely, strapped to a lethal-injection table.

It was a harsh way of looking at things, but it suited my recent mood just fine. I stood up from the school steps and wiped my sweaty face. It was a harsh old world we lived in, after all.

Chapter 27

I TRIED TO BE AS quiet as possible as I came back into the apartment with breakfast, but of course Mary Catherine was already up and at 'em in the kitchen, sewing something in her lap while a pot came to a boil. As I came in and dropped the bagels onto the kitchen's center island, she gave me a look. An extremely Irish, skeptical look.

"Good . . . eh, morning?" I tried.

"I knew it. That's where you were. Running. Again," she said.

"Um . . . I thought exercise was good."

"Usually it is, Mike, but that's all you do these days. Work and run and work some more. You have to stop pushing yourself. You're going to run yourself into an early grave if you're not careful. Have you looked at yourself in the mirror lately? You're getting too thin."

"Too thin?" I said, handing her a latte. "C'mon, that's impossible. Besides, let's face it, with these kids, I'll never be too rich, so what the heck."

She shook her head.

"It's your life, Mr. Bennett. I just work here," she mumbled, going back to her sewing.

Wow, I thought, carefully retreating back into the hallway. "Mr. Bennett?" I must have done something really atrocious for my nanny to be busting out a stone-cold "Mr. Bennett" on me. If only I could figure out what it was.

The front door almost hit me in the back as Brian and Ricky came in, arms filled with dusty suitcases and bags.

"Hey, boys. You're up early. What's the occasion?"

"Just grabbing all the luggage from storage, Dad, for the really wonderful summer vacay we're about to embark on next week," Brian said.

"Yeah," Ricky said. "I can't wait to get up to the old cabin in the woods. And for the rest of the summer instead of last year's two weeks. People think the woods are boring, but c'mon. You have trees and branches and leaves and bark and stuff."

"Animals, too. Birdies and even squirrels," Brian continued. "I mean, who needs PlayStation high-definition gaming when you have the chance to see a squirrel looking for a nut? It's riveting."

I stared at my kids, resisting the urge to roll my eyes. They'd acted the same way the summer before and then ended up having the time of their lives.

"Honestly, Dad. We don't have to go to Hicksville again this year, do we?" Ricky said. "There's nothing to do."

"He means except getting bitten by mosquitoes and getting poison ivy," Brian added helpfully.

I peered at them and scratched my chin for a bit.

"Well, sons. I didn't know you had such huge objections to the trip. Besides, you guys are a year older. Maybe we can arrange something else for you two—like we'll head upstate, and you guys can man the fort down here."

Ricky and Brian looked at each other ecstatically.

"That would be awesome!" Brian said. "The whole apartment to ourselves. You know you can trust us. We're down, Dad!"

They began to step past me. I let them get five feet. Maybe four.

"Oh, wait. I just thought of something. What was it, now? Oh, yeah. I was only kidding. Start packing, knuckleheads, and don't forget the OFF! Next stop for you two happy campers is Hicksville, USA."

Chapter 28

WISPS OF BLUE SMOKE stung my eyes as I lifted the roasted chickens from their foil packets. I listened to the satisfying sizzle as I slipped them one by one onto the grill to finish smoking. The mahogany-colored birds looked awesome and smelled even better—of sweet mesquite smoke and lemon.

"Bobby Flay, eat your heart out," I mumbled as I closed the lid of my trusty Weber grill.

It was my grandfather Seamus's birthday, and I was most definitely doing some grillin' and chillin' for his surprise party this evening. On the table behind me, the Philly cheesesteak sliders were waiting with the rest of the appetizers, the chips, the fruit platter, the beer, and Cokes on ice in galvanized buckets.

Since everything was ready to go, I decided to crack open one of the Coronas to ease my smoky throat.

The whole setting looked as awesome as the food. Colored plastic Japanese lanterns were strung above white paper tablecloths. In the distance, over the buildings and Riverside Park treetops, the Hudson River was sparkling. My West End Avenue building really didn't have a designated rooftop space, but I helped the super out with his traffic tickets, so he looked the other way a couple of times a year when I wanted to have a tar-beach barbecue. I couldn't think of a better venue for tonight's event.

I put down my beer as my phone jangled.

"This is Falcon One. The target is in the box. I repeat, Dumbledore is in the building."

Dumbledore, I thought, shaking my head. Leave it to my nutty kids to turn a surprise birthday party into a covert operation with code words.

"Roger, Falcon One. Keep me posted."

I sipped my beer as I waited for the next transmission. "Falcon One here again. Dumbledore fell for it," Trent reported five minutes later. "Grandpa actually thinks he needs to help Mary Catherine take clothes up to the roof to dry. He must think it's 1912 instead of 2012. Anyway, we have him hook, line, and sinker. They're taking the elevator. We're coming up the back stairs. ETA two minutes."

The other kids and I were huddled together, my youngest, Chrissy, beside me, literally shaking with excitement as the roof door opened.

"Surprise!" we all yelled.

"What?" Seamus said, wide-eyed, dropping the laundry basket he was holding. "Oh, my goodness!"

"He's speechless!" Mary Catherine cried, coming up behind him. "Someone mark the date and time. I think we actually made him speechless!"

We sat down and commenced eating. It was a delicious meal. In addition to the perfectly smoked chicken, we had smoked sausages and German potato salad and slaw. As we joked and bantered, we watched the sun go down and the lights go bright in the city to the south.

As I sat there smiling, one of those perfect

New York moods hit me. Sad and happy and serene all at the same time. I had trouble remembering the last time I felt this good. Definitely before Hughie lost his life. Thinking about him, I lifted my plastic cup to the dark silver sky.

After we dispensed with the paper plates, I popped a bottle of Veuve Clicquot Champagne as Mary Catherine brought over the cake she'd baked.

"How many is it, Father?" I said, filling his glass with bubbly. "How many cases of candles are we going need to light this puppy up? Should I call LaGuardia to warn the air traffic controllers?"

"Please, no candles—and especially no numbers. Not today," Seamus said. "That can be my present from you, Michael. No mention of any numbers."

Jane cleared her throat.

"Before we sing happy birthday, Gramps, we wanted to share with you the top ten reasons why having a priest for a grandfather is great."

"Oh, no. I should have known," Seamus said, shaking his head in mock despair. "First roast chicken, now roast grandpa."

He wasn't fooling anyone. The old man couldn't stop smiling from ear to ear as the kids stood with their index cards.

"Number ten: extra-special 'God bless yous' when you sneeze," Jane said.

"Number nine: front-row pews on holidays," said Shawna.

"Number eight: last rites before the more treacherous amusement park rides," Eddie chimed in.

"Number seven: Roman collar provides excellent grip on horsie rides," said Chrissy.

"Number six: top-notch pet burials," said Trent.

"Number five: reminding Gramps that you're an innocent child of God easily gets you out of trouble," Fiona and Bridget said in unison.

"Number four," said Ricky. "Fear of excommunication is a really great incentive to floss teeth."

"Number three," said Brian. "Sanctity of confessional box keeps Dad in the dark forever."

"Number two," said Juliana. "Lots of chances to wear nifty YOUR GRANDPA LIVES IN FLORIDA BUT MINE CAN EXORCISE DEMONS T-shirt."

"And number one," I said, standing.

The last zinger was mine, of course. Seamus winced.

"Nonstop sermons," I said. "Every darn day of the week."

Chapter 29

AFTER THE BIRTHDAY DINNER, the kids took Seamus to the most recent summer blockbuster while Mary Catherine and I cleaned up. We'd wrapped up the leftovers and were breaking down the tables and chairs when I spotted something.

"Hey, what's this?" I said as I saw something gold at the bottom of an ice bucket. I put my hand into the freezing water and pulled out a second bottle of Veuve Clicquot, which I'd forgotten about.

"Look, a straggler," I said as the ice-water droplets tickled the tops of my flip-flopped feet.

"We can't let this go to waste," I said, putting the music back on. My iPod was jam-packed with fifties and sixties music these days, all the doo-wop crooning and violins and melodies and sweet, soulful love songs I could download off iTunes. I had been playing the songs during the party, to Seamus's delight.

We took the bottle over to the southwest corner of the roof, where we could look out over the West Side and the Hudson River. As we arrived, "Up on the Roof" by the Drifters soon started floating through the warm summer night air.

Millions of tiny lights sparkled in the dark water as the Drifters sang about being up above the bustling crowd and having all your cares sail away. I peeled away the foil on the Veuve Clicquot and untwisted the wire. When the cork popped, it ricocheted off the terra-cotta rim of the building and went spinning out into the night.

"That's a long way down. You think we hit anyone?" Mary Catherine said, looking over the railing.

I stared at her blue eyes and fine-lined face, uplit in the soft glow of the city lights.

"No chance," I said, smiling, as I looked

down. "But even so, I'd certainly take a Champagne cork over your usual New York City 'airmail'—the kind delivered by pigeons, high-rise construction sites, and Macy's Thanksgiving Day Parade balloons."

When I passed her the bottle, she gave me a soft kiss on the cheek.

"What's that for?" I said.

"For celebrating Seamus, Mike. It was really wonderful. The kids love you so much. They love seeing you happy. They've been worried about you. So have I. I know how hard it's been for you since losing your buddy Hughie."

I looked down at the tar paper between my flip-flops.

"I've been pretty pensive lately, haven't I?"

"'Pensive' is a word," she said. "'Silent' is another one."

Unable to deal with where the conversation was headed, I cha-cha'd her around a rusty AC unit as "Up on the Roof" was replaced by Ben E. King's "Spanish Harlem."

It seemed like music from a different world. It was as though the tune came from a different planet—a simple, happy one, where young people longed for adulthood and love.

I knew that getting older meant being skeptical about the music of a new generation, but what I heard on the radio these days was truly new territory. How in fifty years had the human race gone from popular music in which young men sang about things like buying their girl a ring and getting married to popular music in which young women boastfully sang about how much they enjoyed hard-core, dirty sex?

"Ding-dong," Mary Catherine sang. "I'm right here. Penny for your thoughts."

"They're not worth that much," I said, twirling her around. It was maybe another thirty seconds before we heard footsteps behind us.

"Hello? Anyone up here?" a voice said.

We turned as Petey Armijo, the pudgy super of my building, stepped over, swinging a set of keys.

"Hey, Mr. Bennett, if you guys are . . . eh . . . done here, I'd like to lock the roof door."

"We just finished, Petey," Mary said, walking over and turning off Ben in mid-croon before hitting the stairs.

"Exactly, Petey. All done," I said, grabbing a couple of folding chairs. "Your timing is impeccable."

Chapter 30

BY THE TIME I made it back downstairs into the apartment, I heard the dishwasher and the washing machine going. Mary Catherine was in full cleaning mode, which by now I knew meant that she was feeling anxious and emotional, and we'd probably shared our last dance of the evening.

My relationship with Mary Catherine was obviously complicated. So complicated, in fact, that even I didn't know what was going on half the time. There was something deep and special between us, but every time it seemed like we were about to make a solid connection, something—life, the world, one of New York City's unending supply of murderous maniacs, or, most often, my big mouth—would get in the way.

Thankfully, I noticed we'd run out of milk and eggs and bacon for Sunday breakfast, so I grabbed my keys and went out for a breath of what passes for fresh air in New York. Outside my building, I immediately walked over to the NYPD cruiser on the near corner.

"Don't shoot," I said, with hands raised, to the stocky young black cop behind the wheel as he rolled down the window.

The department had assigned nonstop protection to me and my family ever since I'd collared Perrine. And with good reason. In Mexico, during his reign of terror, Perrine had had dozens of cops, *Federales,* and prosecutors killed.

"I'm hitting the deli, Officer Williams. You need anything?"

"No, I'm fine, Detective," the soft-spoken, affable Afghan war vet said as if he were coming to attention.

"At ease, Private Williams," I said, smiling. "Half-and-half, one sugar, right?"

"Okay, Detective. But I thought I was the one

who was supposed to be watching out for you," the rookie said, finally smiling a little back.

"Got it covered," I said, showing him the 9mm Glock in my waistband as I walked away.

I actually had another one on my right ankle, a subcompact Glock 30 filled to the brim with fat, shiny golden .45-caliber bullets. If Perrine's guys came for me, they'd better bring their lunch, because if I thought my life or the life of my family was in jeopardy, I was going to throw down first and ask questions later. I'd already killed two of Perrine's assassins at Madison Square Garden. If killing the rest of them was what this thing took, then, as Paul McCartney so eloquently put it, let it be.

I went two blocks south down West End to the deli on the corner of Ninety-Sixth and was coming back up the hill, balancing a coffee with my bag of grocery loot, when my phone rang.

I glanced at the screen. It was assistant U.S. attorney Tara McLellan, Hughie's cousin, to whom I'd been practically glued at the hip for the last two weeks, prepping for Perrine's trial. I thought it was a little weird to be hearing from her this late, but jury selection on the trial was supposed to start Monday. I stopped on the corner, leaning against a sidewalk construction shed to take the call.

"Hey, Tara. What's up?" I said.

"Mike, sorry to bother you so late," she said. "I'm wrapping up the trial strategy report that I'm going to present to my boss tomorrow, and I was wondering if you could come by and take a look at it and give me some last-minute feedback. Talk me off the ledge."

I could understand her anxiety. Not only was this the biggest case of Tara's career, the whole Perrine thing was a major international news event. This was a very public opportunity for the U.S. to show the world that it was taking on the cartel problem, which had run amok for so long.

"I'd be happy to," I said. "Where are you? Downtown at the office?"

"No. Midtown, actually. I'm at the St. Regis Hotel."

I blinked. The St. Regis on Fifth Avenue was probably the most exclusive luxury hotel in New York, a place where celebrities stayed and where the cheapest room went for eight hundred bucks a night.

"Wow, that's a pretty nice ledge you're sitting on," I said.

"I was late at the office and didn't want to head back to Bronxville, so I decided to splurge. They did say we should shake up our routine for security reasons, Mike."

"Good point," I said. "The St. Regis is certainly the last place a cartel hit man would look for me. Give me thirty to get into my tux."

"Where are you going?" Mary Catherine said upstairs, when she spotted me putting on a suit jacket.

"Work. Last-minute details on the Perrine trial," I said.

"It's Saturday night," she said skeptically.

I tried to come up with one of my patented fast-talking quips as a reply, but drew a big fat zero.

"Tell me, Mr. Bennett. Do all assistant U.S. attorneys look like Fox News babes, or just this one who keeps calling you?" Mary Catherine said as I made my escape into the hall.

"My phone's on. Be back soon," I mumbled as I hit the door.

Chapter 31

IN NO SHAPE TO drive after all that birthday bubbly, I, too, splurged. On a cab to the St. Regis instead of the subway.

I stared up at the dramatically lit, turn-of-the-century hotel as my cab turned off Central Park South onto Fifth Avenue. It was hard not to stare. The iconic French Second Empire–style building was one of the most beautiful in the city—twenty highly embellished stories of glowing limestone columns and cornices topped off by a copper mansard roof.

A doorman ushered me through an elaborate brass revolving door into a lobby of squint-inducing brilliant white marble. Even the furniture was old and French, I noticed, spotting

Louis XVI armchairs with fluted legs backed up against the massive stone columns. This hotel was as imposing, over-the-top, and as expensive as New York City could get, which was saying something.

Tara had already sent me a text message when I was in the cab telling me to meet her in the landmark's famous King Cole Bar. I stepped into the cavernous space, which had a mahogany bar and a massive mural behind it.

Sitting at the bar, Tara looked pretty grand and imposing herself, in a black jacket, ivory blouse, and black pencil skirt. She was wearing her long shiny black hair up a way I'd never seen before. I liked it.

A gaunt old bow-tied bartender, who looked as though he might have served some of the robber barons who built the joint, was waiting for me as I arrived beside Tara.

"What are you drinking, Ms. McLellan?" I said.

"Irish whiskey, what else?" she said with a wink. "No rocks this time."

"Jameson?" I said.

"No, Bushmills sixteen-year."

"Sweet sixteen sounds good to me," I said, giving the ancient barkeep a thumbs-up.

After the relic brought my drink and took away two twenties I'd likely never see again, we clinked glasses and drank.

"So you finished your report?" I said.

Tara put a finger to her lips and giggled.

"Shh. Drink first, work in a minute," she said, slurring her words a little.

She blinked at me, a wide, fixed smile on her face. By the glaze in her eyes, I could tell the drink in front of her wasn't her first.

We chitchatted for a while about the weather and the latest Yankees loss before I realized something. I looked around on the floor beside her bar stool.

"Tara?"

"Yes, Detective?" she said, batting her eyes at me. "May I call you Detective, Detective?"

"Tara, where's your briefcase? You know, your work? All the paper you wanted me to see?"

She smiled mischievously.

"Upstairs in my room. I was just taking a drink. I mean, a break."

"How many breaks—I mean, drinks—have you had?"

"Just the one, Detective, I swear. Please don't arrest me," she said, smiling, as she raised her palms.

"I have an idea. How about we call it a night, and we go over it tomorrow?" I said, grabbing her clutch purse from the bar and gently taking her elbow.

Outside the bar, in the lobby, the grim, middle-aged woman behind the hotel's desk gave me a frosty glare as I escorted Tara unsteadily into a brass elevator.

No fair. I'm the good guy, I felt like saying to the clerk. *Can't you see my shining armor?*

When the door binged closed, Tara turned and touched my face.

"Mike, ever since the wake, I haven't stopped thinking about you," she said quickly. "Did you know that I practically killed about six people to get put on this case? I thought it was for Hughie, but it wasn't. It was so I could spend time with you."

"That's . . . that's . . ." I said, flabbergasted. "I'm flattered."

Tara put her head on my shoulder.

"My husband died in a plane crash, you know. He was a weekend pilot, and he screwed up somehow over Long Island Sound and crashed. We were best friends. We did everything together. When he died, I felt like dying, too."

She pulled away from me and shook her head as she stared up into my eyes.

"I read how your wife died, too, Mike. I know what it's like to lose someone that close. You understand. You're the first man I've met in five years with whom I felt that click. I've just been so lonely. I went on an Internet date a few months ago. Have you ever gone on an Internet date, Mike? My God, the horror."

The elevator stopped on the eleventh floor, and we stepped out into a white, furniture-lined hallway.

"You think I'm a stalker now, don't you?" she said, pouting, when we arrived at her door. "I'm not a stalker, Mike. No, wait—that's what a stalker would say."

I got her room door open with her passkey. Inside, she immediately ran down a short hallway and then through another doorway. Then she ran back out.

"Don't leave, Michael Bennett," she said. "If you leave, I'll come looking for you. You wouldn't want a drunk woman running around the streets of New York on your conscience, would you?"

I stepped in and closed the door.

"Not me. I'm not going anywhere," I said.

She went back into what I assumed was the bedroom. The room was a suite, with a living room window that looked north up Fifth Avenue, toward Central Park. How much money did she have, exactly? I thought. And exactly how drunk was she?

After a minute, I heard water running in the next room. When she came back out a minute or so later, my jaw dropped. Uh-oh. She was wearing a fluffy white bathrobe—quite a short fluffy white bathrobe.

She stopped at the love seat, sat, and tucked her long legs up underneath her.

"There. Okay. Much better. My head isn't spinning so much," she said. "Hey, c'mon. Sit down. Do you want a drink?"

I started laughing at that.

"I think the bar's closed, Tara."

"I like how you laugh, Mike," she said, sounding a little more sober. "I'm so glad you came. Down at the bar, some Eurotrash creep tried to pick me up. When I blew him off, he said some nasty things to me before he left. I got afraid. That's when I called you. That's what you're supposed to do when you're in trouble, right? Call a cop?"

I laughed again.

"And here I am."

"Exactly. Here you are," she said, and stood and undid the spill of her hair.

As I watched it fall, I thought of a fragment of an Irish song from my childhood for some reason.

Her eyes, they shone like diamonds
I thought her the queen of the land
And her hair, it hung over her shoulder
Tied up with a black velvet band.

It was actually her robe that slipped down over her shoulders a moment later, revealing pale tan lines at the nape of her neck. I swallowed. It was a really nice nape.

Chapter 32

BUT AT THE LAST second, as Tara rose up to kiss me, for some unknown reason I suddenly gave her my cheek and turned her embrace into a quick hug.

She stiffened in my arms. Then her head sank.

"Too much?" she said.

She turned, stomping away, and collapsed back onto the love seat.

"I always push it. Always," she mumbled into the arm of it. After a minute or two, she started to sob as if I'd just broken her heart.

I stood there, speechless, in the middle of the luxury suite. What was I doing here? First hugs and kisses, and now tears?

Well, this is another fine mess you've gotten

yourself into, Michael Bennett, I could hear Seamus say.

But as I scrambled for a clue, I finally caught a break. I thanked my lucky stars as the muffled sobbing turned into soft snoring.

After another minute, I lifted Tara up and carried her back into her bedroom, where I laid her under the seven-hundred-thread-count ivory sheets, carefully keeping her robe properly placed at all times.

I stood for a moment and smiled down at her as she slept. I didn't think goofballs came this attractive. Would she even remember all this tomorrow? I wondered. I thought about deleting her text messages to me, but then decided not to. It was what it was. She'd gotten a little drunk and gone a little crazy. I knew how that felt. I was the last one to judge.

"See you at the trial, Tara," I said as I closed the door behind me.

The same stern desk clerk frowned at me downstairs as I stepped back into the lobby. I suddenly remembered who she reminded me of—my fierce seventh grade teacher, Sister Dominick.

"Do you have the time, ma'am?" I said, winking as I passed her.

"Actually, no," the reincarnated Sister D. said, as if she were aching to put a ruler to my knuckles one last time. "Fresh out."

The cop cruiser on the corner hit me with his brights as I got out of the taxi in front of my building back on West End Avenue. Great. It was bad enough that my doorman knew all my dirty rotten nocturnal activities; now my coworkers did as well. There goes the department's Father of the Year award.

When I got upstairs, the house was dark, everyone snug as a bug in a rug. Even Mary Catherine wasn't waiting up for me, which was probably a good thing, considering I smelled like Tara's perfume.

Though when I finally completed the last steps into my bedroom, I did see something. On my bed were lumps. Highly suspicious lumps.

"We miss you, Daddy," one of the lumps mumbled as I took off my shoes.

"Miss you so much," the other cute lump said as I searched for a hanger, gave up, and just tossed my jacket in the corner.

"It's okay. I'm here now, girls. You can go to your own beds," I said to Chrissy and Shawna as I lay down. I felt a whole bunch of smaller lumps flatten underneath me. Oh, criminy, I thought, pulling an itchy fur ball out from under the back of my neck. It looked like the girls had invited their entire Beanie Baby collection to the Daddy's-room sleepover.

"Nugglance?" Chrissy said, pulling on the sheet beside me.

I shook my head. Nugglance in Chrissyese, if I remembered correctly, was a cross between nestling and snuggling.

"Yes, Daddy. We need nugglance," Shawna said, pulling on the sheet from the other side.

"Fine, fine. Have your nugglance," I said, scooting over as I let them burrow in behind me. Giggles started as one of them started to pet the back of my head. With her foot.

I closed my eyes, too tired to protest. More women. I was completely surrounded. Resistance was futile. There was no escape.

Chapter 33

THE HISTORY BOOKS SAY that when the Sun King, Louis XIV of France, entered one of the seven hundred glittering rooms at his Palace at Versailles, his courtiers would fall to their knees and shade their eyes from his royal face as if from the sun itself.

Times change, I guess, because when U.S. marshals led Manuel "the Sun King" Perrine into the federal courtroom in his prison jumpsuit that Monday morning, falling to my knees completely slipped my mind. And instead of looking away, I stared nothing but daggers at the murdering son of a bitch.

I wasn't the only one in a lather at the Thurgood Marshall Courthouse that morning.

One of the dozen off-duty cops and federal agents who had come out in support of Hughie and the other murdered officers stood and began loudly letting Perrine know exactly what he thought of him. The newly appointed federal judge, Susan Baym, banged her gavel, but instead of shying away from the four-letter barrage, the cartel head turned toward the heckler, his double-cuffed hands to his ear, as though he were a TV wrestler playing to the crowd.

Perrine looked thinner now than when I arrested him. A goatee enhanced the angles of his face. Even in his jumpsuit, he carried himself well—head up, broad shoulders back, an almost military bearing. Probably the only thing off about his elegant visage was the sharp bend in his nose, which I'd put there when I'd broken it for him.

Oh, well, I thought, smiling when I saw it. Even into charmed lives a little rain must fall.

Already some in the press were gushing about the man's money and European taste and manners. *Vanity Fair* had done a three-page spread that featured photos of Perrine in several different designer suits.

Despite his obvious elegance, I didn't for a split second forget who we were dealing with here. I'd seen some of the videotaped beheadings and castrations he had ordered, and heard witnesses testify about several of the horrific murders he had personally participated in. In one instance, he had captured a rival drug dealer at a Chihuahua nightclub and killed all the members of his family one by one in front of the detained crowd. I don't know which suit he'd been wearing as he poured a bottle of grain alcohol over the man's wife and lit her up, but I'm sure it was haute couture.

Perrine was living proof that evil existed in the world. Excuse me for not giving a shit about his penchant for stylish cufflinks.

Perrine continued his strut to the defendant's table, where his team of lawyers was waiting for him. The head of his defense team was an affable, bony, middle-aged Washington lawyer named Arthur Boehme. Tara had told me that Boehme had just completed successfully defending a hedge fund manager in an insider trading case for a fee that ran into the tens of millions. I'd read a *New York* magazine article in which Boehme had said that the law was so important to him that he'd represent the devil himself.

I shook my head as Perrine sat down beside him.

The lawyer very well may have gotten his wish.

Perrine leaned back and took in the courtroom as though he were a VIP on a private architectural tour. He peered at the dark mahogany in the paneling, the milling in the high, coffered ceiling, the great seal of the United States District Court, set in heavy bronze above the judge's bench. As he nodded with satisfaction at the august setting, another one of his lawyers, a tall, elegant ash-blond woman, sat down beside him. Perrine leaned in and spoke into her ear, a smile on his lips, his long finger wagging the air to emphasize some point he was making.

After fifteen minutes, the courtroom doors opened and a large group of potential jurors came in for the voir dire. Each candidate stated his or her name and occupation, and the lawyers from both sides took turns asking questions. They asked the candidates if they had any family members who were currently incarcerated, if they knew anyone in law enforcement. At one point, Arthur Boehme asked a hairdresser if she'd ever heard about the "alleged" Mexican drug cartels.

"Alleged" cartels, I thought, wanting to vomit. If only the thirty-five thousand people the cartels had killed in the decade-long Mexican drug war could be "allegedly" dead.

As the process ground on, I noticed something that I'd never seen before. After each potential juror gave his or her name, the lawyers on both sides started typing into laptops. Sometimes they'd read something, then tug at the questioning lawyer's sleeve, and that person would be dismissed. After a while, I realized the lawyers were probably scouring social networking sites to find out about the candidates and their opinions. As a cop, I'd often do it to get a read on suspects and witnesses. Note to self: stay off Facebook.

After an hour or so, only three potential jurors had been selected—a female editor at a university press who lived in Flushing, Queens, a fortyish female occupational therapist from Staten Island, and a heavyset, smiley Hispanic guy who ran the food concessions at the Bronx Zoo.

I checked the time on my phone. I'd love to spend all day watching the total ridiculousness of these expensive lawyers, but it was my day off and I had places to go and multiple children to attend to.

As I stood, I exchanged eye contact with Tara where she sat with the other lawyers on the prosecution side. We'd already had a good laugh about her Saturday night antics. Apparently, she'd forgotten to read the "do not drink alcohol" fine print on some prescription meds she'd just taken and couldn't apologize enough. I told her not to worry about it—with my ten kids, I was an expert at tucking people in.

Tara gave me a quick wave and a smile, and as I turned to leave, I caught Perrine out of the corner of my eye. He was turned around in his seat, facing me. We looked at each other for a beat. I thought one of my molars might crack as I smiled hard at this monster who was in the process of being brought to the justice he so richly deserved.

I yawned elaborately and waved bye-bye before I slowly headed for the courtroom door.

Chapter 34

THE COURT OFFICER BREAK room was in the Marshall Courthouse's hot, musty basement, just off the north stairwell. At four minutes past 10:00 a.m., there were three officers there on break—a white, mustached twenty-two-year veteran officer named Tom Porte and two recent hires, Ronald Pinzano, a short and stout Asian ex-marine, and Stacy Mays, a young black man who'd become a father for the first time three days before.

The armed and uniformed men were used to frequent breaks and delays in the cases they were assigned to and were seated at a table playing a game of hearts when the door opened behind them. As they glanced up from their cards, they noticed a Hispanic janitor smiling at them from the doorway. If there was anything distinguishing about him, it was that he was short and very stocky. Clutched in his wide fist was a coffee mug with the words I SEE DUMB PEOPLE emblazoned across it.

"Help you?" Officer Mays said, eyeing him.

"May . . . I . . . ùse?" the janitor said in halting English as he gestured the mug toward the microwave in the break room's corner.

"*Mi casa es su casa,*" Tom Porte said as he picked up a card.

The janitor nodded and grinned as he quickly crossed the room and put the coffee mug into the bulky old microwave. There were loud beeps as he pressed buttons, followed by a loud hum.

"Hey, buddy. How's ol' Pedro in maintenance doing?" Officer Pinzano said from the table. "Is he back from his knee surgery?"

The janitor turned, smiling blankly, and stared at the officer.

"Thank you," he said, nodding. "Thank you. Thank you."

"Thank you?" the pudgy Asian said, shaking his shaved head in disgust as he threw down a card. "These friggin' illegals. This cat doesn't speak word one of English, and here he is living high on the hog with a government union job. Hell, he probably makes more than us."

"Speak for yourself, Ron," Tom Porte said, raising a white eyebrow. "The way you sponge up the overtime, some of the judges around here make less than you."

The janitor kept smiling as the microwave continued to hum. Two minutes passed. Three.

"Jeez, this guy is really frying that joe," Mays commented as the bell finally dinged.

"You like that coffee *muy caliente,* huh, buddy?" Tom Porte said with a wink.

The janitor had his back to the men as he very carefully removed the cup from the oven. Next to the microwave, a radio played at low volume. The zany percussion of a xylophone, the familiar station ID of a local news channel, filled the small room as the janitor reached out with his free hand and turned it up.

"*Sí. Muy, muy caliente,*" the janitor said, turning deftly with the cup and flinging the boiling baby oil he'd just superheated into the officers' faces.

The scalding oil made a crisp, sizzling sound as it made contact with the men's skin. As Tom Porte screamed, the janitor stepped forward and nimbly removed the .38-caliber revolver from his holster and aimed the gun. Three shots and less than ten seconds later, all three men were down on the concrete floor, flailing in a mess of blood splatter and baby oil and fallen cards.

Officer Stacy Mays shook horribly as he bled out, his ruined head beating against the cement almost in time to the xylophone music. The janitor watched with a bored expression. He counted backward from twenty as he waited for the twitching to slow and then stop.

He turned down the radio and peeked out the door. Nothing. Not even a footstep. He needed to be quick now. He tucked the gun into his waistband and knelt down to remove the weapons from the bodies of the other two men. He would have much preferred something from his own vast collection, of course, but there was no way to get them through the metal detectors.

Getting the guns was the first part of the plan. The second part was to go to courtroom 203 upstairs and put them to use.

The killer's name was Rodrigo Kahlo, and he had been flown to New York on a private jet from Grand Bahama Island the day before. In comfortable semiretirement from cartel work, he had at first declined the highly dangerous American contract offered to him by Perrine's men. Then they had kidnapped his family.

As an assassin in good standing for the Perrine cartel, he never thought that the tables would turn like this. But there you had it. The squeeze was on now with the boss in jail, and the shit had rolled downhill, right onto him.

It wasn't for the lives of his wife or even his children that he had agreed to do this. Living with them 24-7 over the last few comfortable years, he'd learned they were vain, selfish, stupid people, takers and connivers, especially the children. No, it was for his mother, who lived with them, that he'd finally said okay. His mother had lived her hard life like a saint, and he could not let her die as he'd seen so many die—in horror and pain and fear.

He let out a breath and checked the loads in the men's guns. His mind was already thinking ahead to the floor plans he had memorized.

Where the stairs were, the elevator, the layout of the hallway.

Finally, he looked down at the men he had just slain and knelt and said the prayer that he always said before facing danger.

"Most Holy Death," he said in Spanish. "Help me to overcome all obstacles, and may my house be filled with all the virtues of your protection."

He stood and opened the door. Like all good assassins, he feared just one thing now.

Not death, but failure.

Chapter 35

HALF AN HOUR AFTER I left the voir dire session, I was on a bench in City Hall Park, three blocks south of the courthouse, becoming one with nature. Actually, I was feeding the last of my early lunch of an Au Bon Pain croissant to a depressed-looking squirrel, which, for lower Manhattan, is about as Walden Pond as it gets.

I definitely needed the time-out. Like most cops, I pride myself on being bulletproof, body and soul, but I couldn't deny how troubling it was to see Perrine again. I couldn't stop thinking about Hughie, about those last terrible moments in the cramped medical office where he'd given up his life for me. I wondered if I ever would.

So I took an early lunch break with a side of

squirrel therapy. Not exactly textbook, I know, but don't knock it till you try it. It works for bag ladies, right? What I truly couldn't wait to do was embark on my long-awaited vacation to the old Bennett lake house up in Orange County. I love New York City from the Battery to the Bronx, but it grinds on you. You need to get it off of you from time to time or you'll go nuts.

I was finishing my coffee when the first squad car screamed past. I didn't think much of it, but then two more zipped by less than a minute later, sirens wailing. Knowing something was up, I stood and canned the remnants of my lunch and went to the park railing alongside Centre Street, where the squad cars had headed.

I let out a breath and bit my lip. In the distance, I could see that all three cop cars were halted, their roof lights bubbling, in front of the Thurgood Marshall Courthouse, where I'd been all morning. Their doors were flung open, and things most definitely did not look good.

I started walking north, back toward the courthouse. I took out my cell phone and speed-dialed my squad room to see if they had heard anything over the radio. After four rings, I gave up and called Tara. My stomach lurched as I got kicked into her voice mail. I stared at the flashing blue and red lights ahead of me.

Whatever was happening, it was bad. I picked up my pace. I could feel it, practically taste it, in the cloying, warm air.

More cop cars were screeching up to the front of the majestic courthouse steps as I dropped all pretense and sprinted across Foley Square. I grabbed a female cop who was hollering into her radio by the curb.

"What's up?" I said as I showed her my shield. "Is it Perrine? The drug trial?"

"I don't know. Our call was a ten ten in a courtroom on the second floor."

Good God! Ten ten was the code for "shots fired," and Perrine's trial was on the second floor, I thought as I went up the massive stone stairs two by two.

I badged my way through the chaotic crowd in the lobby. People were pouring out of the elevators and stairwells, some talking on cell phones, some crying. It looked like they were in the midst of an evac. My drawn gun set off a buzzer as I hustled through the metal detector against the stream of people exiting the building.

As I was going up the steps, I was almost knocked down by U.S. marshals as they came running down.

With Perrine!

"What is it? What's happening?" I yelled at them, but they just blew past me into a stairwell. That's when I heard several shots above me, followed by screaming.

I topped the stairwell, flew down the hallway, and came through the wooden double doors of the courtroom, preceded by my Glock. Off to the right, by the jury box, cops were yelling and swinging, and piling on top of a man. I saw it was a Hispanic man dressed in Dickies work clothes.

I was almost run down as the potential jurors and journalists and spectators who had ducked down between the benches bolted in a stampede for the door. I looked toward the front of the courtroom and saw the holes in the paneling beside the district court seal, huge chunks blown out of the mahogany. Beneath it, the court stenographer was giving CPR to someone.

I spotted robes and realized it was the judge, Susan Baym.

I jumped to the side as a team of EMTs rushed past me toward the fallen woman. I ran up to the front of the room, frantically looking around for Tara. She jumped up and hugged me when I found her, wide-eyed, hiding behind the over-turned prosecutor's table with the rest of the lawyers on her team.

"Tara, it's okay. It's over. They got the guy. What happened?"

"I don't know," Tara said, staring over to where the EMTs were slipping the judge onto a stretcher. "We were doing the voir dire, and then all of a sudden this janitor was here, firing. He shot the court officer, and then went straight for the judge. He shot her three or four times, Mike. Right in the side of her head. In front of every-body. When more court officers showed up, he barricaded himself behind the judge's bench. Every time someone would run for the door, he'd pop up and start shooting again. We didn't know what the hell to do."

Tara followed the stretcher with her eyes as the EMTs left.

"Perrine assassinated the judge who was going to preside at his own trial, Mike," Tara said, and started crying. "Don't you understand? They do this kind of thing in Mexico, and now it's here, too. Are we safe, Mike? Is my family safe? What the hell is this?"

I stood there, patting her hand like an idiot as my mind reeled.

"It's okay. It's over. They got the guy," I repeated.

Chapter 36

UNBELIEVABLE, I THOUGHT AS I stood in the court officers' basement break room, breathing through my tie.

If there was a word in my vocabulary that I overused, "unbelievable" was it, but was there any other way to describe the sight of three court officers lying dead at your feet, shot point-blank in the head? Not only had they been shot, but it looked like their faces had been scalded or chemically burned.

Day one, I thought, blinking at the carnage. This was only day one of jury selection?

I went back upstairs to the courtroom. The medical examiner team was just about to zip up the green body bag over the assassin when I noticed a ribbon of green tattoo ink on the man's neck.

"Hold up a sec," I said to the medical examiner's people as I unbuttoned the man's work shirt.

I nodded to myself as I squatted over the dead guy. The man had another tattoo, this one over his heart. It looked like a skull wearing a woman's red shawl. I'd seen it before on the chests of both Perrine's driver and the shooter I'd killed at Madison Square Garden.

The tattoo was a depiction of Santa Muerte, or Saint Death, a deity at the center of a religious cult that many of the cartels were involved in. The cult was a weird mix of Catholicism and Aztec religion, and Santa Muerte was a kind of evil Virgin Mary figure. Some of the cartel people would offer blood sacrifices to her in exchange for a peaceful death. Sometimes, Mexican drug dealers would even be found shot dead on altars dedicated to Santa Muerte. It was primitive, out there, very spooky stuff.

I was still squatting and staring at the tattoo when my phone rang.

"Bennett here," I said.

"Hey, pig. How's your morning? So far so good?" a woman said in Spanish-accented English.

No! I thought, immediately jumping to my feet. My heart started beating like crazy. Though I'd never heard her speak, I knew exactly who it was.

I was talking to the gold-eyed witch who had killed Hughie.

"Look around and take in your world now," she said. "Death has come, and she is thirsty. She will not leave until you let him go."

"Ma'am, that's not how it works here in the good ol' USA," I said, trying to recover. "This is how it works. First, we're going to catch every last one of you, and then we're going to put you either in jail or the morgue. Got it? Jail or morgue."

It put a chill down my spine when she laughed. I remembered the unhinged giggle from the moment before she killed Hughie.

"You think you have authority over him because we are in America? You think those bars and walls can actually contain him? You think you are teaching him a lesson, but it is you who will learn. You have offended him. Do you know what happens when you offend a living god?"

"Let me guess," I said. "Um . . . floor seats for the Knicks games?"

"Laugh now. You will cry later, I assure you," she said, and hung up.

"Unbelievable," I mumbled as I closed my phone and my eyes.

Chapter 37

I MADE SOME CALLS and found out they were keeping Perrine in a maximum-security protective custody unit back at the Metropolitan Correctional Center, around the corner from the courthouse.

It was about two in the afternoon, after a lot of favor collecting, when I was allowed to conduct an interview with Perrine concerning the murdered judge.

In an interview room on the second floor, with a one-way mirror along one wall, we sat on plastic chairs on opposite sides of a table. As the guards brought him in, Perrine didn't look concerned in the slightest about the bloodbath at the courthouse. In fact, he looked happy and at ease, as relaxed as a man who'd just gotten his hair cut.

"You wish to speak with me, Detective?" Perrine said in his weird, accented English as he was handcuffed to the cinder-block wall.

The guard left and closed the door.

"It's so nice to have a visitor. What shall we talk about?" Perrine said, crossing his legs and leaning back.

"I don't know. The usual," I said. "Sports, the weather, your upcoming lethal injection."

Perrine laughed.

"You think I ordered this hit of the judge, yes?" he said, rocking his chair back and forth. "But you are wrong. I had nothing to do with it. Some men get excited, and they do things. It is the same with a beautiful woman. People fight over her. Is she to blame if someone is hurt?"

"Interesting analogy," I said, raising an eyebrow. "Since you're such an insightful guy, maybe you could shed a little light on that skull chick you guys keep drawing on yourselves. She's what? A cartoon? Like SpongeBob SquarePants?"

He looked at me hard, with a funny smile on his face.

"I would not take La Santa Muerte, or more properly La Santisima Muerte, so lightly, my friend. Some say the old gods of Mexico are still alive. Who is anyone to dispute it? La Santisima Muerte may seem repulsive to your stale, modern mind, but she and her message and her protections are sound. Death is the only truth in life. Even Catholics believe this."

"Wait a second. You actually worship death?" I said, raising a skeptical eyebrow.

"In a way, yes," Perrine said. "Death wins eventually, always, and every time."

"But I don't get it," I said, shrugging my shoulders.

"Get what?" he said.

"If death is so great, why don't you put your money where your mouth is and kill yourself? I mean, go for it. Please."

He shook his head.

"You do not understand," he said.

"I understand perfectly," I said, raising a finger and pointing it at him. "It's you who doesn't get it. You don't worship death, Perrine. You worship murder. You worship power and evil and hurting people."

Perrine sat up with a loud snap of his chair.

"What I believe and what my men believe is . . ."

He suddenly stopped and caught hold of himself. He smiled as he smoothed his jumpsuit.

"My apologies, Detective. I promised myself that I would not lose my composure, but here I am letting my temper get the best of me."

He dropped his voice into a whisper as he leaned forward, staring into my eyes.

"Now, let us stop fucking around, yes? I have a one-time offer for you, and it is quite a deal, so consider it closely. I give you two hundred fifty million dollars. Let me repeat, that is two hundred fifty *million* dollars, and you get me out of here. Offshore account. My girl's number is already on your phone. You'll have access within two hours."

"What?" I said, stifling a laugh.

"You do not think I am serious?" he said, light flashing in his weird, faded-blue eyes. "I am a man of very considerable means, but what can money do for me here in this place? We need to get rolling immediately. What's the American expression? 'Window of opportunity'? Our window of opportunity here is closing very rapidly."

I couldn't believe what I was hearing. Or, more precisely, I couldn't believe how open and confident Perrine was as he offered his bribe. He truly seemed to believe that I would take his blood money.

Since time was of the essence, I decided to give him my answer right away. My right hand suddenly reached under the table, grabbed one of the legs of his chair, and pulled it. Perrine yelled as he slammed down backward onto the concrete floor.

I heard the guard, watching through the one-way mirror, come running. Perrine cursed a blue streak at me as he tried to scramble to his feet.

"When are you going to get it into that thick skull of yours, Perrine?" I said as the locks on the door clicked open. "You're in the big city now, and no matter how much money or how many freakish drug soldiers you have, I'm going to make you pay for all the evil you've done.

"Do you know why? It's simple. I'm going to do it because it's my job. I'm the garbageman and you're the garbage, so into the back of the truck and on to the dump we go. *Comprenez-vous?*"

As the guards took him away, Perrine tried to spit on me but ended up just spitting on himself. As he began to curse at me again, I smiled. I knew all along that talking to Perrine would be useless. The only reason I'd come up here was to piss him off as much as I could. Knocking his ass onto the floor had been icing on the cake.

Finally, my day was taking a turn for the better, I thought as I headed back toward the room where they were holding my gun.

This was even better than squirrel therapy.

Chapter 38

BRIGHT AND EARLY WEDNESDAY morning, I was finally doing it. Finally and happily hitting the road on the long-awaited Bennett family vacation. It was smooth sailing, too. Well, at least for the first five blocks it was. As I pulled onto the West Side Highway, the air conditioner of the beat-up rented bus I was driving began hosing my knees with ice water.

I wouldn't have minded so much except that the bus had a stick shift, and we were in the middle of bumper-to-bumper traffic. For the better part of an hour, it was clutch and soak and brake and soak and clutch. To make matters worse, all my wiseacre kids were scrunched down in their seats behind me so as not to be spotted by anyone they knew.

When I pulled up in front of our building in the Cheez-It-colored minibus, I guess Trent's cry of, "Hey, look, everyone! Dad bought a dork-mobile!" summed up the general consensus on the transportation. We usually travel in our Ford Econoline van, but with all our luggage, even that was too small for my clan of cave bears.

And the kids were right. The bus was a beat-up yellow eyesore. Luckily for me, though, as a well-seasoned dad, I had long ago become immune to embarrassment on matters of style.

Yet even an incontinent bus and my ten mortified dependents couldn't remove the smile from my face as I made my escape from New York. No price was too high for the privilege of not having to look at or think about Perrine or body bags or my bosses, at least for a little while.

Thankfully, the traffic, along with my kids' complaining groans, finally thinned out after we put the George Washington Bridge and its truly mind-blowing vehicular congestion in our rear-view mirror. I really couldn't wait to get up to the old family house on Orange Lake. This year, we had the place to ourselves for the last two months of summer. I couldn't wait to force-feed a little peace and quiet and country living to my kids, who thought the New York City border was the very edge of the earth.

My mood lifted even more five minutes later, as we came over the span of the Henry Hudson Bridge and I saw the majestic river sparkling far below. Even the kids seemed duly impressed with the massive Hudson and the stark cliffs of the New Jersey Palisades.

"This is it, kids," I said as we finally came through the tollbooth. "Full speed ahead for the SS *Dorkmobile*. Northward ho!"

I put the Bennett magic bus in the left-hand lane and gave her all she had, which turned out to be about fifty-five. About an hour later, I knew we were home free as we got off I-684 onto westbound I-84. I always loved that section of I-84 between Connecticut and the Hudson, where it's nothing but trees and rugged hills.

I was taking in the distant Catskill Mountains vista near East Fishkill when I felt a tap on my shoulder.

"Hey, Dad," Jane suddenly said in my ear. "A

sign back there said Ludingtonville. Is that named after Sybil Ludington?"

"Actually, yes. I believe it is."

"Sybil who?" said Bridget, pulling out her earbuds.

"Sybil Ludington. She was only like the coolest sixteen-year-old girl ever," Jane said, turning to her little sister. "In the Revolutionary War, she got on a horse and warned everyone in the New York militia that the British were coming. She was like Paul Revere, only better because she had to ride farther and faster. This is awesome, Dad," she said, patting me on the shoulder. "I didn't know this was going to be a historical trip."

"I'm glad you're enjoying it," I said.

"Tell me I didn't just hear a history lesson," Ricky yelled from a few rows back. "News flash, Lady Einstein. Just because Dad is making us ride this stupid school bus doesn't mean we're at school."

Eddie raised his hand.

"Ooh, ooh, Teacher Jane! Please finish your lesson about the Ride of Sybil Paddington, and when you're done, may I have permission to open the window and hurl?"

"Enough, ye scalawags," Father Seamus Bennett announced from the last row. "There'll be no hurling on this bus except if it's the sport that Irishmen play."

I looked over at Mary Catherine, who was trying not to grin at me over the Anne Rivers Siddons paperback in her hand.

"Are we there yet?" I whined.

Chapter 39

THE LAST OF MY thoughts and concerns about my job and the city flew away as we crossed the Newburgh–Beacon Bridge. This was always the best part of the trip when I was a kid: the final marker that said good-bye, concrete and crowds and sweating on the subway, and hello, swim trunks and blue sky and summer fun.

"Speaking of road markers," I said out loud, suddenly remembering something and putting on the bus's turn signal.

"Everything okay?" Mary Catherine said as I pulled off the first exit after the bridge into the city of Newburgh. "Don't we need to head up a few more exits?"

"I have to make a quick stop first," I said as I

made a left onto North Robinson Avenue.

We drove through Newburgh. Like many northeastern towns on navigable waters, the small city had had its heyday back in the 1800s, when goods traveled by ship. You could still see that nineteenth-century history reflected in its old oak-lined streets, its red-brick factories, its rambling Victorian houses. I always thought it had a faint resemblance to San Francisco, with its quaint old structures and steep streets that sloped down toward the majestic river.

But as we continued deeper into town, I started noticing changes, and they weren't for the better. The city, even when I was a kid, had never been exactly bustling, but I definitely didn't remember this many boarded-up buildings and businesses. Actually, as I passed a 99 cents store and an Internet café that advertised wire-transfer service to "Centro y Sudamérica," I wondered if I'd made a wrong turn and was now rolling through a grittier section of New York City.

I made some turns and got lost once before I finally found what I was looking for.

Mary gaped out the window as I stopped the bus.

"Hot dogs, Mike?" she said. "We have hot dogs in the cooler."

"These aren't hot dogs," I said. "These are Pete's hot dogs. It's a family tradition. My dad always stopped here first thing to kick off the summer. Just you wait. They'll knock your flip-flops off."

I picked up a baker's dozen loaded with lots of Gulden's mustard and sauerkraut. I sighed as I snapped into the first bite. Tube-steak heaven. The dogs were as perfect as I remembered. Pete's hadn't changed one bit. The kids seemed to like them, too. At least they couldn't complain or aggravate each other while they were chewing.

I closed my eyes as I took a sip of orange soda. When I open them again, I'll be twelve, I thought. My first summer with braces and *E.T.* playing in the movie house down the block.

I opened them, but instead of traveling back to the simpler days of yesteryear, I watched as a tricked-out Acura rolled by the hot dog stand, the thump of its megawatt rap music like a heart under a stethoscope. Not only that, but the two tough-looking Hispanic males in the front seat glared at me and my kids with silent malevolence until the light turned green and they peeled away. What was that all about?

I thought about Perrine for a second before dismissing it. It was just a coincidence. Had to be. I was just being paranoid.

"Okay, kids, back in the bus," I said as I wiped mustard off my chin with a napkin. "This city living is for the birds. Time to get off the grid."

Chapter 40

TWENTY MINUTES AFTER OUR hot dog lunch, we made a turn off a forested road and rolled the bus over a tree-lined gravel driveway to its final stop.

I couldn't stop smiling as the old rambling lakeside cabin came into view. It looked the same as I remembered it, as if I'd traveled back in time. Any second, the screen door would creak open and out would come my grandma and uncles and aunts and all my cousins, waving and smiling and sunburned.

The vacation house had been in the Bennett family for a couple of generations, until Seamus's brother, Cosmo, retired from the fire department and moved in year-round. Cosmo had died a few years before and in his will gave the old girl back to the family as a whole to be used as a vacation place again.

"So what do you think?" I said to Seamus as he stepped over beside me.

Seamus had been a skilled carpenter, among other things, before he had become a priest, and he and his brother, Cosmo, and a few of their friends had built the place over the course of one long summer back in the early sixties.

Seamus took a deep breath as he stared at it. His blue eyes were wet, misted over.

"I remember sitting with Grandma out on the back porch, and we'd hear that sound of tires on the gravel, and you had to see her face light up," Seamus said. "Thirty years would disappear in a second because the family was together, her children and grandchildren."

He looked down at the ground.

"God, she was a beautiful woman. I still miss her. This place brings back so many memories," he said.

"Let's go make some more, Seamus," I said, putting my arm around him as we came up the creaky steps.

Even inside, it looked the same. There was the same massive bay window in the back that looked out over a faded dock and the mile-long lake. I smirked up at the old deer head on the wall, which we used for games of hat toss. My thirst for nostalgia ended abruptly in the kitchen when I realized we would be using the same old hit-or-miss 1960s appliances.

In the family room, I walked over to the wall where some old framed photographs were hanging beneath a mounted boat oar. I took down the one that showed two rows of grinning men above the caption THE SHAMROCK HUNTING & FISHING CLUB.

"Kids, come here. Have a look at this!" I yelled.

Everyone ran over. Seamus rolled his eyes when he saw what I was holding.

"Who can guess who this is?" I said, pointing to a strapping, shirtless, handsome young man in the back row of the photo.

"That's not Grandpa Seamus, is it?" said Mary Catherine in shock.

"Hubba-hubba," said my eldest, Juliana, squeezing Seamus's bicep. "Pleased to meet you, Monsignor Stud Muffin."

Everyone laughed.

"No, Daddy," said eight-year-old Chrissy, shaking her head at the photo. "That's not Grandpa Seamus. Grandpa Seamus is old, silly."

"Yes, Daddy is silly, isn't he?" a red-faced Seamus said, putting the picture back on the wall. "Who's ready for some badminton?" he said, making a beeline for the yard.

Chapter 41

THE NEXT MORNING, AFTER preparing a late breakfast fit for a king—or a dozen starving wolverines—I took to the water. By a little past noon, the only thing between me and my most natural state was an inner tube and my surfer Jams. Sun on my face, heels trailing in the cool water as I floated gently down the lake, my only earthly concern was keeping the adult beverage prepared for me by the great people at Anheuser-Busch upright on my stomach.

I took another hit of my red, white, and blue Budweiser tallboy, squinted up at the tiny clouds high above me, and smiled. The Mike Bennett stress reduction program was going swimmingly indeed.

Off to my right came the occasional sound of my kids laughing and screaming as they cannonballed off the house's faded old dock. Seamus, who had already swum the entire length of the lake earlier that morning, was teaching them how to swim. Or at least how not to drown.

Besides a volleyball tournament scheduled for three, I was planning on filling my day with a massive amount of nothing except kicking back and letting the pristine lake take me hither and yon.

But plans change. Sometimes drastically.

It was about two o'clock, as I lay there in a beery, sun-dazzled state, when I heard the whistle. When I sat up, I saw Mary Catherine waving from the distant dock. I looked over for a panicked moment to see if it had anything to do with any of the kids in the water, but it looked like everyone was in the backyard playing volleyball.

Mary Catherine whistled and waved some more. Something was up.

"I knew it," I said as I started kicking and splashing back toward the house. It had been too quiet for too long.

"Sorry to bother you, Mike. It's probably nothing," Mary Catherine said as I finally made it back and tossed the tube up onto the dock.

Unfortunately, one glance at the concerned look on her face as I pulled my dripping self out of the lake said the opposite.

"Okay. I'm here. What's wrong?" I said.

"It's Brian and Eddie. They left to go to the pizza place down the road about an hour ago, and they're not back yet. I called and texted Brian's phone, but it seems like maybe the battery is dead. I just sent Seamus down the street to see if maybe they went to the neighbor's. They weren't there, but the neighbor said when he passed the pizza place, he might have seen Brian and Eddie talking to two girls and a teenager with a car."

No wonder Mary Catherine was looking concerned. Brian was sixteen but Eddie was only thirteen, and they were hanging around some older kids and girls? It just didn't sound right.

"A car? What kind of car?" I said, pissed. We'd had a big family meeting with the older ones about always making sure to let people know where they were.

"A black convertible," Mary Catherine said, biting at a thumbnail.

"A black convertible?!" I repeated after a frustrated breath. "Oh, well, that's just great. Maybe they'll learn how to drag race. Let me get dressed, and I'll go find them."

"Do you think they're in trouble?" she said.

"No, no, Mary Catherine. I'm sure it's probably nothing. I mean, how much trouble could they possibly get into up here in the sticks?"

Chapter 42

FROM THE BACKSEAT OF the growling Mustang convertible, Eddie Bennett wiped the blowing hair out of his eyes, looked out at the green blur of passing roadside trees, and shook his head.

He couldn't believe it. He thought coming up here into the country was going to be dullsville 24-7, but wow, had he gotten it all wrong. Right off the bat, as he and Brian walked into the country-road pizza place, they met two girls, Jessica and Claire. Not just any girls, either. They were older, pretty high school girls wearing Daisy Duke shorts and tank tops and lots of makeup. They started talking to Brian first, joking with him, but after a little while, they were saying how cute Eddie was and asking him if he liked older women.

"Come on, we're going to go for a ride," the redheaded one, Claire, said, pulling out her cell phone as they came outside in the pizza joint's parking lot.

"Yeah, come on. It'll be fun," added Jessica, who had wild, mascara-rimmed eyes. "Or do you have to go home and ask Mommy?"

"Of course we'll go," Brian said before Eddie could open his mouth.

Then Claire sent a text message, and this guy, Bill, a longhaired dude with tattoos and those freaky flesh-tunnel earrings, rolled up in a rumbling black Mustang convertible. It was hard to tell how old he was. At least twenty. Eddie had gotten into the backseat with Brian and Claire, and now here he was, roaring through these wild country roads with the top down and Mac Miller blasting from the stereo.

> I ain't gotta Benz, no just a Honda
> But try to get my money like an Anaconda.

Who knew life could get this cool? Eddie thought.

"Hey, you dudes havin' fun?" Bill said, turning down the stereo. "Jessica tells me you boys are from New York. That right?"

"Yep," Brian said with gusto. "New York, New York. Born and raised."

"Big Apple in the house!" Eddie tossed out, but then shut his mouth as Brian gave him a glare.

Bill nodded and looked at them in the rearview mirror. He had a long, weird-looking face, Eddie thought, like one of the elves from *The Lord of the Rings*. Kind of cool but also sort of creepy, actually. Eddie looked away.

"That's cool," Bill, the tattooed elf, said. "I love the city. It's good to meet people who are down. Hey, I have an idea. I know a spot over in Newburgh where they sell some primo smoke, you know what I'm sayin'?"

Jessica started giggling in the front seat. She stopped as Bill gave her a long cold look.

"Problem is," Bill continued, "I don't like buyin' on my own. You guys mind if I make a stop there and have ourselves a party? If you don't, that's cool, too. It's a pretty hairy, scary block. I just thought it'd be no biggie since you were from New York and all."

The girls grinned at each other then turned and stared at Brian expectantly. Eddie stared as well, his stomach getting a strange, light feeling in it, as though he were in the first car of a roller coaster right before the first drop.

"Let's do it," Brian said, pumping a fist.

Eddie sat there, blinking, trying to catch up. Everything was blurring by faster than the roadside trees. What had Brian just agreed to? To go buy weed? Dad would kill them. Hell, he was a cop. He'd arrest them first and then kill them. But never mind that. Brian was an athlete. He wouldn't know one end of a cigarette from the other, let alone what to do with a joint if he saw one. He was just doing it because he liked the girls, Eddie realized.

Eddie opened his mouth to say something, but Brian glared him down again.

The Mustang slowed and then chirped to a stop. Eddie slid against the door hard as Bill the elf did a dust-raising U-turn.

"All righty, then, homies. Newburgh, here we come," Bill said.

Chapter 43

THE MUSTANG FLEW OVER a couple of tiny back roads and then bumped over some railroad tracks onto a real road that had businesses on it. A BP gas station, a T.G.I. Friday's, a Home Depot.

As they rolled up a hill into the city where they'd gotten hot dogs, Eddie's stomach dropped again. He wanted to ask Brian why the hell they were doing all this, but when he turned, he could see why. Brian was busy kissing Claire. Great.

Eddie took out his new cell phone and saw 8 NEW MESSAGES pop up on the screen. They were all from his dad, he knew. They were already in trouble. He slid the phone back into his pocket. This wasn't fun anymore. It was crazy.

The Mustang swerved onto a side street that

headed steeply down toward the Hudson. They passed old houses. One of them had plywood nailed over its windows. Was a hurricane coming or something? Eddie thought.

Bill turned down the radio before they pulled onto a narrow road. It looked like something out of Grand Theft Auto IV. Sidewalks strewn with couches and tires, abandoned cars, graffiti all over everything.

When they suddenly stopped, Eddie felt his lungs seize up. On both sides of the street, sitting on parked cars and the stoops of crumbling, haunted-looking houses, were a dozen or more really muscular black dudes. Most of them were wearing red—red ball caps, red do-rags.

These are gang members, Eddie thought with sudden terror. Actual real-life gang members.

Jessica, in the front seat, laughed as she lit a cigarette.

Bill jumped out of the car and walked over to one of the black kids and slapped hands. They talked for a second, and then Bill came back.

"He says I have to follow him into the backyard for a second to do the buy. Will you come and watch my back?"

Staring at Bill, the evil elf, Eddie realized that he was even older than twenty. More like thirty. He was like a junkie or something. Junkies and gangbangers! What the hell had they gotten themselves into?

"Don't do it, Brian," Eddie whispered to his brother. "This is bad."

Brian looked as scared as Eddie.

"Yeah, Brian. Don't do it," Jessica whispered and laughed again.

Brian bit his lip as he looked at her. Then he climbed out of the backseat onto the sidewalk.

"It's okay. Stay here, Eddie," Brian said, blinking nervously at the gangsters across the street.

"No way. I'm not staying here by myself," Eddie said, hopping out after his big brother.

Eddie tried not to make eye contact with any of the gang people as they walked across the street. Bill and the dealer or whoever he was crawled through a hole in a rusted chain-link fence. Following Brian through the fence into an alley strewn with broken bottles, Eddie smelled what he thought had to be weed. He felt like crying. He would never listen to a rap song again. This was so wrong.

They'd just come to the end of the alley, between two crazy dilapidated wooden houses, when it happened. There was a yell, and then Bill and the black guy just bolted, suddenly running behind the house on the left.

Stunned, Brian and Eddie just stood there as a new guy, another black teen, jumped off the back porch of the crumbling house on the right. He had a do-rag tied around his face like a cowboy bad guy. Like everything else he wore, it was red. Red basketball shorts, red Nike sneakers, red tank top.

Blood-red, Eddie thought as the black youth raised his hand, and they saw the gray-and-black gun he was holding.

"Eddie! Run!" Brian said, pushing him back in the direction they had come from.

The guy just started shooting. No warning. No "Get out of here" or "Gimme your money." It was like a nightmare somehow made real in the middle of that bright and sunny summer day. Someone was actually shooting at them!

Eddie fell to the cracked concrete as Brian collapsed next to him, screaming. Eddie put his arm around Brian and felt wetness at his back.

No! What? Brian was bleeding! He was shot. They were getting killed. How could this be happening?

Hovering over his brother and trying to get out his cell phone, Eddie shook as the gun cracked again and again. He'd actually gotten his phone out and opened when he felt something hot and sharp tug at his left shoulder. The phone clattered on the cement as Eddie fell facedown.

He cradled his throbbing arm. It felt scary and weird, like it was hanging on by a string, like it was about to fall off. When he looked up, Brian was hopping toward the street, the back of his white T-shirt splattered with blood and dirt. He fell through the rusted gate and started crawling over the sidewalk, screaming wildly. Eddie had never heard his brother scream so loud. He'd never heard anyone scream so loud.

What had they done? Eddie thought, looking up at the scary house beside him. He cried as he took in its graffiti, its high empty windows. He looked for his phone and saw it ten feet away, its screen cracked, its battery lying on the ground.

Mary Catherine wouldn't find them. Dad wouldn't find them. They were all alone now, Eddie thought. Bleeding and lost and alone.

Chapter 44

SIX O'CLOCK THAT EVENING found me trudging up a thick, wooded ridge a couple of miles east of the lake house. Sweating and swatting at bugs, I stopped on a deer path.

"Eddie! Brian!" I called at the trees for the thousandth time.

I stood there listening for a reply, but there was nothing. Nothing except the sound of crickets and the hot wind pushing the leaves.

I'd already been by the pizza parlor. The owner told me he had seen Eddie and Brian leave with two older teenage girls. That Eddie and Brian would run off with two mysterious older girls wasn't that alarming. What was strange was that the owner said he had never seen the girls before. And why weren't Brian and Eddie answering their phones?

After driving around and spotting no sign of them, I decided that maybe they had all gone to some teen hangout in the woods near the lake. The area, after all, was very secluded. Where else could they have gone?

As I walked through the forest, I had to force myself to stop scanning the underbrush for their bodies. I was being a paranoid cop. Eddie and Brian were just knuckleheads, young male teens in the midst of some hormone-inspired mischief. I would come upon them any moment up here in a clearing, having a beer party or something. We would all laugh about it after I grounded them for the rest of their natural lives.

I picked up my pace, broke into a half jog. Who was I kidding? This wasn't normal. This was incredibly bad. Frantic and now almost physically sick with worry, I was not in a good place. The boys were nowhere. What the hell was I going to do?

The forest ended suddenly, and I arrived at a blacktop road. I looked around and spotted house foundations, a rusted dump truck, weeds growing up between stacks of concrete sewer drains. It was a development, I realized. An abandoned one that had probably run out of money after the real estate bubble burst.

Though it was a desolate place, I was heartened by the sight of it. It was just the kind of secluded place a couple of stupid young teen boys would bring some girls. Or was it the other way around these days?

I was a couple of hundred yards up the road, heading toward a windowless colonial, when my phone rang. It was Mary Catherine, back at the cabin.

"Mike!" she said, frantic. "The police just called."

"The police?!"

"They said it was about Eddie and Brian. They wouldn't tell me what. They said they had to talk to you immediately."

Mary gave me the number as I hit the woods and started back for the cabin at a dead run.

Please let it be something minor, I thought as it rang. Maybe it was nothing. Some vandalism, maybe. Just the cops up here being strict.

"Newburgh PD," came a voice as I crashed through the trees.

I stopped and leaned against a tree, sweat dripping from my face onto the screen of the phone.

"My name is Mike Bennett. Someone called about my sons, Eddie and Brian."

"Hold, please."

Oh, God. Let them be okay, I said to the Muzak.

"Mr. Bennett, I'm Detective William Moss," a voice said a moment later. "Your boys were both shot this afternoon. You need to get to St. Luke's Hospital."

Chapter 45

SCREECHING OUT FROM THE lake house minutes later, I ran every stop sign and blasted through every intersection with my hand on the horn. Coming across the Newburgh city line, I lost a hubcap as I put the bus up on the sidewalk to get around a double-parked pickup.

Dale Earnhardt wouldn't have beaten me to the hospital in Newburgh. Not even with a head start.

"Stop it, Mike. Stop it! You'll kill us!" Mary Catherine yelled, hanging on for dear life in the seat behind me.

I didn't answer her. Hell, I could hardly hear her. Ever since I got the news about Eddie and Brian, I'd become separated from everything, as though I were looking out at the world through a numbing block of ice.

The phrase "Your boys were both shot this afternoon" kept playing and replaying through my head. How could this be happening? I kept asking myself. It was totally insane.

I came a hairbreadth from snapping through the hospital parking lot's gate arm before I stopped in front of St. Luke's emergency room with an enormous shriek of the brakes.

"Eddie and Brian Bennett," I called to the nurse behind the counter inside.

A female doctor in surgical scrubs behind her spun around and waved Mary Catherine and me into an empty examination room.

The slender, fiftyish doctor's name was Mary Ann Walker. She sat us down and made me have a paper cup of water before she explained what was going on.

"They were both shot with nine-millimeter rounds," the doctor explained. "Eddie was shot in the shoulder, and Brian was hit in one of the scalene muscles in his neck, above his clavicle. We were able to remove the bullet in Eddie's shoulder, but left the one in Brian's neck for now."

"Is that a good idea?" I asked.

"Actually, going in to get it would be more trouble than it's worth and I'd just as well leave it in there. They both lost a significant amount of blood, but we were able to stabilize them. Their circulation and breathing and neurological function all seem to be completely normal. Treatment is basically the same as a puncture wound now. Some stitches and clean bandages and in time, they'll completely heal."

"What about internal damage?" I said.

The doctor shook her head.

"Don't worry, Mr. Bennett. We are very vigilant in checking for internal tissue damage. After stabilizing the patient, we do a CT scan, since bullets can ricochet or break up. These, fortunately, did not. No major arteries or blood vessels or nerves were severed."

"Thank God," Mary Catherine and I said simultaneously.

"Your boys were lucky on several counts," Dr. Walker continued. "Gunshot wounds are all about response time. Treatment needs to start before blood loss sends the victim into hypovolemic shock. Your son Brian made a lot of noise at the scene, and about a dozen people called nine-one-one. Your boys were in the emergency room within ten minutes.

"If you need to get shot, Newburgh is the place. We get an incredible number of shooting victims here. Everyone from the responding officers to the EMTs to the ER team is a veteran expert, and everyone did a terrific job."

"Thank you, Doctor. Where are the boys now?" I said.

"We just finished stitching them up. They're in recovery."

"Can we see them?" Mary Catherine asked.

"They've both been sedated after all they've been through. They need sleep now. The morning would be better, Mrs. Bennett."

I let the "Mrs. Bennett" go. So did Mary Catherine.

"We won't bother them. We just need to see them," I said.

Dr. Walker let out a breath. She pulled off her surgeon's cap, showing a spill of red hair. She checked her slim stainless steel Rolex.

"Okay. I'll see what I can do," she said.

Chapter 46

THE BOYS WERE ON the third floor, asleep in the recovery room. Dr. Walker wouldn't let us go inside, so we crowded around the window in the door.

Standing there staring at them, it occurred to me how insane it is to be a parent. You go through this life, and it's hard enough to keep yourself safe. When you have a kid, it's like you take your heart and you just cross your fingers and hand it to each of your kids. I really, really felt like punching a hole through the glass in the door.

I knew I had to be strong, but memories of the death of Maeve, my late wife, flooded back. Still, to this day, I had nightmares about hospitals and waiting rooms. In addition to being ripped up, I was angry. This wasn't fair. Our family had had enough pain. Why couldn't this bullshit happen to someone else? Anyone else but us.

"Oh, they look pale, Mary Catherine. Look at them. Especially Eddie."

She grabbed my hand.

"They're going to be okay, Mike," she said. "The doctor said so."

"I don't know. Look at them. Doctors lie all the time. Look at them."

I teared up then, and when Mary Catherine saw it, she did the same. I don't know how long we stood there like that, holding hands, while the boys slept.

I called Seamus at the lake house maybe an hour later.

"They're going to be okay?" Seamus said. "But they were shot!"

"In the right places," I assured him. "No organs or bones were hit. At least that's what the doctor said."

"Don't listen to these quacks up here in Hicktown, Michael," Seamus said angrily. "You need to figure out what's really going on."

My patience was wearing thin, but I knew the

old man, like me, was just sick with worry.

"Seamus, what do you want me to do? Interrogate the hospital staff?"

"That would be a fine start," he said. "And on that note, what did the police say? Who shot them? And how did they end up in Newburgh, miles from the lake house?"

When I looked up, a thin, middle-aged black man wearing a Newburgh PD jacket was standing in the hallway.

"I'm about to find out, Seamus. I'll call you back."

"Mr. Bennett, I'm Detective Moss," the friendly cop said as he shook my hand. My first impression was that he looked and even sounded a little like the old Yankees player Willie Randolph. "So sorry about your kids. Someone told me you guys are up at Orange Lake on vacation. Is that right?"

I showed him my gold NYPD detective shield.

"I thought I was on vacation, Detective, but it seems like I'm back at work after all," I said.

"Oh, wow. A cop. That's just terrible. I have two girls your sons' ages myself. Please call me Bill. You must be going through hell, Mike. Can you walk me through what happened?"

"I was about to ask you the same question, Bill," I said.

Moss twirled the pen in his fingers as he took out his notes.

"Around six this evening, we received a call of shots fired on Lander Street," he said. "That's actually not a rare occurrence. We get so many shootings there that the locals call it Blood Alley. After the shots-fired call, some nine-one-one calls came in about someone shot on the sidewalk. Our guys got there a minute before the EMTs. Both your boys were down on the sidewalk, bleeding."

I shook my head in terrified disbelief. One second, my kids are splashing in the lake, the next, they're shot down in the middle of some dangerous 'hood. How could that happen?

"It's a drug area, I take it?" I said after another stunned moment.

"Yep. Crack and powder coke and heroin. Gangs run it. Lander is run by the Bloods."

"The Bloods?" I said. "Like the L.A. Bloods gang?"

"One and the same," DT Moss said with a

nod. "The Bloods run the west side. We also have a heavy contingent of the Latin Kings gang to the east. They're at war with each other right now."

"A gang drug war? I vacation up here at my lake house every once in a while, but I had no idea. It's that bad?"

Moss rubbed at his mustache as he nodded.

"Outside of New York City, Newburgh has the highest murder rate per capita in New York State. They're starting to call us the Sixth Borough and the Little Apple, thanks to the heavyweight big-city crime stats. Too bad we don't have thirty thousand cops to keep a lid on it. Anyway, can you think of any reason why your kids were there? I don't even want to ask, but do either of them use drugs?"

"Drugs?! Over their dead bodies," I said.

I saw Mary Catherine wince beside me.

"Sorry. Poor choice of words," I said. "They met some girls is all I know. But how they got from Orange Lake to Newburgh, I don't know. You've probably heard it as many times as I have, but they're actually good kids. My whole family has been worried sick. We thought they'd gotten lost in the woods."

"Well," Detective Moss said, handing me his card. "The doc says they won't be up for questioning until the morning. I'll come back then. If you hear anything in the meantime, please give me a call. As a fellow service member, I'm going to go full press, Mike. Be with your family. We'll find out who did this."

Chapter 47

MARY CATHERINE AND I stayed over at the hospital. I would have said "slept over," except we didn't do any sleeping. We were still too shocked about the whole bizarre, horrible situation. Despite Dr. Walker's assurances, we couldn't help but worry that some horrendous complication would pop up unexpectedly.

As my late wife, Maeve, slowly died of cancer, I remember actually aching with worry— physically aching—as my entire self, body and soul, went around from moment to agonizing moment clenched like a fist. I felt that same full-body ache again as I paced the dim halls of the hospital. Of course I did. Old habits die hard. Just like riding a bike.

Around 6:00 a.m., after the morning shift nurse told me the boys were doing fine, I decided to go out and get some breakfast and coffee. After I picked up some takeout from a twenty-four-hour diner on Broadway, instead of heading back to the hospital, I decided to drive around.

Newburgh really had seen better days, I thought, shaking my head at the blighted streets. I cruised past whole blocks of abandoned two- and three-story row houses—decrepit blocks where the only thing functional on the listing structures seemed to be the jury-rigged satellite-TV dishes.

On one corner, I spotted rows of rum bottles and candles, a faded Mylar balloon tied to a Virgin Mary statue. It was a street shrine to someone who'd been murdered, I realized. There was even a picture of the victim, a handsome young Hispanic man, taped to the telephone pole above a stuffed hippo and a Happy Meal Pokémon toy.

I stopped at the address where Moss had told me my boys had been assaulted. I stared down the alleyway between two dilapidated Victorian row houses. The peeling, weather-battered clapboard on both houses made them look scoured and beaten, punished for some horrible crime. Bent and twisted metal poles from an old missing fence stuck up from the concrete in front of the old houses, as if the area had taken a direct artillery hit.

I turned off the bus and got out. Reluctantly. It was deserted and desolate this early, but it was definitely a scary-looking place. The only comfort I took as I headed down the alley was the Glock on my ankle.

I hadn't taken more than a dozen steps when I saw it. The stain on the concrete. From my sons' blood. Then I wasn't afraid anymore. Just extremely pissed.

Who the hell would shoot two unarmed kids?

When I looked up, I saw someone on the back porch of the Victorian to my left. He was a cute six- or seven-year-old black child, standing there shirtless in his underwear, sucking his thumb as he watched me.

I smiled at him. His happy brown eyes lit up as he smiled back. I'd been a cop for a long time, but it never failed to shock and break my heart when I saw innocents in the midst of such horror.

He took his thumb out of his mouth.

"You're not from around here," the kid said. "Are you a policeman?"

"Yes, I am," I said, showing him my shield.

He peered at my badge.

"Why you driving a bus, then?" he said, pointing down the alley at the street. "Policemen don't drive no bus."

"That's my family car," I said, smiling again. "I have a really big family. That's the reason I'm here. Two of my sons were hurt here yesterday. My two boys. Someone shot them with a gun. Did you see or hear anything, son?"

The little boy's eyes went wide as he nodded. But as I approached him, there was a sound on the porch behind him. A door opened and before I could open my mouth, the boy ran into it. Then the door slammed and its locks clicked.

I let out a breath. No one wanted to get involved.

Who could blame them? I thought, quickly heading back to my bus.

Chapter 48

WHEN I ARRIVED BACK at the hospital, Eddie was still sleeping, but I saw that Brian was awake. Knowing that it's usually easier to ask for forgiveness than for permission, I made a command decision and just opened the door and went in with Mary Catherine.

Brian had an enormous white gauze bandage tied around his neck and under his arm. He looked like an extra in a war movie, which I guess made sense, since he had, in fact, been shot in a drug war. The good news was that he looked worlds better than he had the night before. There was a lot more color back in his cheeks.

"How's it going, buddy?" I said.

He looked at me for a second in complete

relief. But after a moment, his face fell and he stared at the wall.

After a few seconds, I realized he was crying, silent tears streaming down his cheeks.

"What is it, son? Are you in pain?"

Mary Catherine put a hand on his shoulder.

"What is it, Brian? Should we call the doctor?"

Brian looked up at the ceiling.

"All you ever tell us is to look out for one another," he said. "Especially me because I'm one of the oldest. I let you down, Dad. I got Eddie shot. He's going to die, and it's all my fault."

"No, no. He's just sleeping. He's going to be okay. You both are," I said, thumbing the tears off his face.

"But—"

"But nothing, Brian. You're both okay. That's all that matters now," I said. "Eddie getting shot was the fault of the person who shot him. In fact, your hollering saved both your lives. The only thing you have to do now is tell me what happened from the beginning."

He did. He told me about the girls and their friend in the black Mustang, the driver asking them to watch his back only to run away as a drug dealer—a gang drug dealer, judging by Brian's description of him—just started shooting.

The whole thing was bizarre. Why would these older girls take so much interest in Eddie and Brian? Not to mention the guy with the Mustang. Also, why would some dealer just start shooting? He felt threatened by a thirteen-year-old and a sixteen-year-old? It didn't add up.

"Mr. and Mrs. Bennett, what are you doing in here?" Dr. Walker said as she barged in and busted us. "You must leave this instant."

"Mr. and Mrs. Bennett?" Brian said, baffled, as Dr. Walker shooed us out. "You guys got married? Finally!"

Mary Catherine blushed as I winked at him.

"Rest up, wise guy. I'll talk to you later."

But the best surprise of the morning, by far, came as the door closed behind us. Down the other end of the hallway was the whole Bennett bunch, walking toward us and bearing home-made cards and balloons and a "get well soon" banner. I needed a heart lift by that point, and there it was, right on time. The band was back together again.

"We couldn't wait any longer, so we took a

cab," Seamus said. "How are Jesse James and Billy the Kid holding up? What a vacation so far! Are we having fun yet?"

"The hooligans are doing okay, Father. So far, at least," I said.

Chapter 49

PLATINUM LADIES WAS HOUSED in a dilapidated barnlike wooden building a little south of Newburgh in New Windsor, near the airport.

Upstairs in the loft, which he jokingly referred to as his command center, Ramon Puentes hauled his muscled bulk out from behind his desk. He walked to the window that overlooked the stage and slammed down the blinds in order to take his visitor's attention away from the new white girl down below, starting her routine.

The kid who called himself Jay D squared his red Yankees ball cap in frustration.

"Damn. C'mon, G. I was watchin' that," the kid growled.

Ramon groaned as he sat back down. He shouldn't be dealing with this. Ramon was the brains of the operation. The homicidal man-child in front of him was the responsibility of his younger brother, Miguel, no question. But as luck would have it, Miguel was on vacation in Hawaii with his fiancée of the month, so it was up to him to do everything. What else was new?

Ramon and his brother, Miguel, ran the Newburgh Chapter of the Latin Kings, which meant they ran everything. The dope, the whores, the gambling. At least in the eastern, Hispanic part of town. He normally didn't do any business with the Bloods, who ran the west end.

But then again, putting a hit on a cop's kids wasn't normal by any stretch.

"Look at me when I talk to you," Ramon said. "Do you have ADD? Look at me. You think this is a party? Let me answer that for you. It's not."

"You the one making me wait," the kid complained, giving him a look of magnificent insolence. "Pony up the green already, Ramo. I need to get rollin' before someone from the Blood Nation sees me in here."

Ramon tapped a finger to his aching head.

This punk was actually trying to be hard with him? With a whistle, he could have the bouncers, Bartolo and Cricket, up here. They'd teach this kid some manners with machetes before "Hefty-Hefty-cinch-sacking" his worthless ass into an Orange County swamp. He wondered if that was how he should play this. Wipe the slate. It certainly wouldn't be the first time.

"Yeah?" Ramon said. "Deal was half later for getting the job *done*. I was told there was a lot of screamin' after you left the scene. Dead don't scream, last I heard."

The kid waved a hand.

"Don't mean nothing," he said. "I shot 'em up good with my trusty .380. Those kids are done."

A double knock suddenly came from the door behind Ramon's desk.

At the sound, Ramon bent and spun the dial of the floor safe beside his chair. He reached in and took out a manila envelope with what looked like two paperback books in it. He flung it at the kid. The kid took out the twenty thousand dollars that was inside and flipped through the hundreds. He sniffed at the money with relish before he put it back into the envelope and slid the envelope into his knapsack.

When Jay D was gone, the rear office door opened, and the woman, Marietta, from Manuel Perrine's organization entered with her two bodyguards. When she stopped before him, Ramon stared at a spot on the wall just to the left of her exquisite face. Anything that had to do with Perrine or his billion-dollar organization was as touchy as a bomb defusing. Even the tiniest offense or misstep, and—*ba-boom!*

"I'm not sure how successful this has been," Ramon said. "The . . . um, children were shot, but I don't know how badly. Please, let me first apologize to you and then to the great Manuel, who—"

She cut him off with a look.

"That's not necessary, Ramon. What is done is sufficient for our purposes. The policeman will get the message. You have done well. I will let Manuel know that the Latin Kings have as always proven their loyalty to him. He will be very pleased."

Ramon looked away as she left. He didn't even look at the bodyguards. That crowd was from a different planet. Their drugs were pure, their supply line as reliable as Walmart's. But they really believed in all that Santa Muerte stuff. That's why you didn't mess around. He'd heard the rumors. Make the wrong move, and you woke up on a stone altar with some freak spouting mumbo jumbo as he raised a knife over your chest.

Ramon took a bottle of wine out of a drawer. He trimmed the foil and popped it open with a corkscrew. He knew he should probably aerate it and let it breathe, but he didn't give a shit. He found a balloon glass and gave himself a nice pour.

It was a four-hundred-dollar bottle of '89 Chateau d'Yquem that he was saving for a special occasion. Having pulled off his dealings with the Perrine cartel without a bullet to his head qualified as a special occasion in spades.

He sighed and finally closed his eyes and took a sip. Honey, tobacco, some vanilla notes. Happy still-alive day to me, he thought.

DETECTIVE
MICHAEL BENNETT

Book Three

COUNTRY LIVING, COUNTRY DYING

Chapter 50

I WOKE WITH A start in the predawn dark of my lake cabin bedroom, bathed in a pool of cold sweat.

It wasn't an uncommon occurrence of late, unfortunately. In fact, every night of the week since my kids had been assaulted, I kept having a terrible recurring nightmare.

In the dream, I'm running, frantically searching for Eddie and Brian through some dark city streets, and right at the moment I finally spot them in the distance, at the end of some impossibly long alleyway, I hear these awful reverberating cracks of gunfire and wake up with a stifled scream in my throat.

It doesn't take a rocket scientist to interpret

the dream, since I was spending much of my time feeling horrendously guilty for not being there for them, for failing to protect them when they needed me most. Mary Catherine and Seamus told me several times that I needed to stop beating myself up about it, but try as I might, I just couldn't.

I guess if there was any consolation, it was that the boys were home from the hospital and seemed to be healing. Dr. Mary Ann Walker from St. Luke's had been right about there not being any complications with either of my sons' wounds, thank God, but I guess it wasn't the physical damage I was most worried about.

Brian seemed to have come around the emotional corner, already making jokes about how the bullet left in his neck would make him a lifetime TSA target. It was Eddie who was most concerning. Normally the life of the party, he seemed to have drawn into himself like a turtle into its shell. The other kids told me he was also yelling in his sleep, no doubt reliving the horror of what had happened to him.

It just broke my heart to see him like that. Thirteen-year-old boys have enough on their plates in the growing-up department without throwing post-traumatic stress disorder into the mix.

That's why over the last seven days, I'd been meeting up with the Newburgh police. Even though I was probably harassing Detective Bill Moss and his friendly grizzly bear of a partner, Detective Edward Emmanuel Boyanoski, with my constant inquiries, they'd been more than tolerant. In fact, as fellow cops and fathers, they couldn't have been more understanding.

They let me ride along with them on canvasses and even let me sit in on a few interviews. So far, no one in the tightly knit Lander Street drug neighborhood was talking about the shooting, but the two veteran detectives assured me they wouldn't stop until they got to the bottom of it.

I hoped they were right. For my boys' sake and everyone else's.

I finally sat up, yawning. Outside the window, over the still, dark lake, there was only the faintest light in the sky, but already the whippoorwills were whippoorwilling to beat the band.

They actually weren't the only early birds out to get a worm this morning. I had to go back into

247

New York City today. The Perrine trial was resuming after the shooting of Judge Baym at the federal courthouse, and there was a possibility that I might be called to testify. For my departed buddy, Hughie, I needed to go in and do whatever I could to nail the coffin shut on the evil, bloodsucking cartel king Perrine.

I was finally getting to my feet when there was a soft knock on my bedroom door, and Mary Catherine came in with a cup of coffee.

"You're up already. Good," she whispered, quickly handing me the chipped blue mug. "Do you want to eat a little first, or shower?"

If there was anyone worried about our gang as much as I was, it was MC. She was one of those people who, when nervous, gets busy. So from sunup to sundown, when she wasn't directing camp activities, she was a domestic whirlwind of baking and cleaning and cutting the grass. When she went out to paint the mailbox the day before, one of the neighbors asked us if we were fixing to sell the place.

Over the rim of my coffee mug, I noticed the blue glow of the stove light in the kitchen just as I caught a heavenly aroma.

"Bacon?" I said, walking into the kitchen and setting my empty mug onto the countertop. "I thought I told you not to fuss, Mary Catherine. I'm glad you didn't listen to me."

"It's not me who's fussing. That's Seamus manning the stove. He insisted on a hot meal for you before your trip into the city," she said, smiling.

"Wow, I'm really touched," I said, refilling my coffee. "The old codger really does care about me after all, huh?"

"Why? Because he woke up so early?" Mary Catherine said.

"No," I explained. "Because frying bacon is how we stoic Irishmen say I love you."

Chapter 51

FORTY-FIVE MINUTES LATER, clean-shaven and wearing my best trial suit, I waved good-bye to Mary Catherine after being dropped off across the Newburgh–Beacon Bridge at the Beacon Metro-North train station.

As I got onto the Grand Central Terminal–bound 7:21 train a few minutes later, I noticed something odd. Over the tops of their *Wall Street Journals* and smartphones, some of the business commuters sitting near me were giving me double takes. Not warm, fuzzy ones, either. Even though I was wearing dapper attire, they kept glancing over at me suspiciously, as if they thought I was about to star in the latest YouTube subway fight video.

I thought maybe my picture was in the paper concerning the Perrine trial, or maybe there was a huge piece of Irish bacon stuck in my teeth, when I suddenly realized what it was.

Commuting into New York City from the hinterlands of the tristate area is a strange business. Regular passengers on the rush-hour trains see each other every morning or every evening for years and years. Friendships form; floating card games; affairs.

All the fuss was about me being a new face, I realized. Their furtive, spooked glances were a result of the fact that I'd upset their regular morning routine.

You want spooked? I thought. How about cleaning out your young teen's bullet wound? I felt like asking them as I found a window seat and stretched out before closing my eyes.

Though Beacon was sixty miles north of New York City, we arrived at Grand Central Terminal only about an hour and twenty minutes later. I shuffled out with the throng, walking up one dirty underground tunnel until I found another one for the downtown subway.

Instead of heading straight to the courthouse,

the plan was to go over the case with Tara McLellan first. She had sent me a text message, asking me to meet her at an inconspicuous office building on lower Broadway that the federal prosecutor's office was now renting due to the trial's unprecedented need for security.

Running early and dying for light and oxygen, I decided to get off the number 6 train at Canal Street and walk the rest of the way. I walked west to Broadway, and then made a left, going south, down into the Canyon of Heroes.

New York can truly drive you nuts, but every once in a while, you glance around and realize you live in one of the most beautiful man-made places that has ever existed. Washington, D.C., evokes the long line of American presidents, but for me, it's the Canyon of Heroes, with its history of old-fashioned showers of ticker tape, that always reminds me of our country's most shining human triumphs—driving in the golden railroad spike, Edison's lightbulb, the Wright brothers at Kitty Hawk, Armstrong's not-so-small step on the moon.

As I walked, smiling up at the high, massive walls of the majestic buildings, a much more vivid and personal memory suddenly occurred to me. It was the first time I actually came to lower Manhattan with my father, to see the 1977 world champion Yankees in their ticker-tape parade.

Glowing with Yankees pride—and warmed by three or four pints of Guinness from a nearby Blarney Stone pub, packed wall-to-wall with customers—he hoisted me to his shoulders. With me riding on his broad back, we went up and down Broadway, where he pointed out all the landmarks—Trinity Church, where George Washington attended services following his inauguration at Federal Hall, across from the New York Stock Exchange; John D. Rockefeller's Standard Oil Building.

"Look around, Michael. Take it all in," he said, a happy tear in his eye as we finally watched the tape glittering down over Reggie Jackson and Ron Guidry and George Steinbrenner, who were passing by in convertibles.

"Never forget we're the good guys, Michael," he said. "We win. They lose. End of story."

I teared up a little as I thought about that. I thought about my life, the state of the country, the state of the world. I was the man now, and it was my turn to be the good guy, wasn't it? A good father, a good cop, a good man. I'd like to think I was trying to fight the good fight, but I was starting to wonder more and more if the good guys weren't becoming an endangered species these days—if we weren't quickly getting outnumbered, outmaneuvered, outgunned.

No wonder the people on the train were spooked, I thought, shivering in the cool morning air as I walked. I, too, was spooked. Being spooked, I guess, was the only sane response to watching the world come apart at the seams.

Chapter 52

NINE MILES TO THE southwest of the dazzling glass-and-steel skyline of lower Manhattan lie the Maher Terminals in Elizabeth, New Jersey, North America's largest container-ship facility.

It was coming on 8:30 a.m. when the dockside crane along the southern wharf sounded its horn, and the train-like column of trucks idling beside it finally began to move into position.

At the head of the line, a boyish, silver-haired trucker by the name of Norman O'Neill quickly stubbed out his tenth Marlboro of the morning before pulling his rumbling Volvo VN 630 semi beneath the massive steel legs of the towering unloading crane. He felt like lighting up a fresh one as he listened to the overhead cable's shrill whine. Since all the paper and manifests had been stamped hours before, it was looking good, though he wasn't out of the woods yet, he knew. He'd breathe again after he got the box and got the heck out of there.

O'Neill glanced to his right at the rusty hull of the small container vessel, called a feeder, that the crane was starting to unpack. Named the *Estivado*, it was a Costa Rican ship with a French crew that flew a Panamanian flag. Having picked up containers from her before, O'Neill knew there was nothing on the *Estivado*'s cargo manifest, such as machine tools, that would set off any Homeland Security threat-matrix alarms. In fact, most of the nine hundred LEGO-like red metal boxes aboard the ship contained navel oranges and tangelos out of Toluca, Mexico.

Most, O'Neill thought, as the weight of the lowered container settled onto the trailer attached to the truck with a slight thump and a creak.

But not all.

He shifted the five-hundred-horsepower Volvo into gear and pulled away from the crane and around a red-brick warehouse to the end of another line of idling trucks. He nervously drummed the top of the Marlboro box sitting in his cup holder as he sat waiting.

This last part was the gut check. The line he was in was for the Homeland Security vehicle imaging scanner, where the insides of all containers had to be inspected by an X-ray machine before they were allowed to leave. Remembering his very specific instructions, O'Neill waited until it was right before his turn and then immediately sent a wordless text message to a number he'd already preprogrammed into his phone.

He assumed the text was a signal to someone working in the security office, but he wasn't sure and he didn't really want to know. He just held his breath as he slowly rolled between the goalpost-like metal X-ray poles that bookended the security lane.

There was a traffic light with a gate arm on the other side, where you had to wait after you went through the scanner. O'Neill stared at the red light, his heart ticking like a clock attached to a bomb. He was wondering how much prison time they would give him for smuggling several metric tons of coke, and what his clueless wife and daughters would think, and how did one actually hang oneself in a prison cell, when the green light suddenly flashed and the arm tilted up.

O'Neill Zippoed himself a victory cigarette as he clutched and shifted and pulled out.

Chapter 53

AN HOUR LATER, STILL following specific instructions, O'Neill pulled into an I-95 rest stop just south of the New York State line and unhitched the trailer. A minute after he pulled away, a spanking new cherry-red Peterbilt 388 swung in front of the cargo container, and three hard-looking Hispanic men in jeans and denim work shirts hopped out. The largest of them checked the container's seal and locks carefully before nodding to the other two to hook it up.

The final destination of the shipment was a warehouse on the East River in Greenpoint, Brooklyn. Inside, just beyond its open steel overhead door, a white Mercedes S600 sedan with tinted windows was parked beside a large silver Ford van. After the warehouse door was safely back down, an effeminate Hispanic man in seersucker shorts and a butter-colored tennis sweater exited the van and checked the seal and locks on the container. When the foppish man nodded, the driver of the truck, who had been waiting with a pair of bolt cutters, clipped the container's heavy padlocks and swung the doors back.

"*Vámonos!*" the truck driver called.

There was a pause, then out of the mouth of the container came young girls. Sweaty and disheveled, they gasped and squinted at the clean air and light after spending three days in the box. They were dirt-poor Mexican country girls who'd been told they were being recruited for factory jobs in the U.S. fashion industry. Not one of them was over fourteen. One of them was only eleven.

As the men helped them down to the floor of the warehouse, the driver's door of the white Mercedes popped open and out came Manuel Perrine's right-hand woman, beautiful Marietta herself. Even in their exhaustion, the girls marveled at her white Chanel summer pouf dress, the white Chanel purse draping from her slim, cinnamon-tan arm, her white Chanel watch. Beautiful and serene and all smiles, she went among the tired girls with a checklist and a digital camera, taking pictures and pausing here and there to inspect skin and hair and teeth.

She quickly divided the girls into categories and prices. The last shipment had been over-packed, and there had been some damage to the material. A girl had died on the second day, and several of the rest of them had become so ill, they, too, had to be destroyed.

What had Manuel called it?

Spillage. Exactly.

There had been no spillage this time. The sex-slave trade was a new avenue for the cartel, but, as she did with everything, Marietta was picking up the learning curve quickly.

Marietta clopped to the van on her pristine white heels and handed the dapper pimp her checklist and camera. They spoke quietly for a moment, the wiry, almost pretty dark-skinned Dominican nodding thoughtfully at her recommendations before returning his hungry gaze to the line of unkempt girls.

"Who wants a treat?" Marietta called in Spanish as she took a plastic bag of snack-size Milky Ways from her white purse and tossed it into the van.

The famished girls flooded into the vehicle, giggling. In a moment, they were buckled into their seats, chewing ravenously, chocolate on their cheeks and chins. The pimp, already behind the wheel, looked at them over the driver's seat, his soft, seemingly friendly face beaming like a proud father's.

"This is Mateo. He will take you to where you'll be staying," Marietta told them gently in Spanish as the warehouse's steel door rolled back up. "He'll make sure to get you to a phone right away so you can call home and tell your parents that you're okay, okay?"

The girls—like Madeline and her friends responding politely to Miss Clavel—thanked Marietta in unison.

Marietta slipped on a pair of whimsical Chanel sunglasses and stuck her tongue out at them playfully.

"Bye, now. I'm so proud of you all," Marietta called, tossing a wave and a blown kiss over her sleeveless shoulder as she headed back for the Mercedes.

"You made it, girls!" she said. "You really made it. Welcome to America!"

Chapter 54

AT LEAST THE LOBBY security guard wasn't lying down on the job, I thought as I arrived at the U.S. attorney's secret office on lower Broadway. Even after I flashed my shield and showed the guard my driver's license, he made no less than three phone calls before he allowed me to go upstairs.

Tara was on the other side of the elevator door when it opened on the seventeenth floor. I was instantly reminded how lovely she was. She was wearing a crisp Tiffany-blue blouse and a tobacco-colored skirt, her dark hair shining.

She surprised me by giving me an affectionate hug and planting a fat kiss on my cheek. As she guided me through a maze of cubicles into a conference room, I think I might have blushed a little. Or, to be more accurate, quite a lot.

She sat me down at a table stacked with law books and legal pads, and for the next half hour, we drank black coffee as she brought me up to speed on the prosecution strategy. She hadn't seemed to have heard about my kids and what happened to them, so I didn't bring it up. I'm a man who, if possible, always likes to compartmentalize the disasters in his life.

"As you already know, Mike," she said, slipping on a pair of glasses as she showed me the indictment, "Perrine's original warrant for the murders of the Border Patrol agents was put on the back burner while we shifted our focus to the murder of Scott Melekian, the Macy's waiter Perrine killed while fleeing from you."

She suddenly let out a huge yawn that turned into a sigh.

"My bad," she said, blinking. "It's been nothing but late nights since Judge Baym was killed."

"Perfectly understandable," I said, stifling a yawn myself.

"Anyway, we thought it was going to be a

slam dunk at first," she said. "We interviewed fifteen eyewitnesses who were ready to testify that they saw Melekian turn and stumble into Perrine as he was running into the restaurant. Then they saw Perrine grasp Melekian by the head and violently snap his neck with his bare hands, causing almost instantaneous death."

She sighed again.

"That number of witnesses is now down to seven. Only three of the wait staff and four patrons are willing to say what they saw. We're not sure if the witnesses are apprehensive since the courthouse shooting or if Perrine is getting to them in other ways, but people are becoming less and less willing to testify. That's why I need you to be ready to go as soon as the jury is picked. We need to jump right into this with both feet—put you on the stand to set the whole thing up and get the ball rolling quickly. Because the longer we delay, the more witnesses we're going to lose."

I shook my head.

"You're right," I said. "With Perrine's money and global reach, he's already started to go all-in to ruin the government's case through violence. It's unbelievable."

"You don't have to tell me," Tara said. "The Mob used to do the same thing at the height of their power in the nineteen freaking thirties. All they seemed to do was find witnesses and kill them. The most depressing thing about it is that the bloody tactic has a tendency of being highly effective."

She checked her watch and stood, stacking papers.

"Come on. Tempus fugit. We need to get to the courthouse. Grab one of these file boxes for me."

Back at the elevator, Tara smiled at me sort of slyly after she pressed the button.

The last time we'd been in an elevator together was that night at the St. Regis.

I stood there in the pregnant silence, thinking about that night—Tara bringing me up to her room, how nice she looked in her fuzzy white bathrobe. For all its nuttiness, it was actually quite a fond memory. A man could get used to putting this vivacious young prosecutor to bed. In theory, of course.

The elevator binged open.

Tara stared at me, puzzled.

"After you," I said.

She suddenly smiled again as we got into the car.

"Sir Michael Bennett, New York City's last, and perhaps only, chivalrous knight."

Chapter 55

AND I THOUGHT FOLEY Square in front of the federal courthouse had looked like a zoo when the trial first started.

As Tara and I exited our cab and mounted the marble steps, it again looked like a zoo, only this time with open cages. There were reporters, protesters, cops, and sidewalk barriers everywhere. Most of the faces in the crowd looked even more nervous than the ones on the 7:21 out of Beacon. And why wouldn't they be afraid?

The federal court in New York had been around since the days of Alexander Hamilton, and this was the first time a judge had been murdered in her own courtroom in the middle of a trial!

I elbowed Tara gently and pointed my chin up at the NYPD chopper that sailed into view above the courthouse.

"Wow, this is the first trial I've ever been on that required air cover!" I yelled as we moshed our way through the nervous crowd of photographers and newsies at the top of the stairs.

"Come on, Mike. Didn't you read the paper?" she said. "The mayor insists that Perrine's trial will move forward. New York City will not be intimidated by a drug cartel and its boss!"

"Of course. Not intimidated. How silly of me," I said over the deafening rotor wash. "Isn't it funny, though, how *our* job is not to be intimidated down here, at the site of a potential attack, while for the duration of the trial our fearless billionaire mayor will be busy not being intimidated at his Upper East Side town house, guarded by his double-digit-strong security detail?"

Because bullet holes were perhaps not the greatest visual stimulus for potential jurors, the trial had been moved from the majestic courtroom where Judge Baym had been gunned down to a much more modest one on the fourteenth floor.

Perrine was already sitting at the defense table when we arrived. I'd seen a lot of security inside a courtroom before, but this was over the top. There were at least eight uniformed court officers and another half dozen or so U.S. marshals standing in a wide semicircle around him. The men were all huge and intimidating, like an angry, violent defensive squad on a football team waiting tensely for the snap.

But if Perrine was intimidated or even noticed all the fuss, he hid it quite well. His demeanor and posture were as impressive as always, his head canted back commandingly, his crease-free prison jumpsuit worn officiously, as though it were formal military dress.

There was a playful sparkle in his blue eyes as he smiled at something that his thousand-bucks-an-hour lawyer said. You could tell the mass murderer thought the whole thing was a joke, that he was playing us and loving every minute of it.

Chapter 56

THE NEW JUDGE, MARY Elizabeth Fleming, was a tall, elegant black woman with a striking resemblance to Condoleezza Rice. She was just entering the courtroom from her chambers with the court clerk when it happened. There was a sound from outside, a sudden and tremendous window-rattling bang that seemed to increase in volume as it rose up from the street fourteen stories below.

At the massive booming noise, the courtroom broke into complete bedlam. Spectators immediately hit the deck in the seats behind me as the dowdy stenographer screamed. She knocked over her typing stand in a clatter and left a shoe behind as she dove into the witness box for cover.

It was unbelievable how fast all the court officers drew on Perrine, as though it were a Wild West show.

"Hands!" they screamed at him.

A six-foot-five redheaded cop circled in front of Perrine, the chunky device in his freckled hand pointed a foot from Perrine's chest.

"Hey, you deaf? Hands up now or you will be Tasered, you son of a bitch!" he yelled.

The ghost of a smile played on Perrine's lips as he sat as still as a paperweight in his chair. After a moment, he raised his hands in a slow, graceful motion.

"What's that expression? 'Don't Tase me, bro'?" he said in the tense silence.

He turned toward the judge then, laughing softly.

The towering redheaded cop's radio gave off a loud beep followed by the long squawk of a message.

"It's okay. All clear, Judge," the cop said, listening to his radio. "Looks like a truck at the construction site on Centre Street dropped a load of scaffolding."

"How ironic. I almost dropped a load

myself," Perrine said with a girlish giggle.

"Can the comedy routine, Perrine," the judge said. "I mean it. One more word out of you, and I might not Taser you, but I will gag you . . . *bro*."

Closest to the witness stand, I went to help the shaken stenographer up from the floor of the witness box. I exchanged smiles with Perrine at the nearby defense table as I helped right her stenotype. When he gestured me over toward the defense table with his shackled hands, I was more than happy to oblige.

As I leaned in over the table, the drug lord flashed me a grin.

"You don't scare easily, do you, Michael Bennett?" he whispered. "Neither do I. Believe it or not, I like you. With all your antics, I find you a very funny man. This circus needs a clown, and you're doing a great job. Despite your silliness, my offer still stands. You could take a nice long vacation from all this stress, a permanent one, in fact. I hear the Maldives are quite pleasant this time of year."

"The Maldives?" I said, raising an eyebrow as if I were considering it. "They do sound pleasant, but the question is would they be more pleasant than what I'm going to do to you on that witness stand? More pleasant than watching your face when the verdict is read?"

I could see a vein pulse on Perrine's neck as I slowly shook my head.

"Sorry, Perrine. Truly, my apologies," I whispered back. "But even a silly clown like me wouldn't miss that for the entire world."

Chapter 57

THE METRO-NORTH TRAIN BACK to the lake house in Newburgh was half empty that night after nine o'clock. I didn't read a paper or send out any e-mails. All I did for an hour straight was sip the Budweiser tallboy I'd bought in Grand Central as I sat in a window seat on the Hudson River side, listening to the clickety-clack of the train. If I'd had a harmonica, I would have busted into the saddest blues solo ever heard as I stared out at the dark water and chugga-chugga choo-chooed it north up the Hudson Valley.

And I didn't even know how to play the harmonica.

That pretty much summed up how well things *weren't* going in *United States v. Perrine*.

Due both to Perrine's unsettling presence and his legal team's constant stream of delays, I didn't get anywhere near testifying. By day's end, only the selection of the final members of the jury had been nailed down.

The whole day had been nothing but one long, exhausting, frustrating emotional grind. At least for all the good people involved. The worst part was having to watch Perrine sit through the proceedings, sipping Perrier, with his dream-team legal counsel alongside him. Every few minutes, he'd swivel around to give me a little wink along with his arrogant Cheshire cat smile.

After court and a quick powwow with Tara and the rest of the prosecutors, I'd thought briefly about staying over in the apartment, then decided against it. Everyone would probably be asleep by the time I made it back to the lake house, but it didn't matter. The need to be with my guys, especially Eddie and Brian, over the last week was undeniable.

Was it guilt over not being able to protect them?

No doubt it was.

I couldn't stop thinking about what a miracle

it was that they weren't dead, and that we weren't planning their funerals right now instead of finishing our vacation.

As the lonely lights of the Tappan Zee Bridge swung past on my left, I got a text message from Mary Catherine asking me if she should come to pick me up in Beacon. I begged off, texting back that I'd just get a taxi.

Though she'd certainly be a sight for my very sore eyes, I actually had one more stop to make before calling my heck of a long day a night.

I needed to meet up with Newburgh detectives Moss and Boyanoski, who had notified me that there was some potential progress on my kids' case.

Forty minutes later, after exiting the train, I waved over a beat-up Chevy gypsy cab waiting in the Beacon train station's otherwise deserted parking lot. The cabbie was a surprisingly young Hispanic girl with blue hair and earrings in her lower lip and colorful tattoos covering one arm, as though she'd been attacked by a gang of graffiti vandals. I could see that underneath all the junk was a seventeen- or eighteen-year-old young lady with gentle blue eyes who should have been home packing her book bag with paper and sharpened pencils for the new school year instead of out hustling for fares.

"Where to?" she asked before I could ask her if her parents knew where she was.

I shook my head. I had enough on my plate, I decided. Too much, probably.

"The Newburgh police department," I told her, plopping down into the backseat.

Chapter 58

WE ROLLED OVER THE Newburgh–Beacon Bridge back into the run-down town that had almost taken the lives of two of my kids.

I still couldn't get over the dichotomy between the town's Gilded Age history—not to mention its pleasant layout and architecture—and its current decrepit state. Every other house seemed to be a Carpenter Gothic or a Greek Revival or a Queen Anne. These "painted ladies" had definitely seen better days, though, since many of their windows were either missing or boarded up and their gingerbread trim was blistered and rotting.

I continued to shake my head as we pulled onto the four-lane thoroughfare called Broadway.

With its forty-five-degree parking and three-story brick buildings, it looked quintessentially American, like a street scene in an Edward Hopper painting. I was almost expecting a trolley car to turn one of the corners or a soda jerk to walk out of one of the corner stores in a bow tie and white paper hat. But like so many Rust Belt towns in the northeast, Newburgh reminded me of the scene from *It's a Wonderful Life* in which George Bailey gets to see his hometown as it would have been had he never been born.

Talk about wasted potential, I thought. What the heck had happened to this once beautiful place? Staring out at Newburgh's blighted streets, I wondered if George Bailey had maybe caught a bullet in a drive-by.

"I knew I should've taken Water Street," the cabbie said before letting out a loud, slow, scared breath.

We stopped at a red light near Lutheran Street. I leaned forward and watched as a group of teenage black kids crossed in front of the cab. Every one of them was wearing a red do-rag, whether tied to their wrists or peeking out from under their hoods and ball caps. Staring back at their swaggering and arrogant malevolence, I was reminded of Perrine's demeanor in the courtroom. Like Perrine, these kids seemed quite used to driving fear into people's hearts. In fact, they seemed to enjoy it.

I instantly felt myself getting worked up, really starting to seethe. The Newburgh detectives had already told me that the town's drug trade was run by the Bloods and the Latin Kings, and that it looked like it was a member of the rag-wearing Bloods who had shot my sons.

I couldn't take my eyes off them as the group made the opposite corner. I was seeing red, all right. All I kept thinking was that my outgoing son Eddie wasn't so outgoing anymore. That these bastards might have screwed him up for the rest of his life.

By the time the light turned green, I was done. I literally couldn't take it anymore.

"Wait. Stop. Let me out here," I said to the driver.

"What the heck? What are you doing?" my young blue-haired cabbie said. "You don't want to get out on this block. This is like the 'hood, you know what I'm sayin'? The police department

I, Michael Bennett

is only a couple of blocks down."

Instead of answering her, I dropped a twenty into the front seat.

I opened the door with the hand that wasn't holding my quickly drawn and cocked Glock.

Now it was time for some answers.

283

Chapter 59

"HEY, WHAT HAVE WE here?" one of the gangbangers said as the cab sped away. "That Men's Wearhouse two-for-one you wearing says you definitely ain't no pimp. You one of Newburgh's Finest? Or maybe you Bill O'Reilly from the TV?"

The rest of his crew broke up laughing as I approached the north side of Broadway. Every ground-floor business up and down the beat-up block was closed, I noticed. Nothing but steel gates in both directions as far as the eye could see. Everyone had gotten out of Dodge, which was only smart because drug gangs like these Bloods protected their turf with beatings and stabbings and shootings.

The head jokester was a thin, six-foot-three kid of about nineteen. He was relaxed, smiling, enjoying himself. A broad-shouldered youth sitting on the corner mailbox beside him took a toke of the blunt he was smoking and blew the rancid smoke in my direction.

As I approached them, I felt a flicker of fear for the first time as the sane part of my mind began to realize what kind of situation I was putting myself in. There were six of them. Two of them were skinny high school kids, but the others were hardened-looking street punks, tattooed and prison-jacked under spotless XXXL white tees. I could tell at least one of them had a gun in his waistband by the way he was standing a little hunched to one side.

Armed cop or not, I was all alone and didn't even know where the hell I was. What the hell was I doing? You needed backup in an area like this. SWAT, maybe.

But then I did a smart thing. I told the rational Dr. Jekyll part of me to put a sock in it, and let the unhinged Mr. Hyde part of me begin to roll.

"No, no. I'm not Bill O'Reilly," I said with a

laugh as I finally showed them what was in my hand.

They reared back, whoa-ing and raising their hands in unison as I leveled my chunky black polymer Glock in their faces. The gangbangers stood in complete shock, absolutely frozen, as though I'd just conjured up an elephant or a cruise ship out of thin air.

"But I am looking for news," I said. "You guys hear about some little kids that got shot over on Lander Street last week? Speak up, fellas. I can't hear you. I heard the shooter was wearing a red Yankees cap. You guys look like red's your favorite color, like maybe you shop at the same store. I'll ask nice one more time. Who shot those kids?"

They kept staring at me in mute wonder.

The funny thing was, at that moment, I was willing to shoot them, and they knew it. They could see it in my eyes that I was about as far from messing around as one can get.

As a cop, you draw your gun for one reason: to kill someone. You don't wing people, you don't let off warning shots. When you take out your gun, it's for putting bullets into someone's head or chest before they can do the same to you. If you're not willing to go that far, then you leave it in the holster.

"Hey, chill, Officer," the pot-smoking tough finally said. "We didn't do nothing. This ain't Lander Street. This be the east end. Just chill. We got no beef with you."

"Oh, yes, you do, homey," I growled, my knuckles whitening around the grip of my gun. "See, those kids who got shot, they were my kids. I'm not a cop here. I'm a father. Now you tell me right now which one of you red-rag-wearing jackasses shot my kids or by tomorrow morning, your girlfriends and mommas are going to be laying out so many damn memorial candles on this corner it's going to be lit up like Times Square."

That's when I heard it. It was the high squeal of tires behind me. For a second, I panicked, thinking my Irish temper had finally gone and gotten my dumb ass killed. For a moment, I was seriously convinced that I was about to get run over or hosed in a drive-by.

Then over the engine roar of the rapidly approaching car, I heard a glorious sound. It was the metallic double *woop* of a squad-car growler. The flickering blue and red lights made the darkened north side of Broadway look like a carnival as the car screeched to a stop at my back.

The gang kids scattered as I turned around, holstering my weapon.

Two cops got out of the unmarked car and stood behind its flung-open doors.

"Hi, Mike. Um, out for an evening stroll?" Detective Bill Moss said, rolling his eyes.

His partner, Ed Boyanoski, shook his head at me with an expression somewhere between disappointment and awe.

"Well, what do you know? The cavalry, right on time," I said.

"Let me guess. Long day at the office, Mike?" Bill said as I climbed into the backseat.

I smiled.

"It was, but that little meet and greet has rejuvenated me all of a sudden," I said, rubbing my hands together. "I think I just got my second wind."

Chapter 60

INSTEAD OF HEADING TO the police department, the detectives took me to an all-night diner a little north of the city, near the interstate, to meet their colleagues.

At a semicircular red vinyl booth toward the rear of the chrome-and-mirrored space, I was introduced to Sergeant Grant Walrond and Officer Timothy Groover. Walrond was Mike Tyson stocky, a young friendly black cop with a dry sense of humor. Groover, on the other hand, was white and tall, with a mullet hairdo that made him look more like a farmer than a cop. Both of them were extremely dedicated veteran cops and were the major players in the Newburgh PD gang unit.

Bill Moss said, "Sergeant Walrond here received some information this afternoon that the shooter was a Blood, but not from Lander Street."

"The kid we got word about is pretty well known," Walrond said. "His name's James Glaser, but they call him Jay D. He's a Blood from the east end, a low-level punk who jumps from crew to crew because he's a loose-cannon troublemaker. He's eighteen years old, and he was shot on two different occasions last year."

"Got more holes in him than a colander," Groover mumbled over the rim of his coffee cup.

"Crew to crew?" I said. "How many Bloods are there?"

"About a hundred and fifty members altogether," Walrond said.

"In a town of thirty thousand?" I said in shock. "When the heck did all this start? I thought the Bloods were an L.A. thing."

"It's true that most of the gangs, like the Bloods and the Latin Kings, originated in L.A. and Chicago," Groover said. "But because selling drugs is so profitable, members started branching out to expand their markets. Most of the gang members in Newburgh are offshoots of the gangs in New York, primarily those on Rikers Island, which are predominantly run by the Bloods and the Latin Kings."

"Usually, the gang will make contacts among the locals and contract out the street sales," Walrond added. "The locals are brought into the gang, taught its culture and rules, and pretty soon you have yourself a serious problem. The Newburgh kids are like kids anywhere else—just bored teenagers looking for direction and excitement. When the gang rep shows up, it's like a match on gasoline."

"The gangs provide direction, all right," Bill Moss piped in. "How to get to the graveyard before your twenty-first birthday. We had seven murders last year. Six of them were male gangbangers under the age of twenty-five. The seventh was a second grade girl caught in the crossfire."

I shook my head. And I thought New York was bad.

Sergeant Walrond excused himself as he received a text message.

"All right. Here we go," he said. "That's Pops.

He's one of my informants. Why don't you come meet him with us, Mike? He's sort of a street guy, but he actually feels for how bad Newburgh has gotten. He feels especially horrible about what happened to your kids."

Walrond didn't have to ask me twice.

We met Pops a block away, in the empty parking lot of a medical office building. He was a heavyset, kind of goofy, fast-talking black guy with a deep voice who reminded me of the clownish old-school rapper Biz Markie.

"Like I was tellin' you, Sarge," Pops said. "It wasn't the Bloods shot those kids. Shootin' customers be bad for business, 'specially white ones 'fraid to come into the 'hood in the first place."

"But Jay D is a Blood," Walrond argued.

"Aw, he just a peewee. He got no rank," Pops said dismissively. "Plus the kid's just damn crazy. The way I heard it, he was working with the Kings, man. He was like hired out."

"*Hired out?*" I said, my blood beginning to boil for the second time this evening.

Walrond put a hand on my shoulder.

I shut my mouth. Which wasn't easy, considering I just wanted answers. I bit my tongue and allowed the detective to do his job.

"Why would they do that, Pops?" Walrond continued.

"Beats me," Pops said. "All I know is the Bloods ain't happy because tensions already be runnin' high lately between the nations. They say it's that Mexican cartel dude they got on trial. What's his name? Perrine? Yeah, Perrine's been franchising out all that good pure Mexican dope for cheap to the Latin King Nation from South Beach up to Boston. The Kings keep dropping their price, and the Bloods are getting crushed, losin' business like crazy."

Perrine? I thought. Perrine was connected to the Latin Kings who hired someone to shoot my kids? It couldn't be. How could that be right?

Walrond immediately sensed I was about to jump out of my skin.

"Thanks, Pops," Walrond said, sending him on his way. "Keep in touch."

Chapter 61

I HAD A LOT ON my mind by the time Walrond and Groover finally dropped me back at the lake house. Fortunately, Mary had left me dinner, a homemade Italian sub with a side of German potato salad, which I found in the back of the old vintage fridge, deftly hidden from hungry teens. To complete my culinary trip around the world, I washed it down with a bottle of cold Pilsner Urquell beer from the Czech Republic.

Who says the effects of globalization are all bad?

After my late-night dinner, I went into the family room and turned on Leno. There was a box of movie candy on the coffee table called Lemonhead & Friends. I couldn't remember the last time I'd eaten candy, but for whatever reason, I started gobbling up the sweet-and-sour jelly-bean things like they were going out of style.

As I scarfed down the sugary garbage, I watched Leno interview a bullying British celebrity chef who really needed a punch in the mouth. I couldn't stop thinking about what the informant, Pops, had said about Perrine's involvement with the Latin Kings, and the Latin Kings' involvement with my kids' shooting. Was it just street bullshit? His own personal fantasy? The guy did kind of seem like a flake.

It nagged me so much that I found my cell phone and made a call. It was to the DEA SWAT head, Patrick Zaretski, who had been my departed friend Hughie's mentor in the agency. Ever since Hughie had been killed, Zaretski had been doing nothing but delving into the intricacies of Perrine's cartel and trying to find all those responsible for his death. If Pops's story had any truth to it, Patrick would be able to confirm it.

Patrick answered on the fourth ring.

"Hey, Patrick. Mike Bennett. Sorry to call you so late, but I need a favor. I got a guy in

Newburgh, New York, who's claiming that Perrine is supplying the Latin Kings with dope on the East Coast. Does that sound right to you? You think there's a connection there?"

"I don't know, Mike," Patrick said. "But give me an hour and I'll find out."

It actually only took half an hour before my phone rang again.

"Mike, you're spot on. We do have intelligence that the two organizations are working in concert. It started up late last year. Apparently, half the Latin Kings' heroin and almost all their coke is coming from Perrine's people. Perrine is also supplying the gang MS-13 and pretty much all the Latin drug-trafficking gangs in the entire country. That's how deeply these Mexican cartels have penetrated into the U.S.

"I hate to ask, Mike, but does this have something to do with your kids?"

We'd mostly kept the boys' shooting out of the paper, but I'd already told Patrick and a few other law enforcement friends what had happened.

"That's what I'm trying to figure out, Patrick," I said. "I thought it was just a terrible mistake—

my kids being in the wrong place at the wrong time—but the informant up here is claiming that the kid who shot Eddie and Brian was hired by the Latin Kings. Could Perrine know that I'm up here on vacation? He targeted my children?"

"Unfortunately, it's more than possible, Mike," Patrick said. "You've seen the pictures. You know Perrine's tactics down in Mexico. You think you'd be the first cop he's personally targeted? He's a mass murderer, Mike. You put him in a cage. Of course, he'd love to get at you and your loved ones."

I sat there holding the phone. All around me, my family slept safely in their beds. But for how long? I thought. How the hell could I keep them safe with this monster and his organization on my trail?

Chapter 62

MY CELL PHONE RANG early the next morning. Before dawn, in fact.

It didn't really matter, because I was already up with Seamus. I was teaching him how to load and unload the 12-gauge Remington shotgun I'd found behind some canoe oars in the cluttered garage a couple of days before. It killed me to have to teach the kind old man how to lethally defend himself and the rest of the kids. He was a priest, after all.

But what else could I do after my conversation with Patrick Zaretski? It was looking more and more like my family had actually been targeted by Perrine. These were truly desperate times.

It turned out to be Detective Ed Boyanoski on the phone.

"Sorry to call so early, Mike, but we got a witness who just ID'd your boys' shooter. The county DA gave the go-ahead. We're about to go grab him, and I thought you'd want to be there."

"You thought right," I said.

"We'll come to you," Ed said. "Be there in ten."

That's when Mary Catherine came into the kitchen. Her eyes just about detached from their sockets when she saw Seamus in his Manhattan College pajamas with the pump-action shotgun.

"What in the name of sweet holy God is going on here?" she wanted to know.

Seamus smiled devilishly.

"Nothing, really," he said. "Young Michael here was just teaching me the finer rudiments of how to lock and load."

"Give it here," Mary Catherine told him.

She took the shotgun from him deftly and quickly thumbed four shells into the underside loading port.

"What model Remington is this? An eight seventy?" she said, blinking a curl of blond hair out of her eyes.

I nodded, blinking back in shock.

She clicked the safety on before pumping a round into the chamber. She swung the shotgun to her shoulder and aimed down the barrel at the wall, nodding to herself. Then she unloaded it, quickly pumping all the rounds out of the receiver onto the kitchen table, catching the last spinning red shell in her hand.

"Where'd you learn all that?" I said, hiding my smile as she handed me back the gun.

"I grew up on a cattle farm, Mike. There wasn't as much rustling going on in Tipperary as in the Wild West, but we had some. Not at our farm, though."

"I'll bet," I said, and started to laugh. This attractive young woman never failed to shock.

She put her hands on her hips, Wonder Woman–style, which made sense.

"Now, if there's any locking and loading to be done around here when Mike is at work, I'll be the one to do it. Agreed, gentlemen?" she said.

"You win, Annie O'Oakley," I said, making her smile.

Seamus folded his arms, frowning at the both of us.

"Fine. I'm going back to bed," he said after another half a minute.

"I never get to have any fun at all," he whined as he left.

Chapter 63

A BRIEF HORN HONK came from outside a moment later.

"And where are you headed this early?" Mary Catherine said as I clipped my holster to my belt by the front door.

I debated whether to tell her. I decided I didn't want to say anything about bagging the son of a bitch who'd hurt Eddie and Brian until we had him.

"Ah, nowhere, really," I said as I pulled down my shirt over my gun. "Just going to see a man about a dog."

"Well, please don't get bit, Michael," Mary Catherine said. "We have all the Bennetts on the mend that we can handle at present."

"Don't worry, lass," I said, showing her the handcuffs I had in the pocket of my Windbreaker. "I brought a strong leash."

There were two patrol cars in the arrest team besides the unmarked one I rode in with Detectives Ed and Bill, who had brought me a coffee and had laid a Kevlar vest out for me in the backseat.

"Just my size, too," I said, slipping it on. "You guys are the best."

It took about twenty more minutes to roll up to the address in Newburgh. It was actually on a block of pretty well-kept houses on Bay View Terrace. Behind them, there was a pure, stunning view of the Hudson. How much would Newburgh real estate be worth if the city wasn't riddled with crime? I wondered. It was only an hour and twenty minutes away from New York City. I stared out at the sky, just starting to lighten behind Beacon, as we pulled to a stop.

"This is where his aunt lives," Bill said. "He's been hiding out with her ever since he got word we were looking for him."

A dog started barking nearby as we waited for one of the cruisers to get into position on the next block, in case Jay D went out the back. The Motorola in Ed's hand suddenly crackled.

"Heads up," said someone in the cruiser parked behind us. "We have a figure in the alleyway across the street with a long object in their hand."

That tensed things up. There was word that the Bloods had automatic weapons, including AK-47s.

A moment later, an old thin black woman in a tracksuit appeared, mumbling to herself as she began haphazardly sweeping her porch with a broom.

"Stand down. It's just Grandma doing her six a.m. tidy-up," the radio said.

"Or the Wicked Witch of West Newburgh," Detective Moss mumbled after a loud exhale.

Chapter 64

"OKAY. WE'RE SET. WE'RE in position at the back," came word from the other cruiser.

"Roger Dodger," Ed Boyanoski said as he grabbed the battering ram. "We're going in."

It turned out that we didn't need the battering ram. As we came up the stairs, the door opened and a tall middle-aged black man wearing blue Dickies work clothes walked out. He waved his arms over his head.

"Now, now. Calm down. Calm down. You don't need to be bustin' my brand-new door down," he said, eyeing us. "You here for James, I take it?"

"You take it right, sir," Detective Moss said.

"Thank God," the man said, turning and

holding the door open for us. "Hallelujah."

"Woman!" the man called back into the house. "Get that child out here now!"

A moment later, a petite black woman appeared with her arms around a hard-looking, stocky teenager. He was in flip-flops and wore white shorts, a white beater, and a blood-red Yankees cap.

"This is all wrong. All wrong," said the aunt as Ed and Bill frisked and cuffed Jay D on the porch. "James is a good boy."

"I'm sure he is, ma'am," Detective Moss said. "We'd like to go and search his room now if that's okay."

"By all means," Jay D's uncle said. "This good boy's room is just to the right at the top of the stairs. Try not to trip over all the Bibles and choir robes, now."

"I didn't do nothin'," Jay D said after Bill read him his rights and got him into the back of the cruiser. Ed sat in the back with him, wisely leaving me in the front passenger seat, where I couldn't get my hands around his neck.

"This is total bullshit, man," the punk cried as he rocked back and forth violently against the seat. "You only doin' this because those kids shot over on Lander were white kids."

"Now, James, we're not out of the driveway yet, and already you're dropping the race card," Ed Boyanoski said with a tsk. "Didn't we investigate your shooting last year, James? I'm sorry, I mean shootings?"

"Bullshit, man," Jay D repeated. He stomped on the floor of the cruiser. "You don't think I know that the only reason you bugging everybody like this is because those white boys were the kids of a cop?"

Bill Moss and I exchanged a surprised glance before I turned around and stared the punk in his eye.

"You're actually right about that," I said, showing him my shield. "We cops do tend to get a little upset when you shoot up our children. See, I'm in a gang, too. It's called the NYPD. They don't issue us those ratty dishrags you guys like to sport, but we do have some pretty cool hats."

The kid smirked and looked at me sideways. "You him, ain't you?" he said.

He nodded with a sudden smile.

"Bennett, right? Knew it. This ain't just racist-ass bullshit. This is some racist-ass cop bullshit."

"Quick question, James," Ed said. "How do you know who the kids were? I mean that stuff about them being the kids of a cop was deliberately left out of the paper."

"How much did the Latin Kings pay you?" I yelled. "I hope it was worth it, punk, because if you think I'm pulling strings now, this is nothing compared to the favors I'm going to call in to make sure you earn every single goddamn penny of it."

Jay D looked at us one by one. He started biting his lower lip like it was a chew toy. The punk suddenly squeezed himself into the rear seat's corner as if it contained an escape hatch.

"That's it. I want my lawyer," he mumbled. "I ain't talkin' no more."

"You're shutting up?" Detective Bill Moss said as he finally put the unmarked into drive. "Is that a promise, James? Hallelujah! Praise the Lord!"

Chapter 65

WE HAD A COOKOUT to end all cookouts that night. The three-burner grill out on the dock was completely covered with burgers, dogs, corn on the cob, peppers, lamb shish kebabs. I even had an Italian sausage wheel that I'd found in a terrific deli not too far from the lake house, where I also scored some real New York–style Italian bread to wrap around the sausage and peppers. Tony Soprano would have been impressed.

"Hey, Father. How do you say 'fuhgedda-boudit' in Gaelic?" I asked Seamus over the smoke.

Of course we were having a feast. That's what your friendly neighborhood heroes did when they bagged the beast: got the grill going and broke out the mead, like Beowulf and his men after offing Grendel.

But Beowulf actually had to go and fight Grendel's mother next, didn't he? I thought, remembering how Perrine still needed to be deep-sixed. He certainly was a mother, wasn't he?

Whatever, I thought, pulling on the frosty beer at my elbow and wiping sweat off my brow with my grill mitt. Line 'em up, and I'll put 'em down one at a time. No, wait. That was Hughie's policy on shots. Poor Hughie. Man, I missed him.

Half the Newburgh PD showed up. Ed Boyanoski was there with his wife, Celia, and three kids as well as Bill Moss and his wife, Cordelia, and their two daughters. Even the gang-unit cops, Walrond and Groover, showed up with their respective clans.

Walrond's clan included his new wife and beautiful four-month-old baby girl, Iris. My girls —including Mary Catherine, for some strange reason—surrounded Iris's car seat and could not be peeled away during the entire party.

All's well that was ending well, at least for the current moment.

Even the kids' surgeon, Dr. Mary Ann Walker, showed up for a quick ale. It turned out that she and Ed were already friends because they both served on the board of the Newburgh Historical Society. I learned that Ed, a former marine, was also a deacon at downtown Newburgh's Saint Patrick's Church and spent much of his free time coaching basketball at the Boys and Girls Club.

"So many people have written off this town to the gangs, Mike, but I know we can turn it around," Ed said. "This place is my home. I'm never leaving."

Ed was a top-notch guy. They all were. Good people who truly cared about their community and were trying to do their best in a bad situation.

"Man, you know how to toss a soiree here, Mike," a swim-trunk-clad Groover called from a floating inner tube off the dock. He had a sausage-and-peppers hero in one hand and a beer in the other.

"I haven't had too much to celebrate in a while, so I'm pulling out all the stops, my man. You guys deserve it. Now my family can put all this nonsense in the rearview."

"How many kids do you have, anyway?" Groover wanted to know.

I shook my head. "Dude, I lost count a long time ago."

Groover looked down into his beer thoughtfully before raising his plastic cup.

"The more the merrier," he called.

I looked over at my son Eddie, talking and laughing with one of Ed Boyanoski's kids, and raised my own.

"The more the merrier," I agreed with a smile.

Damn right.

It was the Bennett family motto, after all.

Chapter 66

AT AROUND NINE, THE party wrapped up pretty much the way all cop parties do—with some beery high fives and fist bumps and promises to do it again real soon.

It had really been a fun time, even for all our cop kids, who had broken into teams and had wrapped up the night playing an epic game of ring-a-levio. Eddie had been the last one caught as he made a heroic attempt to free his team from jail.

Hearing his squealing laughter again as he was tackled was by far the best part of the night. Hell, the best part of the month.

"These Newburgh guys are all right in my book," I said to Mary Catherine as we waved good-bye to the last set of retreating headlights from the porch.

"Is that just the beer talking?" Mary Catherine asked, eyeing the half-full Heineken in my hand.

"Well, maybe not *just* the beer," I said sheepishly.

Even though the house and backyard and especially the dock looked like they'd been attacked by a host of marauding barbarians, Mary Catherine and I turned our backs on the paper plates. We left all our sleeping, sunburned charges in Seamus's care and decided to take a long walk around the lake.

We ended up taking the secluded forest path I'd frantically scoured the week before when I'd searched for Eddie and Brian. At the top of the hill, Mary Catherine suddenly stopped and turned around.

"Look. It's beautiful," she said.

I followed her pointing finger just above the treetops to a bright, glowing sliver of quarter moon, tinged with pink. All around it, stars—too many to count—sparkled against the seemingly endless navy-blue sky. We could have been the only people in the world, in the universe.

We sat, and I broke out the midnight picnic I'd packed. An old flannel blanket, some Cheddar and grapes, a cold bottle of sauvignon blanc that I had to laboriously work open with the Leatherman tool on my key chain, since I'd forgotten to bring a corkscrew.

I laid out the blanket in the middle of the forest clearing and poured wine into a couple of plastic glasses.

"I thought you weren't supposed to mix beer and wine," Mary Catherine said, leaning back with the cup on her stomach and staring up at the sky.

"Midnight picnics are the exception," I said, sitting cross-legged across from her.

Mary Catherine yawned and closed her eyes.

"You know what would be really great, Mike?"

"What's that?" I said.

"If we could really go on vacation. You know, one where you're not working and actually here?"

I laughed.

"That's quite a concept," I said. "A nonworking vacation, is it?"

Mary Catherine sighed.

"Or how about for once we could go on a real date, Mike? Three or four hours of just me and you. No kids, no phones. Just two adults together alone, enjoying each other's company. I would like that so much. Wouldn't you?"

"You're right, Mary Catherine," I said, feeling suddenly very guilty.

How could I be such an insensitive clod? I had to stop taking this wonderful woman for granted or I was going to be very sorry.

"Enough of squeezing in a moment here and there," I said. "You're absolutely right. I'll arrange the whole thing. We'll put Seamus on duty and go wherever you want. Down into the city. We'll paint the town red. Where do you want to go?"

I waited for a few moments. But even after a full minute, she was still silent. I turned and glanced at her, laughing to myself as I watched her sleep.

"Oh, Sleeping Beauty," I said as I gathered up the remnants of our picnic. "What did I do to deserve someone as lovely as you?"

Chapter 67

IT WAS STILL DARK when I heard the doorbell ring the next morning. Hungover and bleary-eyed, I went ass over teakettle into a beanbag chair as I tripped over an inner tube in the unlit family room. I was still in my boxer shorts, dusting myself off, as I peeked out the window and saw a Newburgh police cruiser in the driveway and a uniformed cop on the porch.

"Good morning," I said, opening the door.

The young, attractive, black female cop smiled and blushed a little when she saw my bamboozled face and skimpy attire.

"Detective Bennett, sorry to bother you so early," she said, quickly recovering. "Detective Boyanoski sent me. He tried your phone, but you didn't pick up. Something's come up. It's about the assailant who shot your boys. The gang member, Jay D—James Glaser?"

"What about him?" I said, rubbing my eyes.

"He was murdered in jail last night," she said.

That got me moving. I threw on a pair of jeans and a polo shirt, grabbed my gun, and took a ride into town with the good-looking rookie cop, whose name was Belinda Saxon. Bill and Ed were already outside waiting for me in the Newburgh PD parking lot. Behind them, the sun was just coming up over the Hudson.

"Let me guess. The party's over?" I said as I got out of the cruiser.

"So's our friend James Glaser," Bill Moss said, opening the unmarked Ford's back door as though he were a chauffeur.

After some coffee and a quick breakfast at the diner out by I-84, we headed to the Shawangunk Correctional Facility in nearby Wallkill, New York, where Glaser had been transferred. The sunny green farm fields we passed had horses in them, rows of corn. I thought about the eighteen-year-old kid we'd picked up the day before and shook my head. How could he be dead on this beautiful summer morning? And how could this bucolic area have a gang problem?

After being processed just inside the steel gate of the maximum-security prison, we were brought into a formidable building to meet with the assistant warden, Kenneth Bozman, in his ground-floor office.

"Twenty inmates from B block went to B yard for evening rec around seven," the well-groomed, round-faced bureaucrat explained as he drummed his chewed-to-the-nub fingernails on a metal file cabinet next to his desk. "Come seven thirty, James Glaser was seen in a scuffle with another black male. Glaser was dead as a doornail upon arrival of staff. His attacker was still hovering over him. The assailant's name is Gary McKay, a lifer. He's been segregated in our special housing unit since the incident."

"How'd he kill him?" Ed Boyanoski asked.

Bozman stopped drumming and pointed to the hollow of his throat above his tie.

"He buried the sharpened end of a broken mop handle into Glaser's clavicle," Bozman said, shaking his head. "Stabbed it all the way down into his heart like a skewer. Unbelievable. What a shitstorm. We're max security, but we run a tight ship. We haven't had a murder here since oh three."

"What's McKay's story?" Bill asked.

"I'm surprised you haven't heard of him," Bozman said. "He's old-school. Drug dealer who used to run the Newburgh drug scene back in the eighties. He's in for a triple homicide and attempted murder of a cop. Now he heads the Bloods here in the prison. I take it this is a Bloods thing, some kind of street beef?"

"You take it correctly," Ed told him.

"I figured," Bozman said. "I mean, McKay's a homicidal maniac, but skewering a son of a bitch is a little excessive for having a newbie look at you funny."

"We'd like to talk to him, if that's okay," Bill Moss said.

"Wait here," Bozman said. "I'll go into the warden and ask." Bozman came back less than a minute later.

"Shit. Sorry, fellas. They actually just took him to the courthouse in Shawangunk for his arraignment. Maybe you can catch him there."

Chapter 68

WE PULLED OUT OF the prison and went into the town of Shawangunk, which, I was told, was pronounced "Shawngum" by the locals. Go figure.

It was a neat and tidy town—hedgerows and farmland, white picket fences. The main drag, as far as I could tell, consisted of a pizza parlor, an industrial building, a water tower, and a field-stone library. The court was in the new town hall at the outskirts of town, a handsome brick building with a recently cut patch of manicured green grass in front.

Inside, we found McKay with his nine-man entourage of corrections officers and state police sitting inside the courtroom. McKay was a rough-looking character, an extra-large tattooed black man with a beard who looked a little like Rasheed Wallace when he played for the Detroit Pistons. Since everyone was still waiting for the judge and McKay's public defender to arrive, we asked the staties to let us interview him. They readily agreed.

We proceeded into a large meeting room adjacent to the courtroom. The room, which smelled as though it had just been painted, was filled with folding chairs and a podium book-ended by the American and New York State flags. McKay, in wrist and ankle shackles, shuffled in, escorted by two state troopers. He parked his ass in one of the folding chairs with a clink of chains and sat, scowling, with his eyes closed.

Without missing a beat, Bill Moss opened a folding chair and placed it down in front of the large prisoner. When the cop sat and opened his notebook, he was almost knee-to-knee with McKay.

The differences between the two black men were stark. Bill was a teddy bear, one of the friendliest, most approachable-looking people I'd ever met. McKay was more like a starving grizzly. Even sitting, he was easily a head taller than Bill, who looked uncharacteristically tired, almost depressed. I felt bad for the thirty-year Newburgh PD vet. He'd actually grown up in the now-rough part of Newburgh, near Lander Street, and you could tell that its recent rapid decline was really taking a personal toll.

"Fuck's this?" McKay said, opening one eye at Bill. "More cops, man? Shit, c'mon. How many times I gotta tell you? I'm tired a this shit."

"I'm Detective Moss," Bill said, as if McKay hadn't spoken.

He took a pen from his pocket and clicked it a few times.

"We're from the Newburgh PD and would like to ask you a few questions."

"Fine. Whatever, man. I told them. I'll tell you. I'll tell everyone. Ma boy, Jay D, was murdered because he was a traitor to the Blood Nation. He worked with the South Americans and made the Blood Nation look bad. I got the call to do something about it, so that's what I did. I did something about it. Now tack me on another life sentence and get it over with already. Sheesh."

Ed and I looked at each other, stunned. The arrogance and complete disregard for human life McKay was displaying was remarkable, even for a hard-core gang member.

Bill, on the other hand, just nodded as he wrote in his notebook.

"Concerning the call you received, who was on the other end of that? Can you elucidate?"

"E-loose-a-what? C'mon, brother," McKay said, closing his eyes again. "This is the easiest case you'll ever have. Write this shit down. Jay D needed to get iced. I iced him. Then I'll sign that shit, and I can get back before lunch. We're havin' grilled cheese, and it's my favorite. We're done now. My statement here is over."

Again Ed and I looked at each other. Bozman had been right about this guy being a maniac. Wow, this McKay was one cold-hearted bastard.

"All right. That's fine. Thanks for speaking with us, Mr. McKay," Bill said, closing his notebook and tucking his pen carefully back into his jacket.

Bill stood and was about to head for the door when he stopped and turned.

"Actually, there is just one more thing, Mr.

McKay," he said, walking back and sitting down in front of the prisoner again.

McKay tsked impatiently as Bill again retrieved his notebook and pen with slow deliberation.

"What now, man?" McKay said.

"Tonight's my fiftieth birthday," Bill said, spinning the pen between his fingers. "I'm going to the Peter Luger Steak House in Brooklyn. Ever been to Peter Luger's? It's the best steak house in New York City. Some say in the whole world."

"Yeah, good for you, dog. I'm trying to sleep," McKay said.

"All my friends and family will be there, including my twin brother. Obviously, it's his birthday, too. My eighty-year-old mom, my kids. After we get up to speed with hugs and kisses and showing each other pictures on our cell phones, I'm going to order a T-bone the size of a phone book and wash it down with a hundred-dollar bottle of Pinot Noir. Then I'm going to go home, drink an ice-cold bottle of Veuve Clicquot Champagne in my Jacuzzi, and make love to my wife on the new Bob-O-Pedic mattress we just bought."

McKay opened his eyes and looked at the cop in stark wonder.

"After I'm done with all that, you know what I'm going to do, Mr. McKay? I'm going to get down on my knees and pray to God Almighty that New York brings the death penalty back so that you can finally be erased like the horrible mistake you are. Society showed you mercy by not executing you for your first three murders, and what did you do with that mercy? You used it to kill a fourth human being with a sharpened piece of wood."

"There a question in there, officer?" McKay said after a long beat.

Bill pointed his pen at him.

"No, more like a moral," Bill said. "Remember a minute ago you called me brother? Well, the moral of my tale is that I'm not your brother and never will be, you murdering sack of goat shit. My brother, like me, has a family, a life, kids, coworkers, people he loves who love him back. What do you have? Victims.

"Before I leave, I just wanted to let you know that if I had the misfortune of having a human disgrace like you for a brother, I'd look for the tallest building I could find and fling my ass off it."

Bill Moss clicked his pen one last time as he stood.

"Now we're done," he said as he left.

Chapter 69

IT WAS A LITTLE past midnight when Newburgh police sergeant Dermot McDonald drove south in his cruiser down River Road in Newburgh. He rolled past the cruddy industrial heating-oil company that abutted the Hudson twice before he pulled into its driveway.

The company was closed, its parking lot deserted. There was just him, some oil trucks behind a tall fence, the railroad tracks, and the big old rolling Hudson River. It was an absolutely perfect secluded spot for a night-shift cop to grab forty winks.

Or anything else that served his fancy, McDonald thought as he looked inside the knapsack in the footwell of the passenger seat.

Inside were three fat, plastic-wrapped, whitish-yellowish bundles that almost looked like large bars of soap. It was cocaine—three kilos of pure uncut nose candy that he had stolen from a Latin Kings drug bust the week before and was looking to unload on his old friend and high school basketball teammate, Dave Crider, one of the current leaders of the Newburgh Bloods.

The fit, middle-aged cop with silver hair and rimless eyeglasses zipped the bag closed. He took out a piece of Nicorette gum from his uniform shirt pocket, popped it into his mouth, and smiled as he chewed. He could practically taste the seventy-five grand in beautiful, greasy, tax-free tens and twenties that his drug-dealing buddy was on his way with right now.

He'd already decided to take his new girl-friend, Amelia, to Ibiza on Labor Day weekend for her birthday to see one of those techno bands she was gaga about. Amelia was twenty-eight to his forty-six; she had dark hair and dark haunting eyes and lines of tattoos running down the fronts of both of her legs from her waist to her toes. Felt like he was doing it with a carnival freak sometimes—conjoined twins or the bearded lady—but damn, who cared if she scribbled on herself? She was young and freakin' hot.

Funny where life took you, McDonald thought. Up until a year ago, he'd actually been the proverbial happily married man. He'd only gotten divorced after he found out his wife had been cheating on him with the neighbor at the end of their cul-de-sac.

Her lover was, of all things, a Turkish physics professor at Mount Saint Mary College, a diminutive, balding man in his fifties who sounded and even looked sort of like the Count from *Sesame Street*. Even now, McDonald sometimes closed his eyes to see the Muppet laughing at him. "I slept with your wife one, two, three, four times. Ah-ha-hah!"

But it had turned out okay. Divorce had changed him, transformed him, made him reevaluate his priorities. He got into truly excellent shape for the first time in his life, started eating healthy, running, lifting, mountain biking, meeting new people, young people. Amelia. The most important change of all was deciding to finally become a full-blown player in the Newburgh drug game and start raking in some real cheese instead of the pathetic sucker peanuts he was paid by the city.

Alimony? he thought, patting the drug-filled bag. Alimony this!

That's why he'd decided to rekindle his old friendship with Dave. Now instead of setting picks at the top of the key, he supplied his buddy Dave with protection and tip-offs, and Dave supplied him with a tax-free two grand a week. He also used the tips Dave supplied him with to stage busts where he could steal drugs from the rival Latin Kings. One of your win-win situations if there ever was one.

Just yesterday he'd earned $5K from Dave. Pulling some strings with a friend in corrections, he'd helped to set up a turncoat in Dave's operation, some punk-ass kid named Jay D, for a jailhouse murder. Amazing the amount of moneymaking opportunities out there once you had a mind to capitalize on them.

To hell with everyone, McDonald thought. His wife, the department, the people of Newburgh. He had finally wised up. He was on his own side now. He was only sorry he hadn't thought of becoming a corrupt cop sooner.

He checked his phone for the second time. That was funny. Dave was late. That wasn't like him.

Sergeant McDonald ruminated on that for a minute and then decided to turn the cruiser around to face the street, keeping his back safely to the Hudson.

Dave was a bud, but it was a dog-eat-dog world out here, and you could never be too careful.

He chewed his gum and pictured his new girl-friend's haunting eyes, lit by strobe lights.

Chapter 70

A LITTLE MORE THAN half a mile northeast of Sergeant McDonald's parked cruiser, a brand-new fifty-foot sport yacht stood at anchor in the middle of the pitch-dark Hudson River, rising and dipping.

So did the night-vision-enhanced crosshairs of the sniper rifle trained on Sergeant McDonald's right temple.

The rifle that the scope was attached to was a CheyTac M200. The almost thirty-pound big bastard of a weapon had an effective range of nearly 1.2 miles and was made in the good ol' USA. The big bastard of a sniper at its huge night-vision eyepiece happened to be a Scot, a fifty-seven-year-old SAS-trained mercenary named Gabler.

Dressed in black fatigues, Gabler was sitting on a camp chair on the forward deck of the five-hundred-thousand-dollar pleasure craft. Beside him, the massive gun was propped on a shooting bench, as though Gabler were a contestant in a competition.

He'd already zoned in the distance-to-target at 826.23 yards, according to the range finder in his bag, and made his windage adjustments. He'd even checked the barometric pressure, 1011 millibars per hectopascal, which would have negligible effect at the range he was looking at. Except for the sway of the boat, it was simple enough.

So easy a caveman could do it, Gabler thought, slipping his finger into the trigger guard.

Gabler turned his signature tweed cap around on his head as he made a minor adjustment to the scope's eye rest. With his pale scrunched fist of a middle-aged Celtic face, he could have been a soccer analyst or a kindly Scottish sheep farmer, a look that was quite useful considering that he was, in fact, one of the most ruthless and sought-after assassin snipers on planet Earth.

Even before the cop car drove into the kill zone, Gabler knew he was working for some serious-as-cancer Mexican dope dealers. Duh, as a thick Yank would say. Wasn't like a knitting circle could fly him in on a private aircraft from his vacation house in Portugal and come up with his four-hundred-thousand-dollar fee.

It didn't matter in the slightest. Like the man he was about to erase from existence, Gabler, too, was in it for numero uno.

The customer is always right, he thought.

"You ready?" Gabler finally asked with a thick Glasgow burr.

At his elbow stood the client, a sexy, light-skinned Latina in a skintight black pantsuit. Gabler didn't like looking at her. There was something terrible and fierce in her pale, striking eyes, something scary, something that said the lass wasn't quite all there. Throughout his preparations, she'd kept unconsciously licking her lower lip, as if she were turned on by what was about to occur.

The wacko, beautiful bitch held up a restraining hand as she thumbed a smartphone.

"The mark is where we were informed he

would be, as planned," Marietta said. "We have a clear shot. Shall we take it?"

"Yes," Perrine said on the line from his downtown Manhattan prison cell. "By all means. Kill the son of a bitch."

Marietta raised a pair of night-vision goggles and trained them on the Newburgh shore. Then she tapped the mercenary gently on the shoulder.

"Do it now!" she said enthusiastically. "Blow the cop's fucking head off!"

Gabler waited and waited, and then just as the boat rose up from a dip, he squeezed the trigger. The shot, even suppressed to the maximum, made a crisp firecracker pop as the big gun hopped up off the bench rest.

In his sight, Gabler watched the satisfying red explosion of the .408-caliber bullet striking home. It was a direct hit. The huge round entered the cop's right temple and came out his left, cleanly shearing off the top of his head.

Gabler let out a proud breath as he ejected the warm casing. It was a nice shot, considering all the factors. A tidy little piece of work, if he did say so himself. Even those Navy SEAL wankers who had snipered those Somali pirates would have been impressed.

"I wish you could see this, darling," Marietta said into her phone. She was still gazing through her night-vision goggles at the carnage as Gabler went below deck with his gear.

"I'm there in spirit, Marietta," Perrine said as one of the bodyguards winched up the anchor and the streamlined yacht's engine softly rumbled to life.

Chapter 71

IT WAS DARK THAT Sunday night when Seamus and I pulled into the almost-full parking lot of Saint Patrick's Church on Grand Street in downtown Newburgh.

No sultry moonlight or romance in sight on this particular summer night, I thought as I got out. Not even close.

The night before, a uniformed on-duty cop had been shot to death in his cruiser. Actually, I guess "assassinated" would be a better term, since it seemed to have been done with a very high-powered rifle. As if that weren't bad enough, beside the veteran cop was a bag with three kilos of cocaine inside of it.

That's why Seamus and I were here. Ed

Boyanoski had told us about a special emergency meeting of several law enforcement, church, and civic groups who wanted to discuss the latest atrocities and see what could be done about them.

As we crossed the parking lot, I looked out on the lights of Newburgh and thought of the big rip theory in physics. Scientists speculate that the ever-expanding universe will reach a point where forces like gravity can't hold things together anymore, and everything in the entire universe will tear apart at the same time.

Maybe that's what was going on, because this killing wasn't just a hard blow to this small city already on the ropes with drugs and gangs and so many young people shooting each other. It was really starting to look like the knockout punch.

After we passed through a battered metal door, we descended some steps into the church's dank basement, where the meeting hall was. The people there were a mix of Spanish-speaking businessmen and laborers, concerned-looking black moms and grandmoms, and blue- and white-collar Caucasians. The Newburgh PD was well represented, too. Ed and Bill were in the center of the front row, with Walrond and Groover and most of the guys from the gang unit. I passed trauma surgeon Dr. Mary Ann Walker sitting in a chair by the front, staring at the floor as she shredded a napkin.

If there was a common thread among them, it seemed to be devastation. There was also some shock, and even more fear.

I walked over to Ed, who was standing beside a plate of cinnamon churros.

"Is this the part where I say, 'Hi, my name's Mike, and I'm an alcoholic'?" I said as I grabbed a coffee.

"I feel like becoming an alcoholic with the way things are looking around here," Ed said dourly.

Okay, then, I thought as I found a metal folding chair. So much for the witty banter.

An older Hispanic woman with brightly dyed blond hair spoke first.

"I have a seventeen-year-old nephew in jail for murder," she said. "My son isn't even in a gang, but he's been shot. It's like the Wild West out there, or Iraq. Please, won't someone help us?"

After she sat back down, a regal young black woman wearing business clothes and carrying an infant in a baby carrier stepped to the front of the room.

"Hi, everyone. I'm Tasha Jennings. I'm nobody, just a citizen of Newburgh like you. I came tonight to tell everyone that this situation is not hopeless. Things were just this bad when I was a kid in Brooklyn in the early nineties. Actually, they were even worse. We used to get like a hundred murders a year in my neighborhood. But they turned it around. I'm not sure how, but they did it. Someone needs to look into those methods. We need to find out what those cops did there and do it here. Thank you."

As she sat, a mustached white guy in an Orange County Choppers T-shirt and dusty jeans stood up.

"She's right," he said angrily. "That's exactly what we need. We need a Giuliani. Some hard-ass who will make the cops do their goddamn jobs instead of stealing drugs!"

That got some hearty applause from the let's-make-the-cops-put-down-the-doughnuts crowd. I looked over at Ed and Bill, who paid informants out of their own pockets and didn't look like they had gotten a good night's sleep in years, let alone taken a vacation.

"Giuliani?" someone called out. "That guy was a Nazi!"

"Damn straight he was a Nazi," Mustache said. "The Nazi who saved New York City."

The rest of the meeting wasn't very effective. There was a lot of yelling, people venting their frustration. You couldn't blame them. The Newburgh residents wanted their city back. They wanted to do the right thing for their town and for their families.

But how?

Chapter 72

THE FIRST TIME SEAMUS spoke was when we got back into the minibus.

"I was thinking about what that nice young woman said," he said after he clicked his seat belt in place.. "About turning around New York. Did you know that Giuliani wasn't the first crusader to clean up New York?"

"What are you talking about?" I said.

"It happened in the late eighteen hundreds. The plight of the Irish in New York City after the 1849 potato famine was far worse than that of the poor people here in Newburgh. The Irish were considered a menace to society, and the run-down parts of the city where they lived were rife with crime and drugs, prostitution and gangs, and deplorable conditions."

"We were the original gangsters?" I said with a grin.

"Exactly," Seamus said in his brogue. "What turned it around was a moral and cultural revolution. A bishop named John Hughes went into the slums and took the people to task, condemning their criminality on the one hand and offering a sense of self-respect and hope through God on the other. Hughes was actually the one who started the Catholic school system. With his efforts, in a generation, all the criminals were cops and the Irish were solid citizens."

"You think that might work, Father?" I said skeptically. "Me and you should walk down Lander Street thumping a Bible? I mean, really? Could I hollow mine out for my Glock?"

My grandfather looked very old as he shrugged and looked out the window.

"It's in the DNA of young male human beings to enjoy acting like hooligans," he said. "Everyone knows that. Nothing will ever stop that. The only effective curb to that unacceptable behavior is the presence of a larger male human being known as a father who will kick the young man's keister when he acts up. Where are the fathers here?"

"So that's it? Fatherlessness is the root of the gang problem?"

"It's not rocket science, Mick," Seamus said. "I don't need to tell you how much hands-on help a teenage boy needs to become a self-reliant, law-abiding man."

"You have a point there," I said.

"Exactly. A mother can't control a fifteen-year-old young man by herself. School can't. So these kids run wilder and wilder until they get killed or the police have to step in."

"They are wild," I said.

"See, the Church emphasizes the family and frowns on premarital sex and divorce, and people laugh and call us killjoys and plug their ears," Seamus said. "There are many ways to raise children and none is perfect, but anyone who says a traditional nuclear family isn't the *best* way is flat-out fooling himself."

He sighed.

"People say it's society's fault, and they're right. In our society, fatherlessness is considered a lifestyle choice. But it's not. To have a child and not be its father is criminal abandonment. You might as well leave your baby in his stroller on the corner and run away, because that's basically what you're doing. Without a father, these kids have been abandoned to the street, and hence the situation here in Newburgh. *Lord of the Flies* with drugs and guns."

"So all of a sudden these gangbangers are going to put away their nine-millimeters and drugs and settle down with formula and diapers? How's that going to happen? And why didn't you say all this at the meeting?" I said. "Put the message out there?"

"They don't want to hear it from an old Irish priest," Seamus said. "They'd shut me out as an interloper before I got to the podium."

"Who should be the messenger, then?"

"I don't know. Jay-Z might be a start, or that P. Diddy fella. The message has to come from someone prominent, someone who already has their respect. Bill Cosby tried to say some sensible things a few years back, but the secular crowd shouted him down. It has to be someone who won't be shouted down by anyone. Someone with fire in his belly."

"Jay-Z, Seamus? C'mon. That's just not going to happen."

"In that case, we need to start building more prisons and graveyards," Seamus said. "Because if someone doesn't come along and somehow convince these young men to live their lives in a different way, they're going to go right on killing each other. Generation after generation after generation."

"As much as I hate to say this, old man," I said as I finally put the bus into drive, "I think you're actually right."

DETECTIVE
MICHAEL BENNETT

Book Four

ALL THE KING'S MEN

Chapter 73

IN THE MIDDLE OF the night—3:00 a.m. on Monday, to be exact—I got a call from DEA chief Patrick Zaretski. It was big news. Good big news, for a change.

A tip had come in on a group linked to Manuel Perrine. Apparently, a team of killers was holed up in a house in Staten Island. It was being speculated that they were there to plot another brazen assault at Perrine's trial. The house was currently under surveillance while an arrest team was put together.

"There's word that there's an attractive brunette at the location," Patrick said. "We think it's that bitch Marietta, Mike. Hughie's killer. We might have finally caught a break on this."

By 4:00 a.m., I was on the New York State Thruway, flying at nearly a hundred miles an hour, with Jimmy Sanchez, a DEA agent from the joint task force who lived in Orange County. His car was an undercover vehicle, a souped-up Dodge Charger, and the bubbling roar of its 6.4-liter HEMI V8 was the perfect sound track to my mounting adrenaline and anticipation. My foot was aching to kick a door down—and even more aching to finally kick some scumbag, drug-dealer ass—as we headed toward New York City like bats out of hell.

We toned it down considerably by the time we got to the rallying point. We rolled up to the wagon train of DEA and NYPD unmarked cars already waiting in the deserted parking lot of a Chili's on Richmond Avenue near the College of Staten Island.

All stops had been thoroughly pulled. There were almost three dozen detectives, DEA agents, and Emergency Service Unit cops helping each other into Kevlar and prepping guns on the trunks of their cruisers. They looked like a pro football defensive squad getting their game faces on, just about ready to mix it up. I know I was ready to trade some helmet paint with Perrine's people. Raring to go, in fact.

It was a strange and sort of wonderful moment there, getting prepared with those men. Though no one said anything, we knew that this was bigger than just a drug raid. The audacious violence of Perrine's men had turned his trial into an international event. The man hadn't just broken American laws, he'd gleefully spat in the face of everything we stood for.

And the rest of the planet was waiting to see what we were going to do about it.

The dedicated cops around me were aching to show the world exactly what we were going to do about it. Because they were tired of the evil and the drugs, tired of the terrorists tearing at the fabric of our great country. We were completely freaking sick of it.

After we divided up the raid duties, a quick prayer was said as the sun came up over the restaurant's giant red plastic chili. I don't know who started it, but mostly everyone joined in. We probably flew in the face of several Supreme Court decisions by actually having the unbridled audacity to bring God into government proceedings, but we just went ahead and did it anyway. I guess we were feeling really wild and crazy that morning as we prepared to stare death in its ugly face. Just completely off the hook.

Jimmy gunned the engine of the muscle car as I got in, the air around me vibrating with every surge of its deep, rumbling thunder. Who needed coffee?

"It's ass-clobberin' time," Jimmy said as he dropped it into drive.

"Amen to that, brother," I said, shucking a round into my tactical shotgun as we peeled out.

Chapter 74

THE TARGET WAS A cruddy stucco two-family house on Hillman Avenue. If it stood out at all on the worn suburban street, it was because of the just-off-the-lot black Chevy Tahoe in its concrete driveway. There were five entrances, including the one to the basement apartment, and the plan was to hit all of them at once, very, very hard, with everything in our arsenal—battering rams, flashbang grenades, tactical ballistic shields.

The word was that the people inside weren't your run-of-the-mill dopers, but highly trained killers and mercenaries. We weren't taking any chances. We parked a block away, and a moment later, thirty armed-to-the-teeth cops were jogging quickly and quietly down the dim, narrow street.

When we arrived at the address, Jimmy and I and our five-man team split off through the house's short alley to the backyard. It was a hot summer morning, and under my body armor I was sweating quite profusely as I knelt in the dirt of a small vegetable garden by the house's rear sliding glass door. I had to wipe my hand on my pants several times to keep the shotgun from slipping.

From a house on the other side of the backyard, I could hear an a.m. news station rising in volume as a clock radio's alarm went off. Don't bother slapping it this morning, buddy, I thought. This whole street is about to hear one hell of a wake-up call.

It happened right before we got the go-ahead. We were crouching there like runners at the starting line when all of a sudden we heard the metallic, clacking *plah-plah-plah* of a machine gun. Our team stared at each other. It was coming from the front of the house, along with a lot of hollering over the tactical microphone.

"What do we do?" Jimmy said. "Go in or go out front?"

I answered him by shattering the sliding glass

door with the butt of my Mossberg and tossing in a flashbang. It went off like a stick of dynamite, and then we were inside.

"Freeze! Police! Police!"

As the grenade smoke cleared, we saw a shirtless Hispanic man, maybe eighteen years old, standing wide-eyed in the kitchen in front of an open closet door. First he put his hands up, but then, snake-quick, he reached into the closet and swung something out of it. Both Jimmy and I shot the kid as he lifted the AK-47 to his shoulder. Our three-and-a-half-inch-barrel 12-gauge Mossbergs were loaded with double-aught buck, and the shooter went down as if he'd fallen through a hole in the floor.

As Jimmy and I entered the living room, we could clearly hear the chopping sound of the machine gun upstairs. Rattles of gunfire were also coming from outside in the street and hitting the house. We crouched as rounds shattered the living room window and thumped into the walls. It was return fire from our guys, who must have been pinned down outside.

"Cease fire on the lower level!" I called into the microphone. "Cops on the ground floor!"

The firing stopped, and Jimmy and I had just shucked new rounds into our guns and were heading toward the stairs when it happened. There was a thunderous ripping sound from above, and I was suddenly airborne. It was the weirdest feeling, almost pleasant, as though I were on some carnival ride.

I grayed out for a second as I landed hard on my back in the kitchen. When I came to, the first thing I noticed was that my shotgun was missing, as well as my shoes. The room and everything in it, including me, were completely covered in plaster and debris. Every inch of my exposed skin felt like it had been slapped. My ears were ringing, and blood was pouring from my nose.

Jimmy rose from beside me, coughing. I just lay there for a minute, trying to reorient myself. The house was roofless, the second floor completely open to the sky.

I smelled fire and grabbed Jimmy, and we ran out into the backyard.

It had been a bomb, of course. Not a large enough one to kill me, but almost. After the FDNY put out the fire, we found two bodies in the charred debris. Another Hispanic man with an AK-47 and a middle-aged white guy with an enormous sniper rifle in his lap.

There was no sign of Marietta. We found the cellar door open right next to where we breached, so she must have escaped during the confusion. The speculation was that there had been bomb-making materials upstairs, and one of our guys must have hit it during the firefight. My pet theory was that Marietta detonated it remotely as a distraction in order to escape.

I certainly wouldn't put it past her to kill some underlings or anyone else in order to get away.

Chapter 75

I'D TAKEN A LICKING, but I kept right on ticking. Well, at least for the moment.

Actually, I thought I'd feel more screwed up, having so narrowly missed buying the farm, but after the explosion I felt strangely exhilarated and energized. In fact, for a few buzzing hours, I felt about as invincible as a sixteen-year-old moto-cross champ, and that's truly saying something.

And why not be joyful? There weren't too many people walking around who had the "experience a truly massive explosion" box checked off their bucket list. The luck o' the Irish indeed!

After the EMTs cleaned me up and the Staten Island crime scene was secured, I went back to my Manhattan apartment for a shower and a change of clothes. I couldn't believe it was only eleven o'clock when I plopped down on my couch. Talk about a full morning.

I checked in with Seamus to let him know I was okay. I was about to tell him that I was planning on crashing in the city tonight until he told me that there was another late-evening Newburgh town meeting being called.

I immediately changed my plans. I had to be there. Because in spite of all their frustration, it was obvious that there was an incredible thing going on with the folks of Newburgh. It might not have been exactly the moral crusade Seamus had been talking about, but it was powerful nonetheless. These good people had had it. They weren't going to stop coming together until their bad situation was changed.

Not only that, but I'd thought of something that might help.

I grabbed a cab downtown and had a long lunch with my assistant U.S. attorney friend, Tara McLellan. I remembered that Tara had been on a violence task force in Boston, where the feds and local authorities had come together and helped several of the violent, gang-ridden communities come back from the brink. I was eager to get her feedback.

"What do you think, Tara?" I said over the remains of the massive, greasy, life-affirming pub-style bacon cheeseburger I'd just devoured. "I know you work in the city, but these people in Newburgh are so desperate. Do you think we could get the federal ball rolling for them?"

Tara lifted her light beer.

"Actually, I work for the Southern District, Mike, which includes Newburgh. I also know full well what gangs do to a community—the insidious fear, the old ladies who can't go outside. I'll do everything I can."

She wasn't kidding. I went back to her office with her, and for the rest of the afternoon, she did nothing except phone old colleagues and call in favors. She even insisted on coming back with me to the meeting and giving me a lift up the Thruway in her battered Jeep.

She looked surprised when I told her to pull over for some Starbucks near Yonkers around six.

"Coffee?" she said. "With the day you've had,

I thought you might want to nap a little on the way."

"I'm fine," I said. "Never better. Just getting my second wind."

"No rest for the weary, huh?" she said, smiling, as she hit her turn signal.

"Not even weary, almost-blown-to-smithereens, workaholic cops," I said.

Chapter 76

IT WAS SEVEN THIRTY when we came through Saint Pat's battered doors and back down into the meeting hall. Several of the people whom Tara had called were already there, including Ann Macaulay, the liaison from the local ATF office, and Larry Brown of the New York field office of the FBI.

We gathered all the feds together with the Newburgh detectives at the back of the meeting hall. After I made all the introductions, Tara gave a brief explanation of how the gang violence reduction initiative in Boston had worked.

"First, we got all the various local agencies together in a room—the prosecutors and cops, the state probation office, the school safety cops.

Then we put our heads together to identify all the gang players. On a huge map, we ID'd the gangs and their turf boundaries. We put together the various beefs they had with one another, which ones in the gangs were the wannabes, which ones were the worst offenders. That was the hardest part."

"Not here in Newburgh, ma'am," Groover said. "We know who the players are all too well. This is a target-rich environment, believe me."

"That's good. Step two is the casework, which in this scenario would be undercover buys."

"Buy-and-busts, yeah, we do that all the time," Walrond said skeptically. "Then they're out in six months with new friends they met in jail."

"Actually, in this plan, all we do is buys with no busts. At least not yet," Tara explained. "We gather ammo on the organizations slowly and surely, until we can prove that what we've identified is, in fact, a criminal organization. That way, under federal law, we can use the RICO statute and prosecute everyone at once to the fullest extent of the law. Clear out all the bad apples in one harvest, so to speak."

"You don't know how good that sounds. Music to my ears," Groover said.

"We also give everyone involved maximum sentences of at least five years, which in federal prison means at least four years before probation," Tara said.

"As an added benefit, in federal lockdown, they're away from their homies, so they can't coordinate anything from behind bars," said Agent Brown. "We break the camel's back with one snap."

"You do know the Newburgh PD has only ninety cops, right?" Bill Moss said. "What you're talking about requires massive manpower."

"That's where we step in," said Brown. "We'll get you manpower, overtime, money, vehicles, and equipment. The whole shebang."

"Federal disaster relief. Finally," Groover said.

"But there are roughly two hundred gang members here," Ed Boyanoski said.

"Not a problem," Agent Macaulay said. "We'll get you all the guys you need."

"This all sounds great, but won't all the wannabes just step in? The second-tier people?"

Detective Walrond said. "Newburgh is the most thriving drug market in Orange County. Won't the demand still be there?"

"That's when we go to phase three," Tara said. "After we clear out the worst offenders, we get social workers, gang members, and community members—along with all the cops—and we do a sit-down. One group at a time, we give the gangbangers a presentation, a little class on what they're looking at if the violence starts back up.

"We educate them fully on the law, the sentencing guidelines, what that's going to do to their lives. We tell them straight up that if someone gets shot, we are coming down with the full weight of the federal government. That's usually enough."

"That's it?" Bill Moss said. "That actually works?"

"Not perfectly, but yes," Tara said. "Violent homicides go down, way down, in every place it's tried. You have to do it one gang at a time and concentrate on one aspect of what they do—in this case, shootings. And you have to back it up. Someone gets shot, you drop the hammer. The gangs aren't stupid. They'll know the jig is up, especially since they know what just happened to the previous leadership. They might not stop dealing, but it'll go further underground. What's most important is that they'll put their guns down and dial it back."

Ed Boyanoski slapped me on the shoulder painfully hard as the townspeople began filling up the hall. He didn't look so depressed anymore. In fact, he looked ecstatic. Finally, you could see it in his eyes and in the eyes of the other Newburgh detectives.

It was hope. Just a glimmer, but undoubtedly there.

"Gee, Mike. Why didn't you just tell us that you had friends in such high places?" Ed said, smiling.

"I'm a humble man, Ed," I said, smiling back. "Unlike you hicks up here, we NYPD detectives don't like to brag."

Chapter 77

SPIRITS WERE STILL HIGH as we headed out of Saint Pat's to the parking lot just before ten.

The attendance at the meeting had been even larger than the night before. Even though the FBI and ATF agents had only spoken briefly and vaguely about their plans to tackle the gang problem, just the sight of federal officials was enough to ease the minds of the people in the seats. Even the most skeptical in the crowd seemed glad that the grave nature of the problem was finally being given some serious due.

Saying my good-byes to my colleagues, I spotted Tara by her Jeep, talking on her cell phone. As I approached, she turned it off, grinning from ear to ear.

"What's up?" I said.

"Reservations," she said. "I just scored us one."

"Reservations? To where? What do you know about this neck of the woods?"

"That's my little secret," she said. "Just tell me you're hungry, Mike."

"Okay. I'm Hungry Mike," I said, smiling back.

"Yay," she said, grabbing my hand and opening the door of her Jeep. "I think you're in for a happy surprise."

She wasn't kidding. She took me fifteen minutes west on I-84 to a place called the Back Yard Bistro, in the town of Montgomery.

But as it turned out, I had a surprise for her.

Before we got out of her Jeep, I started laughing.

"What's so funny?" Tara said.

"I cannot tell a lie, Tara. I've been here before. And you do have excellent taste. I should know. My cousin owns the place."

"So much for my surprise," Tara said, deflated.

"Not to worry," I said. "I don't think we'll be disappointed."

The Back Yard Bistro was a tiny, intimate restaurant. So cozy that Tara and I were almost touching knees under the small table. The waitress couldn't have been more pleasant, and the food was mind-blowing.

The kitchen kept sending out course after course. Tidbits of tuna tartare, foie gras, some rye-crusted pork loin, a truly amazing duck breast. All of it matched with wines. My head and taste buds were spinning.

As we ate, Tara regaled me with family stories of her cousin and my dearly departed pal, Hughie. My favorite was when Hughie and the rest of his ADD-afflicted Irish clan visited a cousin's farm in Ireland. Finding a tiny, deserted-looking house back in the woods, the Yank punks commenced firing rocks through the windows until the tam-o'-shanter-wearing pensioner living there came out with a double-barreled shotgun.

"Wow," I said after our waitress, Marlena, dropped a humongous slice of maple mascarpone cheesecake in front of me and a crème brûlée in front of Tara. "This was fantastic, Tara. I hope you forgive me for ruining your surprise," I said.

"If anyone needs to be forgiven, it's me," Tara said. "After all, I made such an ass out of myself at the St. Regis. Pretty much bare-assed, too, if memory serves me right."

"Were you?" I said. "When was this?"

"Very funny, Mike. I haven't forgotten that night. I probably never will. At least the parts I can remember. You tucked me in. That was so sweet, so genteel. Cary Grant couldn't have been more . . . Cary Grant. But even now, part of me wishes that you hadn't, Mike. Is that wrong to say? Part of me wishes that you had stayed."

I took a sip of the Champagne at my elbow. Low on the speakers, an opera diva was singing a beautiful aria.

The woman in front of me was pretty much flawless. Dark and voluptuous, smart as a whip, tough, and yet caring and kind. There are women you meet in life that you know you could—and probably should—fall deeply in love with. Tara was exactly that. She was a keeper. One ripe for the keeping. All it would take would be for me to reach across the table through the candlelight and take her graceful hand.

And yet, I didn't do it. In the end, I couldn't.

My hand stayed on my glass, the aria ended.

"Ah, Mike. Whoever she is, she's lucky," Tara said, putting her head down and digging into her dessert hard enough to make the plate clink. "Luckier than she'll ever know."

Chapter 78

TARA DROPPED ME OFF in front of the lake house half an hour later. It was pin-drop quiet on the way back. I wanted to explain that it wasn't her. That it wasn't about attraction. But even I knew how lame that would sound. I wisely kept it zipped, for once.

"Thank you for dinner," I said as we stopped in the gravel driveway.

Somewhere between rage and tears, Tara sat motionless behind the wheel, staring dead ahead as her motor ticked. I took the half minute of her complete silence as my cue to get out. Gravel flew as she peeled back out onto the country road. A tiny piece of it nailed me in the corner of my right eye and became pretty much embedded.

Then there was just me and all my friendly chittering cricket friends as I stood there in the dark.

"Way to go, Mike," I mumbled to myself as I climbed, half blind, up the creaky wooden steps to the front door. "Way to win friends and really influence people."

As I reached for the front door, something funny happened. It opened by itself as the porch light came on. I blinked in the light with my left eye as I rubbed furiously at the right one. My crazy day wasn't over, apparently. Not even close.

My kids' loving nanny, Mary Catherine, appeared in the miraculously open doorway with arms crossed over her chest. Even with only one peeper working, I could see that the expression on her face was more than vaguely familiar. It was the same one I'd just seen on Tara's face before she gave me a face full of gravel.

Will Shakespeare was wrong, I thought, rubbing at my eye as moths whacked into each other over my head.

Hell hath no fury like *two* women scorned.

Standing there, I suddenly thought of a dumb

expression from my childhood. It arrived instantly, like a mental text message from Mike Bennett, circa 1978.

Your ass is grass, it said.

"Well, if it isn't Mr. Michael Bennett, finally home, drunk, after his many adventures abroad," Mary Catherine said, clapping her hands together sarcastically.

"That is who just dropped you off, correct?" she said, cocking her head. "A broad?"

She had me dead to rights. Even under the direst of circumstances, I always made every effort to contact her about my status and inquire about what was going on at the house, about the kids. And I hadn't. I'd gone off to work pretty much yesterday, and I hadn't lifted the phone once. Not only that, but I knew full well what Mary Catherine thought of my new friend and colleague, Tara McLellan.

With nothing in the holster, I tried drunken charm.

"Mary Catherine, hello," I said with a courtly bow. "Long time no see. How is everything?"

"Bad, Mr. Bennett," she said, tears welling in her blue eyes. "Bad and about to get worse."

"Mary Catherine, come on. I can explain," I said.

She stood there, glaring furiously at me through her soft, wet eyes.

"Actually, I can't," I said after a moment. "Only that I screwed up. I should have called you."

"And told me what? That you were going to be late tonight because you were out on a date?"

I stood there, wincing, as I remembered what Mary Catherine had said on our walk. The date I was supposed to plan but never did.

"It's not what you think. That was Tara McLellan, the prosecutor on the Perrine case," I said. "It was work, Mary Catherine. She came up to the Newburgh meeting to discuss the feds helping out with the gang problem."

Mary just stood and stared at me, the sadness in her blue eyes really killing me inside.

"You mean the Newburgh town meeting that ended at ten?" she finally said.

Chapter 79

"YES," I SAID. "WE had dinner after."

"Dinner," Mary nodded. "How special. Three hours of it, too. I guess I can toss the plate of ziti the kids and I saved for you. And the slice of cake from Jane's birthday."

"Shit," I said, closing my good eye. "Mary Catherine, I completely forgot. I'm sorry. Let me come in and we'll talk about it."

"Oh, by all means come in," Mary Catherine said, opening the screen door, which gave out a deafening squeak.

I saw then that she was dressed—jeans, a T-shirt, and a backpack on her back. No! Wait. What?

"The house is all yours, because I'm leaving,"

she said. "I'm leaving, Michael Bennett. And I'm not coming back."

"Mary Catherine, come on. I know you're angry, but that's crazy. It's . . . it's one in the morning."

"No," Mary Catherine said, tears streaming down her cheeks. "It's actually two in the morning, and I won't come on. Not anymore."

She stepped forward suddenly. For a second, I thought she was going to belt me one. It was almost worse when she stopped herself and didn't.

She brushed past me and hit the stairs.

I tried to say something, tried to come up with words that would make her stop in her tracks, but there was nothing to say. She walked past me where I stood rooted to the porch and right out into the summer night.

I would have gone after her immediately, but my eye was on fire, so I ran inside to splash water on my stinging face. After I finally worked loose the gravel grit from my burning eye, I rushed back to the front door.

I was convinced that I'd see Mary Catherine there on the porch, her I'm-running-away ploy finished now, ready to give me more of the grief I definitely deserved. But she wasn't there. She wasn't even in the driveway anymore. I jogged out to the road and stood peering left and right into the darkness.

You've gotta be kidding me, I thought. There was no sign of her. She was really gone.

I went back up the driveway and hopped into the minibus. Driving after having had a few drinks was irresponsible, I knew, but I didn't care. Panic was building inside of me at that point, the kind of pure panic reserved for a shit-heel who realizes that he might have just taken advantage of the special woman in his life one too many times.

I almost took out the mailbox as I reversed it out onto the country lane. Trees wheeled by in the sweep of the headlights as I screeched the stupid clunky bus out onto the road. Then I put it in drive and floored it.

At every curve on that twisty rural road, I was sure that I was about to see her. I'd pull over, there'd be some yelling, some tears, but we'd fix it. I'd fix it somehow. The problem was, I didn't see her. She wasn't on the road five miles in each direction. I raced to the parking lot of the pizza parlor and then the bowling alley. I went in and asked the turbaned clerk at the 24-7 gas station if Mary Catherine had come in, but he just shook his head and went back to the cricket match he was watching on his laptop.

I even drove out to I-84 and went up and down it for over an hour, but it was fruitless.

I'd lost her, I thought, near tears as I stared into the roadside darkness. I'd finally done it. I'd finally gone and completely ruined everything.

Chapter 80

I WOKE UP THE next morning on the porch just before dawn. I sat up, my back and neck stiff as plywood from falling asleep on the ancient wicker love seat. Head ringing from my hangover, I lifted my itchy arms to see that I'd been eaten alive by mosquitoes.

Then I remembered the night before, and I really felt bad.

I lurched back into the house. I was hoping that perhaps Mary Catherine had come home while I was asleep and that I'd find her fast asleep in her room. I crossed my fingers as I came through the living room. I even said a little prayer by her closed door, one of those childish if-you-give-me-this-one-God-I-promise-to-be-a-better-person specials. Then I cracked the door and dropped my head in despair.

God must have been off duty this morning, because Mary Catherine's bed was completely empty. "What's going on?" Seamus whispered, suddenly appearing in the hallway beside me in his robe and slippers.

Great, a priest, I thought. Just what I needed. I was going to need last rites when everyone found out I had driven Mary Catherine away.

I stared at Mary Catherine's empty, made bed and then back at him, speechless.

"I heard the yelling last night, Mike. Something happened with you and MC? What is it?"

"Mary Catherine," I said. "She's, um, left."

"What?" Seamus said in shock.

I shook my head.

Rather than wait for an explanation, Seamus put on the coffee and waited patiently.

It actually took two cups of joe and a couple of eggs over easy to give my full confession to the old priest.

"Well, you can't blame the lass, can you?" he said, slathering butter across a piece of multigrain toast. "Running loose with wild women tends to irk the little lady at home."

"The funny thing is, I wasn't running loose with a wild woman," I argued. "I was tempted, don't get me wrong, Father. Sorely tempted, but I resisted. I could never do that to Mary Catherine."

"You're an idiot, Michael Sean Aloysius Bennett," Seamus said. "How many Mary Catherines do you think are out there? Exactly how many good-looking, caring, strong females dumb enough to fall head over heels for the likes of you do you think presently exist? You string people along long enough, the string withers, then it breaks."

"Don't say that. Please don't say that, Seamus," I said, groaning. "I need to get her back. How can I get her back?"

Seamus just shook his head and pointed at the toast stack in front of me.

"Eat some carbs, son," he said. "You're going to need them for all the creative thinking you have to do."

I was in the bathroom rubbing calamine lotion on my skeeter bites after my shower when my cell phone started ringing. I raced into my bedroom, thinking it was Mary Catherine, but of course it wasn't. It was a number I didn't know. Manhattan; 212. I answered it anyway.

"Hello?"

"This is Patricia Reese, Tara McLellan's assistant. Is this Detective Michael Bennett?"

"Speaking," I said with mock cheeriness.

"Detective, Ms. McLellan wanted me to let you know that it looks like your testimony is going to happen today, and we need you in court."

I took the phone off my ear and just looked at it. Of course I had to go to work today. What was I thinking? That I could actually have a day off to repair my wrecked family life? How silly.

"Ten o'clock, Foley Square. Will you be there?" Tara's personal assistant wanted to know.

"Sweetheart," I said, "where else would I be?"

After I found a suit, I went to the powder room, where Seamus was shaving.

"This just in. I'm going to work."

"Work? What about Mary Catherine?"

"I'm testifying today in the city on the Perrine

case. You'll have to be in charge of the brood for now."

"Me?" Seamus said, putting down the razor. "Who'll take care of me? I'm elderly."

"Please, I'm dying here. Juliana and Jane know where everything is. Refer to them. That's what I do when Mary Catherine isn't around. Also, you need to be on the lookout for Mary Catherine. Please text me the second she comes back. If she comes back."

"Ah, don't be too worried," Seamus said, dipping his razor into the sink before passing it down his pale cheek. "I'm sure she's around here somewhere. I have a funny feeling she hasn't just flat-out left the kids. You, maybe, but them? No way. We'll find her, but you have to stop losing her."

Chapter 81

IT WAS HURRY-UP-AND-WAIT TIME when I arrived in the witness room at Foley Square that morning. I was growing more and more anxious until I got a chance to speak to the parents of the murdered Macy's waiter, Scott Melekian, in the courthouse cafeteria during the lunch break.

The Melekians were retired restaurant owners from Bethesda, Maryland, and told me that their only child, Scott, had attended the U.S. Naval Academy before coming up to New York to fulfill his lifelong dream of playing sax for a living.

"He'd worked on cruise ships and sold some stuff on iTunes, but once he subbed for someone at *The Phantom of the Opera,* that was it," the beefy dad, Albert, said. "Down in the pit with the stage lights and all the excitement, he'd found his destiny, he told us. He'd also finally gotten the call from the Local 802 of the musicians' union to work on an upcoming musical. Can you imagine? He'd just given Macy's his two-week notice. Then this bastard kills him."

The round-faced mom, Allie Melekian, started crying.

"He used to play for the whole family every Christmas Eve. 'O Holy Night' and 'Silent Night.' We'd all be sitting around, smiling and crying our eyes out, it was so beautiful," she said. "And whenever he'd come home, he'd always come down into the kitchen and play 'You Are So Beautiful.' I always thought it was a corny joke, but I know now that it wasn't."

The red-faced woman looked up at me, trying to gather her tears with her fingertips and failing.

"Did you ever think, Detective Bennett, that there would come a day in your life when you wanted to die? When you actually longed for it?"

I squeezed the woman's hand.

"I know one thing, ma'am," I said. "I know your son is watching us right now, and he couldn't be more proud of you guys for coming here today to see that his killer never gets a chance to hurt anyone ever again."

When we went back up after lunch, Ivan Vogel, the chief prosecutor of the narcotics unit in the U.S. attorney's office, stood at the front of the small, windowless gray courtroom.

"The prosecution would like to call its first witness," the short, stocky, former collegiate wrestling champ said. "We call Detective Michael Bennett to the stand."

Mrs. Melekian's words still rang in my ears as the court clerk asked me to tell the whole truth and nothing but. Then I lifted my hand off the Bible and turned and stared Manuel Perrine right in his pale blue killer's eyes.

"Would you please state your name and occupation?" Vogel said.

"My name is Michael Bennett, and I am a detective with the New York City Police Department. I have been with the department for the last twenty years."

"Could you please tell us in what law enforcement capacity you were working on the morning of June third of last year?"

"I was working with a joint task force of city

police and federal authorities to facilitate the arrest of the defendant, Manuel Perrine, for international drug trafficking and murder."

"I'm going to have to object there, Your Honor," Perrine's well-heeled lawyer, Arthur Boehme, said, standing with an affable grin. "The federal arrest warrant in question states that Mr. Perrine was wanted to stand trial for the murder of the two U.S. Border Patrol agents. It says nothing about drug trafficking. Also, my client has not as yet been convicted or even tried for those crimes."

"Sustained," the judge said as the Waspy, Jimmy Stewart-looking son of a bitch parked his impeccably tailored ass back into his seat.

I looked at Judge Mary Elizabeth Fleming. Her colleague had been murdered by the homicidal maniac slime at the table five feet away, and here she was, making sure all the hairsplitting bullshit Perrine's mouthpiece was spouting got its due? What a load of ripe horseshit trials could be. Sustained, my ass. Perrine was a stain.

Vogel frowned as he paced in front of me.

"Detective Bennett, how was it that you had information that Manuel Perrine would be in

New York City?" he said.

"Credible information was provided to us by a confidential informant. We set up surveillance at the location where we were told he would be, but after he did not appear, we reevaluated our information and suspected that he was in town to attend the graduation of his daughter from NYU law school. As we attempted to arrest him, gunfire broke out from Perrine's bodyguards, which then resulted in the death of DEA agent Hughie McDonough and NYPD officer Dennis Jaeger."

Perrine's lawyer popped up again like a polished, boyishly handsome target in a game of whack-a-mole.

"Again, Your Honor, I need to object. At this time, my client is on trial for the murder of one Scott Melekian, a waiter at Macy's. There is nothing in the charges leveled against him here today for the murder of any law enforcement personnel."

"I knew we should have put the murders in sequential order, Mr. Boehme," I said into the microphone. "Your client's killed so many people, it gets quite confusing."

Nervous chuckles erupted from the crowd, which would have been fine except for the fact that what I said was actually true.

"Your Honor!" Boehme said.

"Strike the witness's last statement. Please just answer the questions, Detective Bennett. This isn't a stand-up routine."

You're right, I felt like saying. It's a frigging farce.

The prosecutor approached the bench.

"Please, Your Honor. My witness is testifying to his whereabouts and the circumstances surrounding the death of Scott Melekian. That is, he's trying to, but defense counsel is making it impossible."

"The prosecution is right," Judge Fleming said. "Do I have to remind our prestigious defense counsel that he will soon have his very own chance to cross-examine the witness? In the meantime, please do shut up and stop interrupting, okay?"

That's when Perrine popped up.

"Bullshit!" he screamed.

The table before him heaved up and slammed down as he kneed it. Boehme squinted up at

Perrine in abject puzzlement. He looked like he wanted to say something to calm his client, but then thought better of it. He quickly turned his head downward, as if suddenly fascinated by the pattern in the government-issue carpet.

"Bullshit!" Perrine repeated. "These accusations are false, you lying maggot! This is harassment. This proceeding is illegal! I wish to speak to the Mexican consulate. I am not a citizen of this country. I am a Mexican national. Your laws have no authority over me!"

In a moment, no less than a dozen burly court officers, corrections officers, and U.S. marshals rushed forward from their stations. Perrine seemed to calm a little, then he feinted and broke through them, screaming, as he ran directly at me. Immediately, I stood and lifted the metal chair I was sitting on, able, ready, and oh so willing to crush Perrine's skull with it and finish this crap once and for all.

But unfortunately, before I had the chance, the court officers were able to loudly tackle him to the carpeted ground. After a moment, you couldn't even see Perrine beneath the crush of people on top of him. From the bottom of the pile, there were grunts and the click of metal as they cuffed his legs.

"You will regret this, Bennett," Perrine screamed where he writhed like a wild animal on the floor. "You will wish you had been stillborn by the time I am done with you and your family!"

He was still screaming as they took him out by his hands and feet. There was dead silence in the courtroom as everyone looked at each other, trying to recover and catch their breath.

"On that note, I believe these proceedings are done for the day," the judge finally said. "And defense counsel, tomorrow the defendant will be gagged as well as heavily shackled under my order. So I don't want to hear the slightest peep out of you about it. And with the next outburst, I promise you, he'll be tried in a cage."

She brought down her gavel like a blacksmith hitting an anvil.

"This trial will proceed, so help me. This trial will proceed if it's the last thing I do."

Chapter 82

AT A LITTLE BEFORE 8:00 p.m., the Fifth Precinct evening patrol supervisor, Sergeant Wayne Lozada, and his driver, Officer Michael Morelli, parked in their favorite cooping spot, the southeast corner of Canal and the Bowery, facing the ramp for the Manhattan Bridge.

After Morelli put it into park, he lifted a massive binder from the backseat. He flipped through the NYPD Patrol Guide to the section covering the use of the Taser on emotionally disturbed people. Morelli, who was actually quite proficient in the use of the electrical device due to the neighborhood's proliferation of nuts, didn't really need to go over it but was brushing up for a sergeant's test he was scheduled to take at the end of the month.

As Morelli studied, Sergeant Lozada idly listened to the fizz and pop of the radio as he stared at the monumental arch and colonnade at the entrance to the Manhattan Bridge. He never got sick of looking at that thing. Above the Chinese billboards, crappy stores, and skells selling fake handbags on the piss-stained Bowery sidewalk, the intricate baroque stonework looked fantastical, like a Rembrandt peeking out over the rim of a Dumpster.

Lozada, who briefly had been a high school history teacher before becoming a cop, was an architecture buff. After he retired at the end of the year, he was thinking about starting a walking tour.

"You see that thing, Morelli?" Lozada said. "That thing was built by the same architects who designed the iconic New York Public Library. It's called a triumphal arch, and this one was modeled in the tradition of both the Porte Saint-Denis in Paris and the first-century Arch of Titus in Rome. It was part of the City Beautiful movement, started by a bunch of rich folks at the turn of the last century who thought they could promote civic virtue and harmonious social order through beautiful public spaces and grandiose buildings."

"Real nice, Sarge," mumbled Morelli, who couldn't wait for his long-winded boss's retirement party. "Classy stuff, all right."

"A hundred years ago, they erected stunning works of classical art for the opening of a bridge, Morelli," Lozada said with a sigh. "Today, a decade after the nine-eleven attacks, we can't even rebuild two ugly skyscrapers."

"I know, right? Exactly, exactly," Morelli said, flipping a page in the gargantuan binder.

Lozada was still sighing when they heard the sound coming from somewhere off behind them.

"No, it can't be," Lozada said as the lazy *ka-click ka-click ka-click ka-click* came closer.

He glanced in the side-view mirror. A young Hispanic guy was walking up the sidewalk behind the cruiser, shaking a can of spray paint.

The guy stopped ten feet behind the cruiser and commenced painting. They watched in silence as he went to town, bombing the stone wall of the building they were parked beside.

Morelli and Lozada looked at each other for a moment, then broke into riotous laughter.

"Your iPhone charged, Morelli?" Lozada said, grasping the door handle. "Because I believe we either have a vandal with a serious vision deficiency or a contender here for world's dumbest criminal."

Lozada opened the passenger door and put his right foot out onto the sidewalk. He was just standing up when he heard a sudden engine roar and a long tire shriek.

As he glanced forward, he watched as a beat-up white Dodge van veered off the Bowery and stopped directly in front of the cruiser. Its side door rattled open and three squat Hispanic men wearing bandannas over their faces and baseball caps and mechanic's coveralls tucked into construction boots stood there staring at him.

It took him a fraction of a second to register that they had guns in their hands. Long ones.

They were M4 automatic rifles, Lozada knew. He had one just like them in the trunk of the cruiser.

It would be the last thing he would ever know.

The assassins opened fire, muzzle flashes just

visible in the twilight. Lozada was cut down to the concrete immediately as more than a dozen bullets struck his face and throat. Morelli, running from the cruiser at a loping backpedal, managed to just draw his Glock before he, too, was hit with a fusillade of automatic gunfire that struck him in the right side of his head. He was dead well before he and his unfired weapon hit the ground.

The shooters in the van continued to fire on the fallen policemen. When their guns were empty, they reloaded, and fired off another magazine apiece into the cop car.

When they were done, the spray-painter hurdled over the body of Lozada and removed a large red plastic jug from the knapsack on his back. Upending the jug, he poured gasoline all over the cop car's trunk and roof and hood and interior. He tossed the empty jug into the car as he ignited a Zippo lighter with his calloused thumb. He was already in the van by the time the tossed lighter landed on the front seat and the car went up.

The van sped away. The light of the burning NYPD car's flames flickered on the blood-drenched fallen cops and on what had been spray-painted on the side of the bank building next to their bodies.

Dos Por Día Hasta Que Se Libera!

Two a day until he is released.

Libertad! Libertad!
Free Manuel Perrine!

Chapter 83

AFTER THE TRIAL, I went straight out to Woodside, Queens, on the number 7 train to look for Mary Catherine.

Seamus had called and left a message to say that Mary Catherine had called the lake house. It was a cryptic call. She needed to spend some time with friends now, she said, and would call back in a few days. I remembered how she had stayed with friends out in Woodside when she first came to the States, so I took a chance of heading out there to see if I might bump into her.

It was a truly desperate move, the act of a madman, really. With more than eight million people in New York City, human beings don't just bump into each other. I didn't even know if she was staying in Woodside. She could have been out in the Hamptons or on a plane back to Ireland. Needless to say, I didn't find her. All I found out as I hit a few bars and wandered up and down Queens Boulevard was how guilty I felt, and how incredibly lonely.

Officer Williams, the gung ho cop assigned to watch my apartment, flashed his lights and quickly got out of his cruiser as I came up West End Avenue to my apartment house around ten. There were two other squad cars on the block now, I noticed. This couldn't be good.

"There you are! Everybody, and I mean everybody, is looking for you," Williams said. "Don't you turn on your phone?"

"The battery died," I said. "What the heck's up?"

Heck was up, all right. I sat on the hood of his cruiser, my head going lower and lower, as Williams told me about the double cop execution on Canal Street. When he told me about the message spray-painted on the wall, I closed my eyes. The sergeant who was killed had four kids, his oldest girl at Loyola University.

I sat there as the horror of it all sank in like a

dull knife between my shoulder blades. This is what happened now? NYPD cops were being gunned down? Shot to smithereens with automatic weapons? How did that compute? It didn't. How could it? I sat there, dizzy. The world was truly spinning off its axis. How in the name of God were we supposed to set it right again?

I left Officer Williams and went up to my silent and empty apartment. I thought I was lonely before. I couldn't have been more wrong. After some rummaging around, I found a dusty bottle of Smirnoff Lemon Twist vodka with a Christmas ribbon on it in the back of my closet. I cracked the cap and sat on my bed, sipping it.

I didn't bother taking off my trial suit or even my shoes as I propped myself against the headboard. Of course not. When I get shitfaced on discount vodka by myself, I always like to keep it as formal as possible. To cheer myself up, I spun the Christmas bow on my finger and thought about my dead wife, Maeve. I tried to picture her face in my mind, but I couldn't.

I cried for a bit. For Maeve. For Mary Catherine. For those two dead cops. After a minute or two, I tried to break the bottle by slamming it down on the nightstand. But nothing happened, so I took another sip.

This wasn't supposed to happen, I thought. None of it. This wasn't in the original script.

What had I ever asked for? A chance to be a good man. And I had been. Just like my dad, I'd been a cop and put away bad guys. Cleared the streets so that the good people could live their lives, love their wives and husbands, love their kids.

But what was it all for? People weren't even getting married anymore, and if they had kids, they soon abandoned them to the street, to the Internet. It wasn't just the times, either. I was starting to think it was humanity. It was changing. People didn't seem to want to be people anymore.

Ah, who the heck was I to talk? I thought, savoring the warm, lemony, burning Smirnoff. I couldn't even keep my nanny from exiting stage left.

I looked out the window at the lights of the city, at the dark. "Mary Catherine, where are you?" I whispered. "I'm sorry I hurt you. I need you, Mary Catherine. Please come home."

Chapter 84

THE NEXT MORNING, I had the taxi drop me off on lower Broadway, and I walked across Duane Street in a light rain, past the bomb-squad vans, toward the courthouse. Helicopters rumbled overhead. Though I had declined a police escort, I knew I was being tailed anyway by two cars full of undercover cops, watching my back.

Showered, shaved, and rested despite a hangover, I was wearing my best suit. I'd briefly thought about putting a Kevlar vest underneath it, but then gave it a thumbs-down. Perrine was hiring highly trained mercenaries now. If they got a bead on me, they wouldn't waste their time killing me with a torso shot but would do it properly, putting a high-velocity bullet or two directly into my head.

Besides, the bulky vest would have ruined the tailored line of my jacket, I thought as I headed across the plaza toward the courthouse steps. Perrine wasn't the only one who liked to get his *GQ* on.

Because of the cop killing the previous evening, security had been beefed up, even on top of the already beefed-up security surrounding the courthouse. In addition to the guard booths and hydraulic metal street barriers and truck-bomb-proof steel pylons, the entire NYPD Hercules team was deployed. Beside a long line of black Suburbans stood a small army of submachine-gun-toting cops wearing helmets and knee pads and armor-plated vests over their NYPD blue fatigues.

For all the police presence outside, inside the courthouse, past the metal detectors, the halls were pretty empty. That was because all civil and all but the most urgent criminal cases had been postponed for the week due to the incredible circumstances.

Arriving early at the fourteenth-floor witness

room, I declined a coffee from Tara's assistant, but I did accept a bottled water. I didn't ask her where Tara was and, funny enough, she didn't tell me.

As I waited, I checked my smartphone for messages. There was only one that I was looking for—Mary Catherine's, of course. She hadn't contacted Seamus again, and I was worried as hell.

But there was nothing. No matter how many times I shifted all the stupid screens on the phone back and forth with my thumb.

"Detective Bennett?" the assistant whispered as she stuck her head through the cracked door. "You've just been called to the stand. It's time."

All eyes shifted to me as I came through the double doors into the soundproofed, windowless courtroom. The expressions from the rows of seated people were solemn and sort of surprised, as if I were a black-sheep relative arriving out of the blue for someone's funeral.

It was a funeral, all right, I thought. Manuel Perrine's. And it was high time we slammed the lid on his casket.

He was sitting up front, heavily shackled. I

could hardly see him behind a larger-than-usual retinue of cops and court officers. He didn't have a gag on, as the judge had promised, I noticed as I sat. Like all dangerous animals, he definitely deserved one. I would have preferred a dog muzzle or Hannibal Lecter–style hockey mask, at the very least, but there was nada.

I glanced at the judge and shook my head. No wonder trust in the government was at an all-time low.

Prosecutor Vogel stood.

"Detective Bennett, good morning. Yesterday, you were telling us about a gunfight that arose during your attempt to arrest Manuel Perrine. Where did that gunfight take place?"

"In an alley alongside Madison Square Garden."

"Why did you go to the location?"

"We learned that Manuel Perrine had come to New York to see his daughter graduate from NYU law school."

"Exactly!" Perrine screamed. "I come here to this shithole of a country to this utter shithole of a city only to see my daughter, and then I am accused of things I had nothing to do with."

He stood and banged on the table with both fists.

"These are false accusations and lies brought against me. You think I'm afraid of you? Of these trumped-up charges? I'll cut that black lying tongue from your throat, cop. I'll cut it out and feed it to you until you choke!"

"That's it," the judge said. "Strike three. You're out, Mr. Perrine. We're going to try you in absentia. Officers, remove him now."

At first, Perrine resisted, pushing the cops back and forth. But then he suddenly stopped completely. One second he was in a rage, and the next, he was calm, as though he had hit a switch. Strange, I thought. He actually smiled at me as he was leaving.

I sat there as the door closed.

"Thank you, Your Honor," the prosecutor said. "Now back to what you were saying, Detective. You learned that Manuel Perrine had come to New York to see his daughter graduate from NYU law school. Please continue for the jury, Detective Bennett."

I stood, a quizzical look on my face. This didn't feel right. Not at all. Perrine was acting. It seemed like the whole outburst was staged.

"Wait," I said, climbing out of the witness box.

"What in good God are you doing, Bennett?" the prosecutor said under his breath as I passed him.

"This isn't right," I said. "Something isn't right."

Chapter 85

PERRINE AND HIS SCRUM of jailers were turning the corner of the outer corridor to my right, toward the elevators, when I pushed out the doors into the hallway. Not knowing exactly what I was doing, going solely on gut instinct, I hurried after them.

I was next to an ancient pay-phone recess ten feet from the hall corner when I heard it. It was a sudden, heavy *wumpff* sound, followed immediately by the trailing crinkle of breaking glass. It sounded as if, nearby, a giant baseball had just punched a home run into a giant windshield. I felt the floor shake a little under my wingtips as well.

What the hell now?

I barreled around the corner. Perrine and the police were in front of the elevators. The cops must have heard the weird sound, too, because they were all looking around, some with their guns out. Most of them were staring at a doorway opposite the elevators.

"We have a situation here," one said into his radio. "Some sort of situation."

There was the impatient click of the elevator call button being pressed over and over, and then the doorway opposite the elevator bank exploded outward with a concussive roar.

I fell to my knees and drew my gun, my ears ringing. When I looked up, thick yellow smoke was already billowing from the blown-open doorway and filling the hallway. When a waft of it passed over my face, I knew it was tear gas.

Eyes burning, snot pouring from my nose as from a faucet, I plastered myself into a recessed doorway on my right and covered my face with my tie. A moment later, a crisp gunshot went off so close it sounded like a pencil being snapped in my ear. Crouching, I found a doorknob and opened the door beside me, ducking into an empty courtroom.

Then I saw what was in the courtroom's large south-facing window, and I wondered if I was hallucinating.

On the outside of the building, pressed against the window of the room just to the east of me, was a large yellow metal cage. It was a heavy machinery basket being suspended by the tower crane of the construction site nearby. In it, plain as day, maybe ten feet away from me, stood two men in tan construction coveralls, wearing gas masks and holding automatic weapons.

It looked like a SWAT team. But not our SWAT team.

They were trying to break out Perrine, I realized. Literally trying to break him out of the building from the fourteenth floor!

Without thinking about it, without saying "Freeze," I lifted my gun and started shooting at the two men through the window. My Glock's 9mm rounds sprayed holes through the heavy window glass, but the bullets were either deflected by the glass or the metal grate of the basket, because neither of the two armed-to-the-teeth men went down.

All I did was get their attention. A moment

later, I backpedaled as they raised their weapons over the metal rim of the basket. I dove back into the hallway as the window and half of the empty courtroom's wooden pews were ripped to shreds by automatic gunfire.

I peeked through the doorway a moment later when I heard a high-rpm hum. Through the shattered window, I saw the yellow basket on the move. The tower crane arm above it swung as it pivoted the metal rig away from the courthouse. I also saw, sitting in the basket between the armed men, a light-skinned black man in a prison jumpsuit.

The audacity of it was stunning, literally amazing. This couldn't be happening, and yet it was.

They were really doing it, I thought, staring up at the basket as it started to ascend. As hard as it was to believe, it was happening before my very eyes.

Manuel Perrine was actually getting away.

Chapter 86

THE TEAR-GAS SMOKE was clearing as I ran down the hallway among the fallen cops. Half of them were shot up pretty bad.

"Gun!" I yelled to a burly black federal cop who was holding his hand over a bleeding thigh. I caught his SIG Sauer as I turned the corner, hit the stairwell door, and went up.

There were another ten floors to the roof, but I didn't feel them. With my adrenaline pumping the way it was, I could probably have ascended the stairs on my hands. The next thing I remember, I was out on the roof and running across to the south side of the building.

I arrived at the edge just in time to see the crane dropping the yellow cage onto the roof of the building across from the courthouse. A moment later, as I was trying to get a bead on the men with my handgun, I heard the close sound of a helicopter. Turning, I thought it would be the overhead NYPD chopper, but incredibly, it was an NBC News chopper!

"Get lost, you idiots!" I screamed at it. "Get your damn scoop somewhere else!"

But I was wrong again.

The chopper swooped down and descended right onto the roof! It was part of the escape plan!

I started firing as Perrine and his gunmen clambered aboard the chopper. I emptied the SIG Sauer at the pilot's-side door. I must have missed, because a moment later, the nose of the chopper lifted, and it swung in a lazy circle westward, over the courthouse, and disappeared behind the FBI headquarters on Federal Plaza.

I couldn't believe it. Perrine had done the impossible.

The Sun King had gotten away!

Chapter 87

IF THERE WAS ANY consolation in the wake of the whole fiasco, it was that no one had been killed. In addition to the federal cop, three other corrections officers had been shot, but they were all in stable condition and would survive.

I was livid. I'm talking bed-bath-and-beyond pissed. Obviously, the drug boss was able to buy off people everywhere outside and inside the justice system, probably even inside the damn courthouse itself.

Back downstairs in the street, I went immediately over to the construction site near the courthouse. The leader of the NYPD Hercules team was already there talking to the workers and the site's general contractor, a man named Rocco Sampiri.

"He claims the tower crane operator was on a break," the ESU cop said. "No one on the site saw who got into the basket."

I stared at Sampiri. He looked pretty well groomed for a construction worker—silk-screened T-shirt showing off his tan, muscular arms, spotless designer jeans and boots. With his gold Rolex and tidy manicure, it seemed like the only work this musclehead really did was at the gym, lifting dumbbells while gazing lovingly at himself in the mirror.

"Really?" I said to Sampiri. "A guy climbs up three hundred feet into that cab and swings up a bandito SWAT team into the courthouse and no one saw? What kind of break was this? A nap?"

"That's funny, Officer, but really, we didn't see nothing," Sampiri said, his steroid-deepened voice sounding like it was coming from the bottom of a barrel.

"Come on, guys," I said, turning toward the laborers standing around. I pointed at the sky. "You know who that guy was who just got away? He's a mass murderer who's declared war on this country, no different from a terrorist. Please, anyone. I need some help here. Didn't anyone see anything?"

In my peripheral vision, I watched Sampiri glare at his workers. They all seemed to put their heads down at the same time.

"See? Like I said. No one on my crew saw shit," Sampiri said with a shrug. "We don't know what the hell happened. Maybe you should be looking for this guy instead of busting our crank. He sounds really dangerous."

I stared at the general contractor. I didn't need to type "Rocco Sampiri" into an FBI database to come to the conclusion that he might've been involved in organized crime. Or to make the jump that the Mafia would be more than willing to help out Perrine for the right price. This musclehead had probably given the person who had swung the cage over to the courthouse a cup of espresso before he busted out Perrine. And he was actually smirking a little. Even with all this heat, Rocco couldn't help but enjoy telling bald-faced lies to us idiot cops.

That's when I guess you could say I lost it. It was the smirk that did it. There aren't too many things I truly hate, but the Mafia is one of them. People acted like the Mob was cool—*The Sopranos, The Godfather*. They only kill their own, everyone said. But that's the problem. The secrecy of it, the conspiracy of it. As they were at this work site, normally decent people are induced through intimidation to "not see nothin'," allowing evil animals like Perrine and Rocco here to just go to town.

"Okay, Rocco. You win. I guess I'm done here, then. Thanks for your help," I said, turning.

"Actually, there is one more thing, Rocco," I said, taking the collapsible baton off my belt and flicking it out by my leg as I turned around.

The next thing I knew, the metal baton and Rocco's crotch had collided violently. I must have tapped something important, because he immediately went down on one knee like he was about to propose, tears springing onto his suddenly beet-red cheeks. I quickly slipped the baton into my pocket and put a hand to his gym-chiseled shoulder.

"Jeez, Rocco. You all right? You don't look so good. Can I get you something? A glass of water?" I said.

"You son of a bitch," he finally got out in a gasping voice, which was much higher than it was before. "You prick. Why did you do that?"

"I'm not sure, Rocco. Everything happened so fast, I didn't see anything," I said into his ear. "Weird, isn't it? That I-don't-know-what-the-hell-happened shit really seems to be catching around here."

Chapter 88

OVER THE NEXT COUPLE of frantic hours, I tried to position myself front and center on the Perrine escape investigation, but my, oh, my, how the attempt failed.

Almost immediately, a young FBI special agent in charge by the name of Bill Bedford had taken charge of the scene. I'd heard about Bedford. Tara had told me that Bedford was an up-and-comer in the Bureau, a former running back at Duke University who never hesitated to plant a cleat or two between the shoulder blades of his blockers on the way to his touchdown dance.

After I introduced myself, Bedford took me into an empty courtroom on the Foley Square courthouse's ground floor for a few questions. It was more like a grilling than an interview. The fair-haired agent's demeanor was reserved, but a few times, I caught something in his eyes. Something angry, the shining surface on a well of hostility.

After I was quite professionally interviewed about everything that had happened, I was told he'd be in touch.

"But wait, Bill," I said as he started thumbing his BlackBerry at the speed of light. "I can help you on this. I know Perrine. I've been on this from day one."

"I'll call you," Bedford said without looking up.

Yeah, right. I'd heard that before. I was being completely boxed out, I knew. It was obvious the feds didn't want me anywhere near the investigation. Even when I tried to get some assistance from the higher-ups in the police department to bring me on board, I was told in no uncertain terms that the brass didn't want me on the case, either.

For once, I could hardly blame anyone. Because I'd had Perrine. Had him and then lost him in the worst, most publicly embarrassing way imaginable. My boss, Miriam Schwartz, even let me in on a few nasty rumors she heard—a few whispers that maybe I was actually in on the escape, since I had spoken to Perrine in court and interviewed him alone in prison.

In my defense, I thought about bringing up Perrine's quarter-billion-dollar bribe, which I'd rejected, but then I came to my senses and kept my lip thoroughly buttoned. It was obvious the brass was already sizing me up for a scapegoat suit. Why pour more fuel on my own bonfire?

There was no way around it. I was toxic now, a bad-luck charm. Standing around in Foley Square with no one to talk to, I felt like a little kid at the moment he realizes he hasn't been picked for either side in a game of sandlot baseball.

And the tacit message coming in from my law enforcement colleagues was just as clear.

You suck, kid.

Go home.

Chapter 89

SO THAT'S EXACTLY WHAT I did. I hightailed it out of Manhattan on the Beacon-bound 6:12, went back up to Orange Lake, and stayed away for the next two weeks.

I thought I'd be stressed out with Perrine in the wind and all the bad stuff hovering over me, but I surprised myself by having a really fun time hanging out with the kids. These were the last weeks of summer vacay, and we didn't waste a second of them. We did something fun every day—go-kart racing, miniature golf. To the girls' delight, one morning we got up at dawn and drove to a farm over in rural Sullivan County and rode horses.

The best time of all was driving up to

Massachusetts for a day to check out a massive state fair called the Big E, at which all the New England states were represented. My city kids' heads were spinning at all the Ferris wheels and tractors and petting zoos. After we gorged ourselves on massive stuffed baked potatoes on the midway, we even attended a blue-ribbon cattle show just for the hell of it. I stood at a rail, shaking my head, as bright-faced young country boys wearing bow ties came into the tent, walking cattle on a leash as though they were in a dog show.

"Now there's something you don't see on West End Avenue," Seamus said, standing beside me. "Why are we here again?"

"Well, Gramps," I said. "My career as a city cop seems to be coming to a close. I might have to look for another line of work, so why not farming?"

It goes without saying that being so close to my guys wasn't just about fun and games. I knew my friend the Sun King wasn't done with me. Even though he was free now, I'd seriously inconvenienced his arrogant ass. Not only had I caught His Highness, I'd actually broken his nose for him and laughed in his face. I knew there probably weren't too many people in this world who had screwed with him as much as I had.

Not living people, anyway.

So throughout all the summer fun, I had my guns attached to me at all times. I'd even illegally sawed off the barrels of the lake house shotgun so I could keep it handy under the seat of the bus. I kept it there with the mirror I used every morning to see if there was a bomb attached to the underside of the bus's chassis. Paranoid, I know, but sometimes it's the little things in life that count most. This kind of crap never happened to the Partridge family, I bet.

After the cattle show, we went into one of the Big E tents and listened to some country music. I was getting into it, too, had almost forgotten all my troubles, when the cowboy-hatted singer started a sad tune about losing his girl.

Talk about bringing things down. I didn't need this. My life had become a country music song. If I hadn't been the designated bus driver, I would have ordered a beer to cry into.

Because just like Perrine, Mary Catherine was still MIA. No calls. No contact. I wasn't the only one missing her, either. Despite all the fun vacation activities, I could see the kids were quite confused and upset.

So even with the sad-sack serenade wailing from the stage, I didn't leave the music tent. Even after the kids went off with Seamus to go to the hay maze, I sat there and listened to every word as the cowboy sang about broken hearts and empty beds and watching the red taillights on his girl's car driving away.

Chapter 90

THAT NIGHT AFTER THE fair, we arrived back home after midnight. I checked the house as I always did, namely, from stem to stern with my 9mm cocked. After placing all my sunburned, carb-stuffed guys into the loving arms of Morpheus, and after enjoying a nightcap with Seamus, I played messages on the house phone.

My boss, Miriam, had called and said that the *Times* wanted to speak to me, as did someone from ABC News. Even though I'd been pretty much unplugged, I knew Perrine's escape was front-page news not just across the country but throughout the world. Some British politician said it was just another example of the decline of U.S. dominance in world affairs.

Gee, thanks, old boy. I always knew I'd make history one day. What was worse was that some of our own talking heads were agreeing with him.

Another message popped up.

"Mike, hi. Bill Bedford here. I need to reinterview you concerning a few things on the Perrine escape. Specifically about an incident at the federal lockup. Some sort of scuffle between you two? I can be reached at . . ."

I promptly hit the erase button. Screw this guy. He wanted to talk to me as though I were a suspect in the Perrine escape. I wasn't about to make it easy for him. The handsome Duke-educated prick could drive up here to the sticks in his shiny G car.

A moment later, I was actually about to unplug the phone when it rang. I stared at it for a bit and, against my better judgment, finally answered it.

"Hello?" I said.

"Mike?" said a woman's voice.

For a split second, I thought it was Mary Catherine. My heart kicked against my chest. She was okay. She was coming back.

But it was just wishful thinking.

"Mike? Hello? It's me, Tara. Are you there?"

"Hi, Tara," I said wearily. "How's it going?"

"Mike, listen. I'm sorry about the silent treatment at the trial. I've been a complete jackass, and I apologize. I've made a resolution to stop being nuts, okay? Cross my heart, hope to die, stick a needle in my eye."

"Okay," I said, startled.

"Still friends?" she said.

"Always, Tara. Always."

"Good," she said. "Now, did you hear the news?"

"No, what? They bagged Perrine?" I yelled, sitting up.

"No, no. I wish," Tara said. "I'm talking about the progress in your neck of the woods. This afternoon, the U.S. attorney just signed two RICO-statute federal indictments aimed at taking down the Bloods and Latin Kings in Newburgh. We've already reviewed the open gang cases and are red-balling more than eighty arrest warrants. We're amassing a huge multi-agency strike force. A couple of days from now, we're going to take down both gangs at once. You interested in helping us out?"

"I'd love to, Tara, but I guess you didn't get the memo. I'm persona non grata with you *Federales* these days."

"Bullshit, Mike. I already spoke to my boss and told him how you lit the fuse on this thing. He's agreed. It's only fair that you be front row center when the fireworks go off. What do you say, Mike?"

This was good news. Not for me. For Newburgh.

"I do love fireworks," I said.

Chapter 91

TWO MORNINGS LATER, AROUND 4:00 a.m., Newburgh detectives Moss, Boyanoski, and I rolled up on an imposing old castle-like brick building on South William Street.

As we parked and crossed the darkened lot of the old National Guard armory, I thought I was hearing things. Even before we got to the steps, you could hear voices coming from inside the thick stone walls. It was an amazingly loud rumble of voices, as if maybe a midnight session of the New York Stock Exchange were under way.

When Ed opened the front door, I just stood there for a moment, as if nailed to the floor of the brightly lit, cavernous space. In the indoor drill shed of the old building, where the state National Guard had once trained their horses, stood the largest gathering of law enforcement personnel I'd ever seen. There had to be nearly five hundred federal, state, and local cops. Wearing raid jackets and faded, drab SWAT fatigues, they stood in clumps before whiteboards or in semi-circles around warrant folders laid open on the hoods of black SUVs.

I knew Tara had said that this was going to be a mass operation, but holy moly. There were folding tables everywhere, laptops, phones going off. It looked like some kind of strange college open house. But instead of young Republicans and glee club representatives, the tables were manned by people standing behind placards that said things like MUG SHOTS and FINGERPRINTING and EVIDENCE CONTROL.

"Newburgh hasn't seen anything this big since Washington's Continental Army was here," Ed said in amazement.

"And wouldn't you know it? The bad guys are still wearing red," Bill Moss said.

We came across Tara behind one of the folding tables. In her official blue Windbreaker, with her dark hair pulled back in a ponytail, she was busily collating one of the nearly eighty arrest packages that were being put together.

"Bill, Ed, Mike," she said with a nod. "Glad you could make it. You wanted some action from the feds, right? Well, how'm I doing so far?"

"Well, if this is all the guys you could get," I said with a shrug, "then I guess we'll just have to make do."

Ed Boyanoski started laughing. It didn't look like he was going to stop. No wonder he was so mirthful. He had worked so hard for so long to try to effect some change in his hometown, and it finally looked like it was going to happen. Both he and Bill were practically speechless, not to mention unbelievably pleased.

"I've been waiting on this for a long time, Ms. McLellan," Bill Moss said, looking out on the army of law enforcement. "Longer than you know."

"Let's not count our chickens before they're hatched, gentlemen. You still have a teeny-weeny bit of work to do," Tara said, handing us each a folder. "You bag 'em, we tag 'em. You'll find your fellow team members on the assignment sheet two tables down. Happy hunting."

Chapter 92

HAPPY HUNTING IT WAS!

Two hours later, just before dawn, I was kneeling in my hunting blind, which in this case was a gutter on Benkard Avenue in southeast Newburgh.

I peeled away the shirt where it was clinging to the back of my sweaty neck and looked through the night-vision scope. Across Benkard, under a streetlight the color of a chainsmoker's grin, was our target, the end unit in a decrepit row of dust-gray town houses.

I panned my scope up the unstable stack of bricks that held up its stoop—an arrangement that looked like something out of a Dr. Seuss book—and checked the door and windows.

Nothing. No movement in the house. No movement in the street, which we had just blocked off with two unmarked black SUVs.

If the task force had come up with a deck of cards showing the faces of the most-wanted criminals, Ed, Bill, and I would be holding the ace of spades. The town house we were about to raid belonged to Miguel Puentes, the city's most ruthless dealer and chief Latin Kings enforcer, who ran the drug trade on the southeast end of town. His brother, Ramon, had already been picked up at the strip club they owned out by the airport.

Talk about getting ready to rumble. I really couldn't have been more psyched as I crouched, squeezing the gummy rubber grips of my drawn Glock. Things were just where I liked them. God was in his heaven, the happy, amphetamine-like buzz of caffeine and adrenaline was in my bloodstream, and a bad guy was snoozing behind a poorly locked door.

I felt a hand on my shoulder.

"Alley and rear are clear. What do you think?" Bill Moss said in my ear.

"I think," I said, lowering the scope, "it's time for a Puentes family reunion."

A moment later, it was showtime. The word "go" came crisply over the tactical mike, and we went.

The next seconds were a delicious blur of sounds and sights. The sharp crack of a police battering ram against a lock, and then the sound of wood splintering. We poured inside, flashlights raking the doorways of the darkened house.

I was actually the one who found Miguel in a back bedroom, off the kitchen. I saw him immediately as I came through the doorway, a muscular, bug-eyed tough with the word "magic" tattooed on his neck. He was in his skivvies, scrambling up off a sheetless king-size bed that barely fit the room.

"Hands! Let me see your hands!" I screamed.

"No hablo inglés!" he screamed back, leaping for the closet to the right of the huge bed.

I jumped up on the bed, took a step on the mattress, and tackled him. We both whammed into the cheap closet door almost hard enough to crack it. Miguel continued to struggle a little, but then stopped as I stabbed the barrel of my gun as hard as I could against his tattoo.

"No English, but he seems to understand German pretty well, don't he, Mike?" Ed Boyanoski said as he came in the room and body-slammed Miguel back onto the bed.

"*Sprechen sie* Glock, Miguel?" he said as he clicked a pair of handcuffs on him.

"My arm! That hurts, you fuck! I want my lawyer. I want my goddamn lawyer!" Miguel said as Ed lifted him onto his bare feet.

"And I want a goddamn Advil," I said, rubbing my knee where it had slammed into the closet's door frame.

Chapter 93

BY EIGHT IN THE morning, we were done. In addition to our new buddy Miguel, we rounded up another two Latin Kings and two Bloods.

"This catch is full," Ed said, smiling, as he slammed the sliding door of our Ford Econoline paddy wagon near Lander Street. "Let's bring 'em back in and get another list."

"I can't tell who you look like more, Ed—my kids on Christmas morning or my kids on Halloween. This is supposed to be work, buddy. You're having way too much fun."

"Love what you do, and every day is a vacation, Mike," my big Polish-American friend said, knocking on the hood of the van.

We headed back toward the armory. We

honked and waved at another passing arrest squad and spotted several more up and down the side streets off Lander. Talk about kicking ass and taking names. Newburgh was under siege. And by the good guys, for once!

No wonder Ed was so ecstatic. It was the first time I'd ever driven down Lander Street when I didn't want to run all the red lights.

As I looked into the rear of the paddy wagon while Ed drove, the thing that struck me most about the gang of fools we'd just bagged was how sad, cheap, and dumb they looked. With their bedheads and their cheap hoodies and baggy jeans, they didn't look dangerous. They looked sloppy, like a not-so-merry band of young, tired losers.

Staring at them, I thought what a shame it was. What an incredible mess they had made of their young lives. Miguel Puentes, who was going to be charged with three murders, was pure evil, but the rest of them were low-level, B-team knuckleheads, morons who had seen too many rap videos. They looked stunned and scared, mired in self-pity. The thing they always feared would happen was happening. I felt like asking them if staying in high school or getting a degree in AC repair or joining the army would really have been that bad.

I guess the only thing going for them was that they were young, mostly in their early twenties. Some of them were looking at serious time, five or ten years, but maybe in the end, it would help them. Maybe they could get out at thirty, when they wised the hell up. Who knew? Like everyone said, hope springs eternal.

Speaking of hope, by far the best part of the day happened when we were pulling back into the armory.

A group of about thirty people was standing in the parking lot. I recognized a lot of faces from the meetings we'd attended. As I exchanged a wave with Dr. Mary Ann Walker from St. Luke's hospital, I spotted a coffee urn in the back of a pickup beside a tray of pastries. All these moms and construction workers and business owners must have heard about the unprecedented police effort and had come out to support us.

They cheered as though we were rock stars when they saw the arrested gang members in the back of the van. They even offered us refreshments as we passed, just as they would hand them out to marathon runners. Everyone laughed as Ed opened his mouth to accept a jelly doughnut.

"We're so proud of you," a smiling old black woman in a yellow tracksuit said to us as we frog-marched the punks up the steps of the armory. "My grandkids can play in the street this evening. At least for one night, my babies won't die."

Proud of us? I thought, looking wide-eyed at the group. It really was a touching thing. It reminded me of right after 9/11, when so many regular people lined the West Side Highway and handed out water and food to cops and utility workers heading down to Ground Zero.

I exchanged a stunned look with Ed, who seemed equally touched. We didn't have to say it. This spontaneous and unprecedented outpouring of humanity from the good people of Newburgh was one of those brief moments in a cop's career when it's all worth it. All the pain and bullshit and nut-cracking and nonsense and slogging through the mess. I wouldn't have traded it for the world.

Chapter 94

THAT SAME NIGHT, AROUND 7:00 p.m., Lady Gaga's "Born This Way" was pumping at deafening levels from the overhead speakers as neon disco lights alternately circled and strobed all around me.

Over the pounding dance track, a DJ suddenly urged me to throw my hands in the air and shake it like I just don't care. And I would have, except I didn't want to drop the Hannah Montana sheet cake I was carrying through the middle of the Tarsio Lanes bowling alley.

Nope, I wasn't out clubbing. The disco lights were for "cosmic night" at the bowling alley, and the party people in the house tonight were me, Seamus, and my ten kids, here to celebrate the twelfth birthday of my twins, Fiona and Bridget.

The kids' birthday wasn't the only reason to party. We'd put away a grand total of seventy-two criminal gang members that afternoon. In eight hours, we'd cleared the town of just about every bad guy. And not one cop had been hurt. It was an insanely successful day.

I spent the next few hours after we left the armory doling out pizza and tying bowling shoes. Which was a lot more fun than it sounded. The kids had never bowled before and were having a complete panic. Especially when Eddie and Trent stood on their plastic chairs beside the ball return and did a spirited square-dance routine to the song "Cotton-Eyed Joe."

"Hey, Dad! Dad! You have to see this. It's Grandpa Seamus's turn," Ricky called as I was setting out the paper plates.

"Ladies and gentlemen, behold Seamus Bennett, legendary master of the lane, as he bestrides the golden hardwood," the old man said in a mock TV announcer's voice as he lifted his ball.

"What a perfect approach," he said. "What perfect form."

"What a perfect load of malarkey," I called out.

Eyes locked on the pins in concentration, Seamus swung the ball back, stepped forward, and let her rip. His right foot swung dramatically behind his left during his release. He actually was pretty graceful.

"Go, Twinkle Toes," I said, clapping.

"Come on, baby," Seamus yelled as the ball hooked. "Cruise in the pocket! Cruise in the pocket!"

Cruise in the what?

Wouldn't you know it? It was a devastating, pin-crushing strike. Seamus pumped his fist and high-fived everyone as the kids went crazy.

What the…? Who knew the old codger was a good bowler?

I was up next. My ball made a lot of noise, but instead of a strike, it was a four–ten split that I missed completely on my second roll. Worse than that, I received nothing but crickets from the kids.

"I thought you said you played this game before," Seamus said, licking the tip of the pencil he was using to keep score.

"Granddad is better than Daddy. Granddad is better than Daddy," Shawna called out to everyone.

"That really was awesome, Granddad," Brian said. "Who taught you how to bowl?"

"A nice American fella I met when I first came to this country from Ireland," Seamus said.

"Wait, it was a tall guy, right?" I said. "White wig, wooden teeth? George Washington?"

" 'O beware, my lord, of jealousy,' " Seamus said, holding up the pencil. " 'It is the green-eyed monster, which doth mock the meat it feeds on.' "

I held my hands up in defeat.

"Now he's busting out Shakespeare? Okay, okay. You doth win, Father. I know when I'm beat. You're firing on all pistons tonight."

We cut the cake and sang "Happy Birthday" as Fiona and Bridget blew out their candles. I scanned the kids' faces. They seemed happy. Sugar-crazed and binging around like pinballs with all the treats and dance music, but happy. A large contingent of safe, content, well-adjusted kids.

I thought of what the woman had said outside the armory.

At least for one night, my babies won't die.

Exactly, I thought. What else was there? I couldn't have said it better myself.

That's when someone pointed it out. The eight-hundred-pound gorilla in the corner of the disco-pumping bowling alley.

"I wonder where Mary Catherine is right now," Fiona said as I handed her the first slice.

That did it. The party was over right there, right then. Though the music still raged, the laughter stopped as everyone looked down at their bowling shoes.

At least they weren't looking to me for the answer. Because for once, I didn't have the slightest clue.

Chapter 95

AT LONG LAST, THE dreaded moment had arrived. It was packing-and-cleaning day at the Bennett vacation compound.

Sunday was still two days away, but with Mary Catherine still AWOL, I thought it best to start the herculean task of moving my family back to the city as early as possible. I thought getting my guys to get their stuff together was going to be like pulling teeth, but I was in for a surprise.

Not only had Mary Catherine devised an effective system for the care, organization, and cleaning of everyone's clothes and possessions, she had taken pains to teach it to the kids. In no time flat, the guys were working the dishwasher and the washing machine and rolling their little suitcases out into the hall one by one like a troop of seasoned business travelers.

If anyone was having trouble finding their stuff, it was yours truly. I was under my bed, scattering dust bunnies as I looked for my flip-flops when my cell phone rang. Still on my belly, I managed to retrieve it from the pocket of my shorts.

"Yeah?" I said into the hardwood floor.

"Mike? It's me, Tara. I have big news. How fast can you get to Shawangunk prison?"

I flipped over on my back.

"Well, Tara, we hicks up here pronounce the prison 'Shawngum,' and I can get there fast. Why?"

"Cleaning out Newburgh is starting to pay unexpected dividends, Mike. Huge ones. You know the Puentes brothers, Miguel and Ramon?"

"The gentlemen who run the Newburgh Latin Kings?" I said.

"Yep. It seems like those fine young men want to play ball. I just got a call from their lawyer. They claim Manuel Perrine is still in the States. Not only that, they say they know where he's hiding out and are willing to tell us in exchange for immunity and witness protection."

I smiled up at the multitude of cracks in the lake house ceiling. I couldn't believe it. Actually, I could. The connection made sense, since the Latin Kings were supposedly being supplied with drugs by Perrine's cartel.

That's exactly how it happened in cases sometimes. You'd be beating your head against a wall for months with no clue about a murder or a felony, and then one day, the phone would ring with a willing eyewitness or an out-of-the-blue confession.

"What do you know, Tara? Dumb luck happens to cops sometimes, too," I said. "Have you contacted my pal Bill Bedford, the special agent in charge of the Perrine escape investigation, for his take on the latest development?"

"He's number two on my call list," Tara said. "The race goes to the swift, Mike. This was your case originally so I thought I'd give you a head start to get back in on it. You game?"

"See you at the prison," I said, pulling myself up off the floor.

Chapter 96

TARA WAS WRONG.

It turned out the meeting with the Puentes brothers wasn't actually at the Shawangunk prison, because Shawangunk is a state facility. Since the charges were federal, it turned out that the seventy-plus Newburgh gang arrestees were being housed in the federal lockup in Otisville.

Driving up to the second prison I'd visited during my summer vacation, I sighed. With all this running around in the country, I could write a fairy-tale romance novel for middle-aged cops, I thought. Call it *The Prisons of Orange County*.

I arrived at the white-brick bunker of the administration building first. An affable black female assistant warden showed me the conference room where the meeting was to take place. It was surprisingly unlike a prison—a windowless room with a carpet, a conference table, coffee service, and even a whiteboard.

I was pouring my second cup of joe when Tara came through the door with a mannequin from the men's clothing store Jos. A. Bank. Actually, it was my tall, slim, nattily attired friend Bill Bedford, the FBI agent.

"Tara, Bill," I said, turning, with a smile of pure innocence. Bedford seemed to have some trouble preserving his unflappable demeanor.

"What the hell is he doing here?" he barked.

"Oh, did I forget to mention Detective Bennett, Bill?" Tara said. "He was part of the arrest procedures in Newburgh last night. He was the one who arrested Miguel Puentes. You know, the suspect we're here to deal with?"

I nodded at Bill helpfully as I sat back down. What Tara failed to mention was that Miguel hadn't spoken to me personally. But ol' Bill didn't need to know everything. What would be the fun in that?

"But why is he here?" the special agent in charge wanted to know.

"What do you mean, Bill? Not only is Mike already a part of the federal gang task force, he's been an integral part of the Perrine case from the get-go. So of course I took the liberty of including him in this meeting."

Bedford made a noise.

"I'm sorry, Bill. I didn't catch that."

"Yeah, uh-huh, whatever," Bedford said, kicking out a chair and sitting. "Where are these Puentes people already?"

Tara had her video camera set up when the Puentes brothers came in a few minutes later. I waved to Miguel, who was now wearing prison coveralls over his boxer briefs. His larger brother looked like he'd just taken a huge bite of some bad meat. Their lawyer was a large, bald Dominican gentleman in a gaudy banker's suit who looked like he could make a go at professional wrestling if the law thing didn't pan out.

Everyone remained silent, sizing each other up as two corrections officers securely cuffed the Brothers McPuentes to a steel rail along the wall.

"You understand that my clients are putting themselves and their families in grave danger by speaking with you," the lawyer started out.

"Bullshit," Bedford said with over-the-top venom. "What I understand is that your clients here are looking at life in jail for murder and drug trafficking. Save the medal of valor application and cut to the goddamn chase, counselor."

The lawyer opened his mouth for a moment, and then closed it, the overhead fluorescent lights gleaming off the brown wrecking ball of his head.

"I was told we were here to make a deal for my clients," he said. "Maybe I heard wrong."

"Exactly. We want immunity. Full immunity," Miguel cut in.

"And witness protection," said Ramon.

"Oh, is that all?" said ever-helpful Bill Bedford. "No problem. How about we toss in a flying pony that shits bars of gold?"

Chapter 97

"ENOUGH, OKAY? WE GET it," Tara said, suddenly jumping in before Bedford could do any more damage. "You want to skate. That's a very tall order. What do we get?"

"We know where Manuel Perrine is," Ramon said. "I'm talking right now."

"No," said Miguel, eyeing his brother. "He doesn't know shit. I do. *I* know where Perrine is."

"How would you know anything about Perrine?" I said.

"We've been doing business with his people for quite some time, purchasing cocaine and heroin from their distributor in the Bronx. People from the Perrine cartel contacted me three weeks ago and asked me to lease a house for them in a secluded location where a helicopter could land without looking suspicious. I was also asked to supply a staff of cleaning people and a chef who could cook French cuisine.

"The chef is an old friend of mine. He confirmed to me that Perrine is at the location, that he arrived the night after the escape. I was able to contact my friend this morning, and he confirmed it again. Perrine's still there as we speak."

"There was an attractive, dark-haired woman with Perrine," I said.

"Marietta?" Miguel said, looking at me. "Yes. She's there as well."

"Why the hell is he still hanging around?" Bedford said.

"Arrangements are being made to get them out of the country, back into Canada, where they had been living before Perrine's arrest, but there's some sort of problem," Miguel said. "We need to move on this before my arrest is made public. Once that happens, he'll send a kill team to wipe out me, my brother, and our family. That's what he does.

"He told me many times that sweet death is the noble price every man should happily pay for failure. He thinks of dealing drugs as a religious calling and himself as a messiah figure. He's incredibly insane. Please, you need to help us. You need to grab this sick bastard. It's our only chance."

"Okay, okay," Tara said, standing. "We'll confer out in the hall for a moment."

"What do you think, Mike?" Tara said after the door closed. "This info sounds credible."

"Extremely credible," I said. "Especially the part about Perrine being incredibly insane."

"I agree," Bedford said, trying hard not to lick his chops. "These two are sharks, but Perrine is Moby Dick. We need to make the deal."

"I will, Bill, on one condition," Tara said.

"What's that?" Bedford said.

"That Mike is brought back in on this for Perrine's arrest and capture."

Bedford glared at her and then at me, but behind his eyes, I could see the calculator in his brain being furiously punched.

"Okay, fine. I'll have to talk to my boss, but I think we can work that out."

"Okay, then," Tara said, winking at me as she grabbed the doorknob. "Let's go back in there and make a deal."

Chapter 98

AROUND 6:00 P.M. THAT summer evening, I was an hour and a half north of Newburgh in upstate Greene County, New York, standing on the shoulder of a two-lane country road.

As I glanced at the seemingly endless ribbon of blacktop curving upward through the gold-tinged pines, the free-spirited maverick in me felt like sticking out my thumb and lighting out for the territories. But then I suddenly remembered that I was a cop instead of Jack Kerouac, and I followed the FBI agent I was with past a freshly road-killed porcupine into the bucket of a tree-service cherry picker.

I held onto my borrowed yellow hard hat as the bucket hummed upward through oak leaves and pine needles. Halting just at treetop level, about seven stories up, I was greeted with 360 degrees of stark, breathtaking Catskill Mountains peaks and shale ridges. Since there was no man-made structure to be seen, the experience was like going back in time.

To the seventies, maybe, I thought, since on the way up, I'd actually passed a faded old billboard bearing a picture of Smokey Bear in his Park Service hat with the words ONLY YOU CAN PREVENT FOREST FIRES.

We were three miles due south of Perrine's rented wooded estate on West Kill Mountain, along a section of the Catskills called Devil's Path, which made a lot of sense, considering we were here to find the devil himself. In the five hours since we had gotten the location of Perrine's hideout from the Puentes brothers, earth and sky had most definitely been moved. In the space of the afternoon, a sixty-member contingent of the FBI's Hostage Rescue Team and all their equipment had been mobilized up from their headquarters in Quantico, Virginia, to Stewart Air National Guard Base, just outside of Newburgh, on two C-130 military cargo planes.

I met with HRT briefly at the base when they arrived, and they were formidable indeed. Think of an armored, and armed to the teeth, professional football team. Only they brought their own helicopters and were dressed like ninjas. The feds didn't just *want* to capture Perrine after they got egg on their faces down in Foley Square. They *needed* to.

In the bucket beside me, HRT leader Kyle Ginther handed me a Canon SLR camera with a huge high-power zoom lens. Thirtyish, dark-haired, and boyish, Ginther looked friendly, like the young dad next door. Only when this dad wasn't leaf-blowing his lawn, he was emptying sniper rifles and automatic weapons into range targets.

I glassed the terrain to the north with the camera. After a moment, I spotted the roof of Perrine's hideout halfway up the south slope of West Kill and super-zoomed it in. Through hanging motes of pollen, a shingle-and-beam chalet-style lodge house came into view. It had river-stone chimneys and a massive deck out in front to soak in the view. I'd already seen the photographs, taken an hour earlier, of Perrine and Marietta on that same deck sharing a drink.

"We've received the building plans from the architect and have a shoot house mocked up," Ginther said. "We know that there are two other guesthouses on the property, along with a barn. We also just learned that Perrine's quarters are on the lower level of the main house."

I blinked at him in shock.

"How did you find that out?"

"Intel from the Puentes brothers," Ginther said. "Getting the phone numbers of the people up there with Perrine was gold, Mike. With the help of the phone company, we sent software into the targets' cell phones that turned them into microphones. Their phones don't even have to be on. Ain't technology grand?"

"How many people do you think are up there?" I said.

"Twenty-five to forty, as far as we can tell," Ginther said. "They're armed mostly with shot-guns, but we have seen a few assault rifles. The men we've observed patrolling the perimeter seem professional, definitely trained. We're going to have to watch our step."

"How are you going to do the raid?" I asked.

"Wait till it's dark, put our snipers in a tight perimeter around the facility, then cut the power and fast-rope in onto that deck from our Black Hawk and Little Bird helicopters. With snipers covering the outside with suppression fire, the airborne assault unit will split into two teams, one securing the main and upper levels, the other the basement, where Perrine is at. We'll be ready to go by tonight."

I wiped sweat out of my eyes as I thought about things for a minute. On the way up to Greene County, I'd stopped at a country store to answer a text message and spotted a crow moving at the parking lot's edge. It took me a second to realize with horror that it was plucking the feathers out of a smaller dead bird. For some reason, I couldn't shake that sickening image— the large dark bird holding down the smaller one with his talon, fastidiously plucking out its feathers one by one—as I stood there sweating on the cherry picker.

"Something bothering you, Mike?" Ginther said.

"Despite your confidence and HRT's obviously incredible abilities," I said, "Perrine has the high ground. He brought heavy weapons to the midtown Manhattan shoot-out we had at the beginning of the summer, so he's bound to have some more up here. Hell, I wouldn't be surprised if he had RPGs. And he knows special operations tactics. The bad guys actually used flashbangs on us when my partner was killed. I wouldn't be at all surprised if they had night vision, too, so a full-frontal assault, even in the dark, sounds dangerous to me. This bastard has sent me to enough cop funerals, thank you very much."

"Okay, I'm listening. You have any ideas?"

That's when it hit me. I did have an idea. At least the germ of one. I let it settle in for a beat, and then I grabbed the camera and looked back up at the house peeking out between the treetops.

"That driveway is the only way in or out?" I asked.

"By car, at least," Ginther said.

"Smokey Bear," I mumbled.

"What was that?"

I handed the commando back his camera.

"Take us down," I said. "I think I have an idea."

Chapter 99

TWO HOURS LATER, JUST after the sun went down, Ginther and I sat in the cab of a truck, looking out at the silent mountain twilight as we waited by the radio. We sat up when we heard the radio scratch.

"Okay, this is Rabbit. We're in position," came the word from the first HRT infil team.

I glanced over at Ginther as he checked his watch. We waited some more.

It took another three minutes before the second team crackled the mike.

"Okay, this is Merlin. We're here."

"Okay," Ginther said back. "Pop 'em all, fellas. Everything you got."

"Roger that, Cap," Merlin said. "Affirmative. Fire in the hole."

We waited, our eyes glued north, toward Perrine's house. After a minute, we smiled in unison as an enormous column of black smoke rose into the pale, twilit sky.

But having two HRTs pop dozens of smoke grenades into the woods below Perrine's hideout was only phase one. As the smoke billowed, Ginther made another call to the fire station at the base of West Kill Mountain's north slope. A moment later, a blaring air horn sounded in the distance.

My last-ditch plan was under way. Perrine might suspect something fishy was up once he heard the siren and saw the smoke, but how could he be sure if it was a real forest fire or not? The answer was that he couldn't. Because deception is basic to the art of war, we needed to cause as much confusion and chaos as possible as we went in. In fact, we needed to bamboozle the living shit out of Perrine if we were going to capture him without heavy resistance.

"Okay, buckle up. This is it," Ginther yelled as he started one of the two fire trucks we'd borrowed from the nearby towns of Hunter and Roxbury. I slipped on a yellow fire helmet. I and the dozen other HRT members riding in the two trucks were already wearing firemen's gear over our automatic weapons. I crossed my fingers.

Please let this work.

A second later, our blue and red lights started flashing and we were rolling along the country blacktop, sirens blaring. I held onto an overhead strap with my right hand and the strap of a borrowed M4 assault rifle with my left as the roaring, rumbling truck swung off the mountain road and onto the driveway of Perrine's hideout.

We saw it almost immediately. After we had gone up the steep driveway for about a minute, we didn't see just smoke anymore. Not good, I thought, staring open-mouthed out the front passenger-side window.

Tall orange flames were now engulfing the woods on both sides of the driveway. I stared out at the growing fire. On each side of the driveway, there had to be half an acre of forest already in flames as the fire climbed up the slope toward Perrine's mountain retreat. Bits of burning black-and-orange embers were falling everywhere.

Like confetti in a Halloween parade.

Our fake forest fire had somehow just become a real one!

Ginther halted the truck and lifted his radio.

"Rabbit! Merlin! This was supposed to be a pretend fire. Are you effing kidding me? What's going on?"

"Those smoke rounds get hot, sir. Seems like too hot in this case," replied Rabbit. "We didn't realize how dry the forest floor was."

Ginther shook his head at the flames, his face grim. I could almost see visions of the FBI Waco standoff dancing through his head.

The radio came alive with a metallic squawk.

"Ground one, this is air one. Do I see real fire down there?" asked the already airborne assault team.

"Man, is Smokey going to be pissed," Ginther said, glancing at me. "Screw it. Accidents happen. Can't worry about it now. We use it.

"Full speed ahead," Ginther called into his radio. "All forces assault now. We're going in. I repeat. We're going in."

"Through a forest fire?" I said.

"Hey, you're the one who wanted to run this

flea-flicker. Besides, worst-case scenario, we'll exfil on the choppers," Ginther said.

The crazy commando shrugged and gave me his all-American smile as he put the truck into gear and gunned it *toward* the flames.

"Come on, Mike. Get into it," Ginther said. "This is what it's all about. Improvise. Overcome. And by the way, welcome to HRT."

Chapter 100

TWENTY SECONDS LATER, AS we passed through the massive wall of flames, a hand banged hard on the roof above Ginther.

"Cap," said one of the FBI commandos on top of the truck. "Twelve o'clock on the driveway ahead. We have a vehicle approaching."

"Follow my lead, but be ready for anything," Ginther said to his guys.

He didn't need to tell them to lock and load, I knew. These elite commando types woke up locked and loaded. They probably couldn't tell you where the safeties on their guns were.

My gaze shifted from the flames we'd just passed to the vehicle coming down the road. It was a black Jeep Cherokee with four hard-looking Hispanic men in it. It stopped in front of us.

"Private," the driver said, waving his arms as he hopped out. "You need to turn around and go back. This is a private area."

"Private? Are you out of your cotton-picking mind?" Ginther yelled, thumbing back his fire helmet as he stepped out onto the driveway. "See that hot orange stuff heading our way? That's a forest fire, son. Winds are coming up from the south. You don't have a minute to spare. You need to get yourself and anyone else up at that house off this mountain now."

The Hispanic guys conferred quickly. One of them lifted a phone and started speaking rapidly into it.

Ginther lifted his own phone.

"Okay, Central. This is hook and ladder thirty-eight," he screamed, loud enough for Perrine's guards to hear. "We can't get access to the fire site. You're going to have to bring up the water chopper. I repeat. Bring in the water bird."

Water chopper? I thought, remembering the already hovering HRT helicopters.

It's going to rain in a minute around here, all

right, I thought, glancing at Perrine's thugs. It's going to rain cops and lead.

The head Hispanic tough was putting away his phone when the four HRT commandos with us rolled off the top of the truck and put assault rifles in the bad guys' faces. In a fraction of a second, the bad guys were facedown by their Jeep, hog-tied, with white plastic zip ties around their wrists.

"Oh, my God, Mike. Look at this," Ginther said, showing me the back of the Jeep.

It was filled to the brim with military hardware. AK-47s, sniper rifles, three pairs of night-vision goggles, fragmentation grenades. They even had claymore mines.

"What did I tell you?" I said. "These jacks think it's World War Three."

After Ginther told his men to transfer all the weaponry onto our truck, he lifted each of Perrine's thugs one by one and kicked them in the ass to get them moving down the driveway, toward the main road.

"*Ándale*, assholes," Ginther said. "You have about five minutes before that driveway melts. Run, if you want to live."

Chapter 101

GINTHER LEAPED ABOARD THE rig and got on the radio to update the rest of the teams about the weapons cache. Then he hit the siren again and put the fire truck into gear. We could hear the buzz of helicopter blades as the truck stopped on the circular driveway next to the house.

"Evacuation! This is an evacuation!" Ginther bellowed over the fire truck's loudspeaker. "A forest fire is in the area! I repeat. A forest fire is on its way!"

As we exited the fire truck, I was greeted by the glorious sight of the HRT Black Hawk hovering over the house, commandos fast-roping onto the deck. I was congratulating myself at getting this far in without resistance when the sound of gunfire erupted inside the house. Ginther told his men to watch the perimeter as we both shucked off our fire coats and raced over the driveway toward the house.

The closest entrance we found was a sliding glass door under the enormous deck. The finished basement was extremely elaborate—a pool table, a wide-screen TV, a bar with wine bottles stacked within two huge glass coolers. In a split second, the door was shattered with Ginther's rifle butt and we were inside.

I turned to look back through the sliders when I heard a crackle. I paused, blinking. About thirty feet away, the woods below the house were completely on fire. There was so much smoke you could hardly see the sky. It was amazing how fast the forest fire had moved.

I felt like running back and grabbing some fire gear, but instead, I quickly followed Ginther through a door near the back of the room. I was in for another shock. Beyond the doorway was a huge indoor lap pool and a glass wall running along the entire width of the house.

Not only that, but there was someone in it. A pale form under the water.

The water bulged, and Marietta herself appeared with a splash at the end of the pool closest to us. She wasn't wearing a stitch, and for a moment, Ginther and I stood arrested in place, staring at the water sluicing off her curves, at the long, black, wet wave of hair that clung to her shoulders.

Instead of being shocked, she was smiling, as though she'd been waiting there for us.

Then we heard the sound of engines. There were lights in the trees beyond the window. Then three or four ATVs blew past, roaring up behind the house, up the mountain.

"Freeze!" Ginther said.

I looked away from the window to see Marietta moving along the pool's edge.

"No. My robe. I need to cover myself. I just want my robe," Marietta said, reaching toward a white robe on a chaise longue beside the pool.

Waiting for her, my eyes pinned on her hands, I saw black and shot just as she was bringing the machine pistol up. The triple burst of my M4 rifle was amplified by and reverberated violently off the pool-room tile. I hit her in the side of her neck, and her gun clattered onto the concrete deck. I watched her go stiff and fall straight back into the pool in a move we used to call the Nestea plunge when I was a kid. For a long dumbfounded second, I stared at the glow of the outside flames, their pink reflection on the tile, Marietta's blood making a pink cloud in the water.

"Where's Perrine?" Ginther roared into his tactical microphone. "We heard ATVs going north. What the hell is going on? Tear this place apart!"

"We can't, Cap. We're done. The deck just caught," came back one of his men. "You need to get the hell out of there. We need to exfil now. Everyone needs to head to the LZ behind the house."

That's what happened. We retraced our steps and went back outside. The heat was incredible; it felt like we were standing at the door of the world's biggest convection oven.

The Black Hawk was filled by the time we got there, so we had to leave on one of the puny Little Birds, which reminded me of those toys you see at the mall. Ginther strapped me in and we lifted up. When we swung around the front

of the house, I saw that it was completely
engulfed. The living room curtains, the rugs, the
furniture. Everything was burning.

The Devil's Path, I thought, staring down as
we sailed over the burning mountain through
the smoke-dark sky.

Chapter 102

THE HRT RALLY POINT was the parking lot and field behind a rural post office in nearby Lexington, New York. When we landed between the tents, it was already chaos. About a hundred or so state troopers, local cops, and FBI agents were running around, coordinating a massive manhunt. I even spotted a few of the firemen we had borrowed the trucks from. It was going to be fun when we told them we left their new rigs behind in the inferno up on the mountain.

And this was the calm before the shitstorm, I thought as Ginther unclipped me from the chopper. We'd lit the world on fire to get Perrine, and it was looking like he'd still gotten away.

Ginther took me aside in one of the tents and

handed me a baby wipe and a bottle of water. When I collapsed onto the bumper of their SWAT truck and wiped my face, it came back black. I poured the water over my head and watched it drip onto the beaten dirt between my boots.

I'd definitely had better days at the office. I was tired, filthy, and smelled like a smoked chicken. And I'd just killed a beautiful naked woman. A completely insane, homicidal maniac of a beautiful woman, but still. Actually, I didn't feel bad about it, considering that the witch had killed my good pal Hughie. It was pretty much the highlight of the raid, since Perrine was still on the run.

"Mike, whatever happens, this was *my* plan," Ginther said. "They want to transfer me to Alaska, I don't give a shit. Because you were right about the night vision, about the weapons they had up there. We would have been sliced to ribbons if it wasn't for you. We didn't get this animal, but all my guys came back safe. That's all I care about."

"Thanks, brother," I said, looking up. "But I have a funny feeling the blame-layers aren't going to be satisfied with just one crucifixion. And screw the pencil pushers anyway, Kyle. They're like eunuchs in a harem. They know how it's done. They've seen it done every day, but for some reason, they just can't do it themselves. We gave it our best shot, and we're going home alive. Tomorrow's another day."

"For me, it's looking like tomorrow's going to be another day in the land of a thousand suns. We torched an entire mountain and got jack shit to show for it," Ginther said. "I mean, I never even heard of that."

I started laughing a little then. He was right. I'd been involved in disasters before, but this took the cake.

"But our heart was in the right place, Kyle," I said. "Isn't that what really counts?"

My phone started vibrating then. I had a funny feeling it was going to be doing quite a bit of that in the next few hours.

"Bennett," I said.

There was a pause, then a strange voice.

"You killed her, Bennett, didn't you? You killed Marietta."

Chapter 103

I COULDN'T BELIEVE IT. It was Perrine. I could tell by the stupid Pepé Le Pew accent. I jumped up and frantically waved at Ginther and pointed at my phone.

"Hey, buddy. You're the one who left her there," I said. "I would have said 'high and dry,' but you actually cut out and left her doing the backstroke in the pool."

Ginther ran and grabbed an FBI phone tech, who whispered that she needed my cell number. I grabbed her offered pen and wrote it on the back of her hand.

"She was my wife. Did you know that, Bennett?" Perrine continued. "We were married right after my escape. My child was inside of her.

You set that fire to smoke me out, didn't you? You killed my pregnant wife."

For a moment, I almost felt sorry for the drug-dealing, murdering son of a bitch. He sounded depressed. You could tell the pain in his voice was real. He sounded like he really did love that crazy chick.

"Pregnant? Didn't show, Manuel. Do you always let your wife swim in the buff?"

The sound of pain and outrage that erupted from the phone a moment later was something I was unfamiliar with. There was something primal about it, something Jurassic. The cry of a pterodactyl caught in a lava flow.

"Oh, I see how this works," I said, hearing Perrine's cries turn into sobs. "You can kill anybody in your path and that's fine and dandy. But someone close to you takes a bullet to the back of the head and all of a sudden it's Greek tragedy time? How does it feel, you piece of garbage? Choke on it. Boo-hoo, you fucking crybaby."

Was what I said cruel? You better believe it was. But then again, Perrine had taught me all about cruel. I'd never said anything as remotely hurtful to anyone in my entire life, but this monster had killed my friend Hughie, and had actually put a hit on my kids. It was safe to say the gloves were off. I'd stab him in his broken heart with the cheap Bic pen in my hand if I got the chance.

"Do you know where I am right now, Bennett?" Perrine finally said with a sniffle. "Right this very minute? I'm in front of your house at the lake. I'm about to kill your family, Bennett. I'm going to tie everyone up and gather them around and make everyone watch as I carve out their little hearts one by one. Chrissy, Jane, Juliana, even the priest. All their heads will be on sticks by the time you get here. Just remember. You did this. You did this to yourself."

Then he hung up.

Chapter 104

AN HOUR LATER, I was racing south down the Thruway in a borrowed FBI SUV, lights and siren at full strength. I threw it onto the shoulder without touching the brake as traffic backed up. I was still tearing ass when I threw the vehicle up on a grass berm around both the state police car and the ambulance at a highway accident scene that was causing the backup.

In my rearview mirror, in the red light of the road flares, I could see the trooper glaring at my taillights, as though he wanted to empty his service revolver at me, but that couldn't be helped. I punched the SUV back off the berm onto the dark highway in a cloud of dust and continued south.

I'd already spoken to Seamus, who assured me that everything was fine. I'd even contacted Ed Boyanoski, who had sent a Newburgh PD squad car to watch the house. And yet I frantically needed to get back to the lake house. Perrine's words, his promise to hurt my family, wouldn't stop replaying in my mind. Perrine was capable of absolutely anything.

It was about twenty-five minutes later when I finally fishtailed the truck into the lake house driveway. The first thing I noticed was Ed's Toyota beside a Newburgh squad car out in front. All the lights were on in the house as I flew up the steps through the open door.

Ed was in the hallway. He caught me as I almost ran through him.

"It's okay, Mike. Everybody's okay."

I finally looked over his shoulder and felt like crying as I saw he was telling the truth. Everyone was sitting around the dining room table in front of several pizza boxes.

"Is everybody here?" I said. "Is everyone here?"

I scanned faces.

Jane: check. Eddie, Ricky: check. Juliana,

Brian, Trent: check. Little Shawna, with Chrissy —thank you, dear God: check.

"Fiona and Bridget," I said. "Where are the twins?"

"Right here, Daddy," Fiona said, coming through the kitchen doorway with a bowl of salad, followed by Bridget, who was holding a two-liter bottle of Coke.

"Why is Daddy's face all black?" Bridget said.

"Good question, Bridget," Trent piped in over his slice. "What I want to know is, why is he acting nuts?"

"You mean more nuts than usual?" Eddie said.

I smiled at my motley crew as I let out a breath. What Perrine said was a bluff. Of course it was. Thank you, God.

"Oh, we're all here, Detective Bennett," Seamus said from the foot of the table. "Everyone is present and accounted for. And I do mean everyone."

That's when the kitchen door opened.

And Mary Catherine came in with a bunch of napkins in her hand.

Chapter 105

WHEN SHE SPOTTED ME standing there, she stopped in her tracks, the napkins in her hands fluttering to the floor. My jaw was already there waiting for them.

It was one of those movie moments. I waited for a sappy eighties love ballad to start playing so I could lift her up where we belonged or something. All the kids started giggling. Actually, that was the girls. The boys were too busy rolling their eyes.

"Okay, Bennetts. This is where I take my leave," Ed Boyanoski said.

"Hi, Mike," Mary said.

She bent down and started picking up napkins.

"Here, let me help," I said, just about hurdling over the table and grabbing some napkins off the floor. Then I grabbed her hand and pulled her toward the kitchen.

I kicked the door shut behind me, and before I really knew what I was doing, I lifted her up off her feet as I bear-hugged her. My arms tingled where I held her to me.

The door started opening behind us. I blocked it with my foot.

"Hey, what gives?" Seamus said. "What's going on in there? And what's wrong with the door?"

"It's, eh . . . the napkins," I cried as I held the door fast with my foot. "They're jammed in the hinge. You should call a cop or something."

"But you are a cop, Daddy," Chrissy squealed.

"Um . . . it's nice to see you, too, Mike," Mary Catherine said, suddenly pushing me away.

"Sorry about that," I said. "I guess I'm a little overwhelmed. I truly never thought I'd see you again. It's just . . . it's just really good to see you, Mary Catherine, and . . ."

"Just wait, Mike. This is hard, so just let me say it," Mary Catherine said, staring at me levelly.

"It's not what you think. I'm not *back* back. I'm just willing to come back to handle all the back-to-school stuff for the kids. Then you have to find a replacement for me."

I stood there trying to keep my heart from jumping through my chest. As if replacing her were possible, I thought as I stared at her. Why had I destroyed everything? I wondered. A replacement for her? God, that hurt.

"Of course," I finally said.

But Mary Catherine was already on the move toward the dining room.

Cancel the eighties love ballad, I thought as I watched her walk away.

Chapter 106

THAT NIGHT, WE WENT back to New York in the most brutal end-of-summer traffic imaginable. To add some fun to the mix, Trent, after having probably one too many Cokes, barfed sausage pizza chunks all over the back of the Bennett bus.

Pulling the bus off the West Side Highway, we were greeted with more grief. Cops had West End Avenue completely cordoned off. In the distance, beyond the blue sawhorses, I could see a bunch of blindingly bright portable light carts positioned in front of my building.

Was it a movie? I thought, pulling up to the NYPD blockade.

"Hey, moron. Read my barricade. Move this

hunk now," a tall, helpful, uniformed New York City peace officer screamed at me.

"That's Detective Moron to you, Sarge," I said, showing my gold shield as I got out of the bus. "That's my building there. Didn't they cancel *Law and Order*? What's up?"

"Supposed to keep it under wraps, but looks like the *T* word, Detective," the white-haired cop said, nodding. "They found a truck bomb. Can you believe it?"

"What?" I said.

"You heard me. Some mother parked a Penske truck filled with ammonium nitrate and diesel fuel in the middle of the block. Bomb guy just told me it was bigger than the one that took out the Murrah Building in Oklahoma City. They got the detonator or whatever licked, but they still gotta tow it out of here. Watch the potholes, right? If a sharp-eyed doorman hadn't seen something and said something, the freakin' West Side would be a crater."

I stared at him, my mouth open. Then I stared down the block.

Perrine, I thought, shaking my head. Had to be. He wasn't going to kill just me and my family.

No, that would be far too common. In order to get to me, he was actually going to kill everyone on my entire block.

"Hey, Detective? You okay?" the cop said, but I was already on the move, scanning the street in front of me and the street behind as I jogged back to my bus.

"What is it, Mike?" Mary Catherine said.

"Um . . . gas leak. We can't get back into the building. We need to hit a hotel tonight," I said, popping it into gear.

Chapter 107

I TURNED AROUND AND drove out of the city and checked into a hotel over the New York State line just outside of Danbury, Connecticut. On the way up, I had Mary Catherine confiscate everyone's cell phones. Remembering what Ginther had said about cell phones being potential microphones, I even had her remove all the batteries.

For the next hour, as the kids watched TV in the other room, I exchanged calls with Tara McLellan and my boss, Miriam. About an hour or so after that, a team of FBI agents and U.S. marshals arrived at the hotel in unmarked cars.

"These gentlemen are from the gas company, I take it?" Mary Catherine said skeptically.

I nodded and left with them for a meeting in the lobby.

An hour later, I came back to the room, my head spinning. What I'd just been told made a lot of sense, but I still had trouble swallowing it. Talk about a shock to the system.

"Mary Catherine," I said grimly. "I have news. Could you gather everybody together for a family meeting? Actually, have the twins take Trent and Chrissy and Shawna into the other room. I need to talk to all the bigger guys."

"What is it, Mike?" Mary said.

"I'll tell you in a second," I said. "But you really might want to reconsider your position when you find out what it is."

"What is it, Dad?" Brian said as they squeezed into the room.

I looked at their faces one by one where they sat on the chairs and the desk and the double bed.

"Well, what's going on is, well . . . we're moving," I said. "We have to move."

The kids stared at each other, giant-eyed.

"What? Why? Huh? Why?" everyone wanted to know at the same time.

"Quiet down, children," Seamus cried.

"Our block was cordoned off because a criminal, a drug lord, a man named Manuel Perrine, whom I caught and who then escaped, planted a bomb in front of our building. He wants to kill me and hurt you guys because of how much I love you. That's why we need to go somewhere where he can't find us. Now. Someplace safe."

"But what about school?" Juliana said.

"And Mass?" Seamus said. "Father Charles is out sick. I have to say Mass tomorrow morning."

"We're going to have to figure all that out, guys," I said. "The U.S. marshals are sending over a team right now to take us to our new location."

"What about our stuff?"

"They're going to go by the apartment and pack it up for us. We can't go home. It's too dangerous."

"We're leaving New York?" Seamus said. He seemed flabbergasted.

"At least for now," I said.

"But all our friends. Our lives," Brian said. "How can this be happening?"

My sentiments exactly, I thought as I let out a breath. This sucked, and it was about to get worse. I didn't even tell them we might have to change our names.

Chapter 108

THE WITNESS PROTECTION TEAM arrived at four in the morning. Four more FBI agents and about a dozen U.S. marshals in cars and vans. Though they tried to keep their weapons under their Windbreakers, out of the kids' sight, I spotted more than one submachine gun.

This was no joke. They wouldn't have gone to all this trouble if we weren't serious targets. This was about as serious and scary as it got.

"Okay, Mary Catherine," I said to her in the lobby as the agents were walking the kids out into the waiting vans. "I guess this is good-bye for now."

One of the female FBI agents who was co-ordinating our transport turned around from

498

the front sliding door as she overheard us.

"Excuse me," she said. "Good-bye? What are you guys talking about?"

"It's okay," I said. "This is Mary Catherine, my nanny. She's not coming with us."

The brown-eyed, red-haired agent thumbed her smartphone.

"Mary Catherine Flynn?" the agent asked.

"That's right," Mary Catherine said.

"Yes, well, Ms. Mary Catherine Flynn, you can't go anywhere. Not if you value your life. You need to come with us right now."

"What do you mean?" I said.

"We traced the rental truck used for the bomb in front of your building. It came back to a Dominican drug gang affiliated with Perrine. We raided them last night. They had photos of all of you. Folders with information about where you guys work, where the kids go to school, the works. Mary Catherine here was with all the rest of you. Perrine is paying top dollar to take every one of you out. She's a target as much as you are. She can't be left behind."

"But—" I said.

"It's okay, Mike," Mary Catherine said. "I'll

go along for now. You're going to need my help anyway with the children. They're all so upset. We'll figure it out."

How? I thought as I stood there helplessly watching my world, my family's world, and now Mary Catherine's world turn upside down and inside out.

How would we be able to figure any of this out?

Chapter 109

THEY DIVIDED US BETWEEN two vans. Mary Catherine and me with the girls. Seamus in the other vehicle with the boys.

We drove west, back into New York State, and straight on through into Pennsylvania. Neither of the jarheaded U.S. marshals sitting in the front seat told me where we were headed, and I didn't ask.

I didn't even want to know, I was still so depressed. As we drove along, I asked myself if I regretted pissing off the drug lord so much on the phone, and quickly decided that I didn't. To hell with his evil ass if he can't take a joke. Besides, he'd have come after me anyway.

If I had any regrets, it was that Mary Catherine had been roped into it. Especially with the mess I had made of things. Not only had I driven her off, now I'd put her life in danger. I didn't know how to begin to apologize to her.

I fell asleep as the sun was coming up and when I woke, it was noon. We were somewhere flat. Ohio. Indiana, maybe. I stared out at the side of the highway into empty farm fields, wondering if I was dreaming. Despite everything, it felt good to be in the middle of nowhere and moving. There was something instinctual about it, that feeling of safety in motion.

I heard a strange sound and realized it was the new phone the marshals had given me in exchange for my old one. I looked at the 212 number as I clumsily thumbed it on. Tara, I thought.

But it wasn't.

"Mike? Hi. It's Bill Bedford."

He was slurring a little, I noticed. In fact, he sounded drunk.

"Hey, Bill," I said. "I take it you heard about what happened at my building?"

"I did, Mike, but that's not why I called," Bill said. "I don't know how to tell you this. I just got off the phone with NYPD Homicide. Tara's dead. They just found her."

I sat up.

"No, no, no," I said.

"They must have gotten her on the street on her way to work, Mike," Bill said, sniffling. "She was taken to a motel in the Bronx, and God, Mike, they tore her apart. They found her head floating in the bathtub."

I closed my eyes and let out a breath.

"Perrine did it himself, too," Bedford said. "They have him on the motel's security video waltzing through the door with a big grin on his face. He's not human. That fucker isn't human."

"No, he isn't," I agreed as my mind spun.

"I'm so sorry, Mike," Bill said.

He sounded completely wrecked. I thought about Tara at the St. Regis, how she'd said I'd saved her.

"Me too, Bill," I said after a bit. "Thanks for calling. It couldn't have been easy."

Mary Catherine stirred beside me.

"What is it, Mike? What's wrong?"

"Nothing," I said, looking back at my kids, then out at the fields, up at the sky.

"It's okay," I lied as I fought panic and tears. "Go back to sleep, Mary Catherine. Everything is going to be fine."

THE NEW ALEX CROSS THRILLER,
AVAILABLE FROM NOVEMBER 2012

Merry Christmas, Alex Cross

James Patterson

Detective Alex Cross is ripped away from his family on Christmas Eve – and that's nothing compared to what awaits him on Christmas Day.

It's a snowy Christmas Eve, and Detective Alex Cross is at home celebrating with his family. Nana Mama's famous pecan pie is in the oven and the kids are hanging their favourite ornaments on the tree. Just as Alex's wife Bree emerges from the kitchen with a bowl of homemade eggnog, his phone rings with news that shatters the night: at a nearby home, a family has been taken hostage – and the situation is spiralling out of control fast.

Alex rushes to the scene and confronts the unthinkable: a father is threatening to murder his own children and his ex-wife. Then just as the insanity peaks, a second horrific situation explodes – one that no one could have foreseen and that puts millions of people at risk. This is a red alert of the darkest kind, and Alex is forced to make a decision that could end as many lives as it saves – including his own.

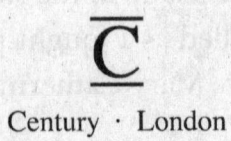

Century · London

Turn the page for a
sneak preview of

**MERRY
CHRISTMAS
ALEX
CROSS**

THEY SAY IT'S GOOD luck if it snows on Christmas Eve. I didn't usually buy into that kind of folk wisdom, but if it turned out to be true, well, this was looking like it'd be one of the best Christmases ever. A nor'easter was churning its way up the Carolinas at the same time as a cold front was diving south out of Ontario, all the makings for a monster storm along the Eastern Seaboard.

Sampson and I brought Lewis in and booked him. Since there were no arraignments scheduled until the day after tomorrow, it looked like the man of the year would be waiting for Santa in a holding cell this Yuletide season.

It was nearly eight by the time we finished up the paperwork and left.

"Merry Christmas, Alex," Sampson said outside.

"You too, John. Feel like stopping by for a holiday beverage tomorrow?"

"I'll check with my scheduler," Sampson said.

I took a cab home. As the taxi moved through DC, I looked out at the decorations glowing everywhere. The pace of the snow hadn't increased much yet, but the size of the flakes had. They were each about the diameter of a quarter, and thick, making the city look the way it does in those snow globes tourists buy at Union Station and the airports.

By the time I reached our house on Fifth Street in Southeast, it was close to eight thirty. The air smelled of pecan pie. Bree and the kids were busy finishing trimming the tree, which was in the alcove by the window at the front of the house. And of course, the official sergeant-of-all-holidays, Nana Mama, was supervising every little task on her to-do list.

"Don't put two green ornaments right next to each other, Damon. Show some style when you decorate a tree," she scolded with all the authority of the vice principal she'd once been.

Bree was hooking a faded crayon drawing of the Three Wise Men up on one of the branches. According to legend, I had made that ornament when I was in kindergarten, and Nana always dragged it out on Christmas.

"Well, look who's come in from the snow-storm," Bree said, and she walked over and gave me a kiss on the lips. "Hello, sweetheart."

Nana decided not to look in my direction. All she said was "Is there a faint possibility, Alex, that you might spend a few minutes of the holiday season with your family? Or are we asking too much?"

I should have had the wisdom to say nothing to Nana, to just give her a Christmas kiss, but I'll never learn. She pushes my buttons like nobody else on this earth.

"Thanks for the guilt! All wrapped up in a bow for Christmas," I said, dispensing hugs to my daughter, Jannie; my son Damon, who was home on winter break from prep school; and then Ava, the foster child Nana had recently brought under our roof.

"You're getting a dose of sense, fool," Nana Mama snapped.

"Nana, this morning, when I got that jingle from Father Harris, he told me that *you were the* one who suggested he call me to help catch the poor-box thief," I said. *"Which I did."*

"Father Harris said that?" Nana asked.

"He did. He said that he hated to pester me on Christmas Eve, but you told him it would be no bother. Wouldn't take any time at all for your grandson to solve the case of the poor-box pilferer."

"Humph," she said, shaking her head. "Imagine a priest making up something like that. Father Harris of all people. Then again, you never know." She reached in a box, turned to Ava. "Here you go, sweet thing. Put this porcelain Baby Jesus on a low branch, so if it falls, it doesn't fall far."

"So you're saying that Father Harris lied to me on Christmas Eve, Nana?"

She scowled, squinted at me. "I'm saying it's a pitiful state of the world when a man can't be with his family on Christmas Eve. Even a high-and-mighty homicide detective such as yourself needs to be home with his loved ones the night before Jesus's birthday."

Everyone was chuckling at Nana giving me

such a hard time. I was holding back a smile myself. So was she.

"Kind of sucks Ali's not here," Jannie said, speaking of my six-year-old son.

"It does," I replied. "But his mom celebrates Christmas too."

Bree said, "I'll be right back," and left the room. I had to admit that the tree looked pretty great against the snowy picture window. Then Bree reappeared with a big glass bowl of homemade eggnog, another Christmas Eve tradition in our house.

The eggnog had big globs of nutmeg-sprinkled real whipped cream in it, so rich and sweet, each cupful would probably register a couple thousand calories. She set the bowl beside a plate of shortbread cookies that also probably registered a couple thousand calories each. But, hey, it was the Christmas season. I helped myself to two rounds of both. Damon got a Christmas-music station up on Pandora, whatever that was, and old Nat King Cole was crooning that all our troubles would soon be out of sight. Even though Nana wouldn't let up about me working on Christmas Eve, it was looking like it'd be a warm, wonderful night.

When the song switched to Mariah Carey's

"All I Want for Christmas Is You," Jannie and Ava and Bree started dancing. Damon began telling me about an incredible true story he was reading at school, about Teddy Roosevelt going up the Amazon River with his son.

Then my cell phone rang.

Not even Mariah's transcendent voice could stop that sound from sucking the joy right out of the room.

I hung my head, avoided eye contact, went into the hall, and answered. It was deputy chief of police Allen Chivers. "Am I interrupting Christmas Eve?"

"Yup," I said.

"Hate doing this, Alex. But we've got a bad one. The kind of thing that only you seem able to handle."

I listened another full minute, leaning my head against the wall, knowing just how silent the house had gone. "Okay," I said. "I'll get there." I clicked off, went back. Nana rolled her eyes. The kids looked away from me with here-we-go-again expressions on their faces.

Bree shook her head and said, "Well, there it is, then. Merry Christmas, Alex Cross."

AS I DROVE THROUGH the almost-deserted DC streets, the snow that had looked so beautiful an hour ago now seemed downright ugly. It was depressing to leave my house and family, and I didn't blame them for being angry and upset with me. Hell, *I* was angry and upset with me. And with my job.

Goddamn it, I thought. There was only one person in the world who should work on Christmas Eve. And he wore a goofy red suit and drank way too much fattening eggnog topped with nutmeg and real whipped cream. Damn it, and damn Santa too.

As I was driving into Georgetown on Pennsylvania Ave., the snow really began to fall.

A bus in front of me hit the brakes in a half inch of slush. I skidded and almost rear-ended it. Goddamned DC public-works folks were home with their families. Let the plows wait, right?

My windshield wipers were icing up as I looked for the address on Thirtieth Street in Northwest, a neighborhood in the city that was completely the opposite of mine. This was the land of milk and honey, and power and money, and the trophy homes to prove it.

Number 1314 was a beautiful limestone town house lit up like the White House Christmas tree. But I quickly saw that most of the lighting effects came from police cars, flashlights, floodlights, and TV-camera lights. I parked, opened the door, looked down at the slush, and cursed.

I had left home so quickly and in such a pissed-off state that I hadn't had the sense to bring along a pair of snow boots. As I slogged toward the crime scene tape, my ankles got cold, and little chunks of ice and wet snow wormed their way into my shoes.

I showed my badge to the patrolman working the barrier, ducked the tape, and started toward the two MPD vans parked on the front lawn of a

Georgian brick mansion across the street. A car door on my side of the street opened. A middle-aged man in a green ski parka and a red ski hat got out and walked right up to me. He pulled off his gloves and held out a puffy red hand.

"You're Alex Cross, aren't you?" he said.

I thought I knew most cops in DC, but this one with the sea of freckles and bits of wavy red hair sneaking out from under his ski hat was new to me.

"I am," I said, shaking his hand.

"Detective Tom McGoey. Six whole days with the MPD. Originally from Staten Island."

"Happy holidays, Detective. Welcome to Washington. I got just a brief summary from Deputy Chief Chivers. You want to tell me all of it?"

"God-awful Christmas gift for you. And me."

I sighed. "Yeah, I already figured that much. Let's hear the gory details."

WE GOT IN HIS car, and McGoey turned the heater on high and fleshed out the story for me. I soon realized that it clearly *was* a god-awful situation, one with the potential to turn into a full-scale tragedy.

The beautiful town house used to belong to Henry Fowler, a top-flight attorney who'd fallen on hard times. Fowler's ex-wife, Diana, now owned the home and lived there with her new husband, Dr. Barry Nicholson, and her three children: eleven-year-old twins, Jeremy and Chloe, and six-year-old son, Trey.

"Henry Fowler's got them all in there," McGoey said. "He's armed to the teeth and said he is fully prepared to die tonight."

"It's a wonderful life," I said.

"And it only gets better," the detective said. "Melissa Brandywine's in there too." He gestured down the street to another, similar townhome. "She's the neighbor, wife of Congressman Michael Brandywine of Colorado."

"The chief told me," I grumbled; then I closed my eyes and rubbed at my temple. "Where's he? Brandywine?"

"At Vail with his two kids, waiting for her to come join them for their ski vacation. She was supposed to fly out this afternoon but made the mistake of bringing Diana a box of homemade cookies before she left."

Funny what a nice small-town gesture can get you in DC.

"He giving you a reason? Fowler?"

"He's only spoken to us once, and that wasn't part of the conversation," McGoey said. "We wouldn't have known anything if Mrs. Brandywine hadn't used the toilet and texted her husband about what was going on inside."

"The congressman was the first to report it?"

"Yeah, really lit a torch under everyone's ass."

Mentally I began to compartmentalize, to

push aside all my frustration at having to leave my family on Christmas Eve and focus on the task at hand. "Tell me about Fowler. His divorce. Whatever I should know."

"Headquarters isn't exactly loaded up with personnel tonight, so we're still waiting on most of the background check. But we know the Fowlers divorced two years ago. She filed, found the new hubby within two months, or maybe before, and moved on. Fowler not so much, evidently."

"Any idea what Fowler's got for weapons?"

"Oh yeah," McGoey said, going to his notebook. "He gave us the breakdown the one time he picked up the phone."

Fowler claimed to have two Glock 19s. The Glock 19 is the standard-issue service weapon of the MPD, which means I carry a 19. The good thing about a 19 is that it holds sixteen rounds. The bad thing about a 19 is that it holds sixteen rounds. Fowler said he also had two twelve-gauge pump shotguns, two AR-15 rifles, and multiple clips and boxes of ammunition for each weapon.

Two of everything. What was that all about?

I wrote it all in my notebook, jotted down *Long lead time*, and drew an arrow to the list.

"That everything?" I asked.

"Far as we know. Well, except for the peanut butter and jelly sandwiches."

I frowned and said, "Didn't know PB and Js were deadly weapons."

"Only to someone like Fowler's youngest kid," McGoey said. "Peanut allergy. One bite and he'll have about ten minutes to live."

Also by James Patterson

ALEX CROSS NOVELS

Along Came a Spider • Kiss the Girls • Jack and Jill •
Cat and Mouse • Pop Goes the Weasel • Roses are Red •
Violets are Blue • Four Blind Mice • The Big Bad Wolf •
London Bridges • Mary, Mary • Cross • Double Cross •
Cross Country • Alex Cross's Trial (*with Richard DiLallo*) •
I, Alex Cross • Cross Fire • Kill Alex Cross • Merry Christmas,
Alex Cross (*to be published November 2012*)

THE WOMEN'S MURDER CLUB SERIES

1st to Die • 2nd Chance (*with Andrew Gross*) •
3rd Degree (*with Andrew Gross*) • 4th of July
(*with Maxine Paetro*) • The 5th Horseman (*with Maxine Paetro*) •
The 6th Target (*with Maxine Paetro*) • 7th Heaven (*with Maxine
Paetro*) • 8th Confession (*with Maxine Paetro*) •
9th Judgement (*with Maxine Paetro*) • 10th Anniversary
(*with Maxine Paetro*) • 11th Hour (*with Maxine Paetro*) •
12th of Never (*with Maxine Paetro, to be published February 2013*)

PRIVATE NOVELS

Private (*with Maxine Paetro*) • Private London (*with Mark
Pearson*) • Private Games (*with Mark Sullivan*) •
Private: No. 1 Suspect (*with Maxine Paetro*)

STAND-ALONE THRILLERS

Sail (*with Howard Roughan*) • Swimsuit (*with Maxine Paetro*) •
Don't Blink (*with Howard Roughan*) • Postcard Killers (*with Liza
Marklund*) • Toys (*with Neil McMahon*) • Now You See Her (*with
Michael Ledwidge*) • Kill Me If You Can (*with Marshall Karp*) •
Guilty Wives (*with David Ellis*) • Zoo (*with Michael Ledwidge*) •
NYPD Red (with *Marshall Karp*)

NON-FICTION

Torn Apart (*with Hal and Cory Friedman*) •
The Murder of King Tut (*with Martin Dugard*)

ROMANCE

Sundays at Tiffany's (with *Gabrielle Charbonnet*) •
The Christmas Wedding (with *Richard DiLallo*)

FAMILY OF PAGE-TURNERS

MAXIMUM RIDE SERIES

The Angel Experiment • School's Out Forever •
Saving the World and Other Extreme Sports •
The Final Warning • Max • Fang • Angel •
Nevermore

DANIEL X SERIES

The Dangerous Days of Daniel X (*with Michael Ledwidge*) •
Daniel X: Watch the Skies (*with Ned Rust*) • Daniel X: Demons
and Druids (*with Adam Sadler*) • Daniel X: Game Over
(*with Ned Rust*) • Daniel X: Armageddon
(*with Chris Grabenstein*)

WITCH & WIZARD SERIES

Witch & Wizard (*with Gabrielle Charbonnet*) •
Witch & Wizard: The Gift (*with Ned Rust*) •
Witch & Wizard: The Fire (*with Jill Dembowski*)

MIDDLE SCHOOL SERIES

Middle School: The Worst Years of My Life (*with Chris Tebbetts
and Laura Park*) • Middle School: Get Me Out of Here!
(*with Chris Tebbetts and Laura Park*)

CONFESSIONS SERIES

Confessions of a Murder Suspect (*with Maxine Paetro*)

GRAPHIC NOVELS

Daniel X: Alien Hunter (*with Leopoldo Gout*) •
Maximum Ride: Manga Volumes 1–5 (*with NaRae Lee*)

For more information about James Patterson's novels, visit
www.jamespatterson.co.uk

Or become a fan on Facebook

I'm proud to support the National Literacy Trust, an independent charity that changes lives through literacy.

Did you know that millions of people in the UK struggle to read and write? This means children are less likely to succeed at school and less likely to develop into confident and happy teenagers. Literacy difficulties will limit their opportunities throughout adult life.

The National Literacy Trust passionately believes that everyone has a right to the reading, writing, speaking and listening skills they need to fulfil their own and, ultimately, the nation's potential.

My own son didn't use to enjoy reading, which was why I started writing children's books – reading for pleasure is an essential way to encourage children to pick up a book. The National Literacy Trust is dedicated to delivering exciting initiatives to encourage people to read and to help raise literacy levels. To find out more about the great work that they do, visit their website at www.literacytrust.org.uk.

James Patterson